COMPLICITY

COMPLICITY

A NOVEL BY
ELIZABETH COOKE

LITTLE, BROWN AND COMPANY
BOSTON   TORONTO

FIRST EDITION

Library of Congress Cataloging-in-Publication Data

Cooke, Elizabeth.
  Complicity.
  I. Title.
PS3553.O5554C6   1988   813'.52   87-3121
  ISBN 0-316-15507-1

10   9   8   7   6   5   4   3   2

The characters, places and events portrayed in this book
are fictitious. Any similarities to real places or persons, living or dead,
are purely coincidental and not intended by the author.

RRD-VA

*Published simultaneously in Canada
by Little, Brown & Company (Canada) Limited*

PRINTED IN THE UNITED STATES OF AMERICA

For Ellen and George
who remind me of love

Except it be for this one voice,
that I cried standing among them

ACTS 24:21

# COMPLICITY

❧ ONE ❧

ELEANOR had two faces.

The right side, in sleep, showed life in the tight wrinkles, the shivering closed eyelid, the pinched frowning mouth. The left side, without life, showed wrinkled skin falling from the high cheekbone, the corner of the mouth without a pose. On the left side the eyelid was flat, the eye socket appeared empty, the lashes like bits of ash that could disappear in the wind.

Amanda's eye followed from Eleanor's two faces to her thinned and lengthened bird neck, to her small body, flattened beneath a white sheet and a pale blue blanket. One arm lay strapped to a board by her side, a needle taped to the grey-blue skin; the other arm rested by her side under the sheet.

Eleanor opened her right eye wide; the other showed a crack and a watery darkness. The open eye rounded, and Amanda noticed, in leaning closer, black specks on the green iris.

"I've changed my mind," Eleanor worked the words out of a small hole formed in the right side of her mouth.

Amanda leaned closer, frowned, pulled back. These were her mother's first words in over two weeks.

"I have," she whispered, "I have changed my mind." The hole closed and Eleanor breathed in through her nose, the right nostril quivering.

Amanda wondered if she should call a nurse, reached for the cord that hung over a corner of the bed, and held her thumb against the red button. But she did not press the button, just held her thumb there, and waited.

"Is that you, Amanda, are you there?" she asked, the right eyelid fluttering, searching.

Amanda did not answer, just watched her mother, her lips tight in a line.

"I've decided to tell you the truth," Eleanor rasped.

Amanda ran her fingers along the cord, watched the fingers strapped to the board begin to move, first one, then the others. Age spots covered the veined hand, its joints swollen.

"What's wrong with my arm?" Eleanor continued.

Amanda knew there was nothing wrong with that arm, that it was the other arm, and the whole left side of her body, that was the problem. She figured that Eleanor did not know the left side was gone, so she said nothing, watched the fingers that were strapped to the board grope in the warm air.

Eleanor opened her green living eye, and the right side of her face crinkled, the wrinkles twisting to make peaks in the skin. A low groan echoed in her chest, the sound coming from some hidden place. Amanda realized Eleanor was crying without tears and her eyes widened; she could not remember seeing her mother cry before.

"It's about your father," she went on.

Amanda pushed the metal chair back, it scraped on the tan linoleum floor, and the cord dropped from her hand, the buzzer rattling to the floor. She stood up, reached over the cocoonlike blanket, and with her left hand, she squeezed the tube that ran through the needle into Eleanor's arm. Eleanor's eye remained closed.

"It's about when you were born."

Fifty-eight years ago, Amanda thought, and now she decides to tell me. Silent for fifty-eight years, and Amanda thought she screamed the word *silent* into the morning sun that streamed through the one window in the room. Her heart jumped, the beats irregular, and she reached a hand to hold her breast, letting go of the tube.

Eleanor's body jerked in a spasm, the left arm lurching under the bed covers.

"I told him, Amanda, I told him he was not to touch you, not to speak to you, ever."

Amanda shut her eyes and tilted her head back, feeling the pounding of blood in her temples. She ran a hand through her hair, held her hand over her closed eyes.

"He was gone, Amanda, during the months I carried you."

Amanda waited for her heart to calm. She concentrated on its beating.

"He didn't even know I was carrying you." A series of jerks ran through Eleanor's body, and her right arm clanked against the metal rail beside the bed. "You were five months old when he came home." Eleanor's one eye opened, the green almost black as it stared up at the ceiling.

Amanda listened to Eleanor's words through the pounding in her head. She imagined her heart growing larger with each beat. Her grey eyes grew cloudy. "You told him not to touch me," she repeated Eleanor's words.

"I had to. I had to, Amanda, because he was gone all that time, and your brothers never stopped asking, where was he, they asked, and when he came home, they climbed all over him, they forgot all those days and months, and Amanda —" Eleanor breathed in slowly through her nose, exhaled, her chest rising and falling with the effort.

Amanda watched Eleanor's fingers fan out in the air, watched her lips shape more words, as the light on the floor receded.

"Amanda, he did not know you were even alive until you were five months old and he came home." Eleanor breathed in again. "He had no right, after what he did."

Amanda did not know just what it was he had done, did not want to know, fought the fluttering in her heart rather than try to know. She fought a memory, a picture of her father on the porch at Land's End, when she was only three, and she remembered standing by the door to the steps, repeating the sound da-da-da-da, as if she was even younger than three, as if she was first saying his name, and Amanda remembered wanting him to look at her. But his blue eyes fixed on the lake, his hands quiet in his lap. "You told him not to touch me," the words fell out of her mouth, as her mind shifted to a vision of her enlarging heart.

"It was for your own good, Amanda."

Amanda leaned over to pick up the buzzer, fingered the button; and waited.

"And you should face the truth about his death," she added as her neck lifted farther out of her shoulders in an effort to see her daughter with her own eye.

Amanda stood up, walked to the window, felt a tightening in her chest as her heart beat in sudden bursts, and she closed her eyes to the vision of her father after he was retrieved from the lake, his face swollen with water, his jaw loose, his two feet turning together to one side. She shook her head, concentrated on the pulse of her heart, turned to watch Eleanor's fingers tapping the board. "He couldn't have drowned; he loved that lake," and her hands drew together at her waist.

A tremor ran through Eleanor's slight frame. The tendons on one side of her neck stretched tight, the flesh on her face bluing, her right eye bulging as it searched for Amanda's face. Her lips rounded again as the words, "You never could stand the truth," spat from her mouth. Amanda walked to the end of the bed, stood with her hands clasped, as she watched Eleanor's green eye meet hers. Her head fell back, the eye closed into the socket, sinking down, as her mouth opened to breathe in. She exhaled, all the breath in her lungs leaving her, and then she was still.

Taking a couple of steps, Amanda came to the side of the bed, leaned over Eleanor's body to look down at her face. She whispered to the sunken eye, the frozen jaw, "He loved that lake; he could not have drowned." She reached a finger to touch the angled jaw, to close the mouth, but it opened again. She touched a finger to the fine white hair that was brushed carefully away from her mother's forehead, ran her finger across the top of her head. Realizing that she had not been this close to her mother since she was a child, she held her pose, studied the face, touched the lashes and the dry skin on Eleanor's cheek.

Then she drew her hand away, pulled back, sat on the chair, and studied Eleanor's face from that distance. The green eyes were gone in their sockets, gone forever from Amanda's view. She could not remember her mother's face, alive.

Later, when the nurse came for the morning round, she found Amanda sitting erect in the chair by the bed, her grey eyes gazing out the window, her fingers working the cord in her lap.

"Why didn't you push the buzzer, Mrs. Rhoades?" she asked when she saw the death in Eleanor's face. "Why didn't you call me?"

Amanda just shook her head left to right. "I didn't buzz you because I didn't know I needed you," she said. "I watched her through the night, she never moved once, not a flicker, until her jaw opened once, and then it stayed there. I tried to close it." Amanda twisted the cord around her fingers, feeling her breath high up in her shoulders as she watched the nurse cover her mother's face with the sheet.

"She was not a dramatic person," Amanda told the nurse. "She was usually silent. As now. There was not a violent moment ever," and her voice lilted.

The nurse patted the sheet where it covered a hand. "Of course not," she said, "she was a fine old soul."

Amanda nodded. A fine old soul, she thought.

When she called Maggie to tell her of the death, she also told her of a plan she formulated after her mother died, before the nurse came. "I've decided to go to Land's End, to see my father's grave."

"To the grave? Now? What about Grandmother's funeral?" Maggie asked.

"Oh Margaret," Amanda answered, "I shall wait till the summer is over, till the fall comes. The lake is lovely in the fall, so many colors, and only the locals are left."

"Let me come with you, Mother," Maggie suggested.

"Margaret, that's a kind offer, but it's a trip for me to make alone. I'm old, this will be my last visit," and her voice grew small and came from within her chest.

"Mother, you're not old, you've got to stop this —"

"Never mind, Margaret, I know when I'm old."

"I'm going with you then, I insist. It's only just the two of us now. Let me come too. You shouldn't go back there alone. After eight years. It would be too hard —"

"We'll talk about it at the funeral," Amanda concluded.

At the funeral Amanda told everyone of Eleanor's peaceful death. "Typical, don't you agree," she said, "for her to leave the world in silence." The others nodded, yes, and the minister agreed, yes, Eleanor Elliott was a silent woman. Amanda told the story, of how Eleanor died peacefully in her sleep, and she told it so many times that she believed it herself, and her mother's words faded into the ground with her burial.

Maggie unzips the blanket case. She pulls out the red plaid blanket and lays it carefully on the newly cut grass.

"This is probably the last time this year they'll have to cut here, don't you think?" she asks Jeremy as she kneels on the edge of the blanket and flicks off her white leather shoes.

"Maybe," he answers. His dark eyes are directed toward the river. His white shirt reflects light in the late afternoon sun that still heats the air, even under the shade of a cherry tree. "This heat," he announces, wiping the back of his hand under his chin and behind his head on his neck. "I've had enough of this."

Maggie shifts to a seated position, pulls the skirt of her blue dress up over her knees, runs her hands over her stockinged calves, and stretches her feet out, wiggling the toes. She pats the blanket beside her. "Come sit," she tells him. "We'll feel cooler if we sit. Just walking from the car has made us hot."

Jeremy turns and looks back toward the museum, its ochre walls rising above the greenery that is carefully groomed down to the Schuylkill. A slight breeze hits his face as he undoes the cuffs of his shirt and begins to roll them up over his forearms. He runs his fingers through the thinning hair at his temple, leaving sprigs of it sticking into the air.

"Come sit," she repeats, patting the blanket again. "And tell me, what'd you think of the show?"

Jeremy sits beside her on the blanket, lays back onto the ground, rests his arms under his head, and closes his eyes. "You did a good job, Maggie." Before he can go on, Maggie interrupts him.

"You think I had the sea series in the right place? I mean, for lighting? Because they were hard, since the artist requested —"

"Maggie, it was right. Everything you did for that show was right. You could see all the big shots were there, and Morris said it was the best show you've done. Right?"

Maggie bites her lower lip, turns to look at Jeremy's damp face, his eyes still closed. She lies on the ground beside him, keeps her eyes open to peer through the branches, the sky pale blue, in the spaces between the leaves. She turns her head, sees pink in the sky over the museum, rolls to her side. She touches the skin on his face, touches his shoulder, feels the wet underneath the cotton, seeping through. "Well, it was nice of you to come. I mean, I'm glad you were there."

Jeremy's black eyes flash open.

Maggie waits, then repeats herself. "Yes, I'm glad you were there."

Jeremy reaches a hand over to her arm, strokes it. But his eyes waver, won't look directly at her. "That's what I mean."

Maggie's eyebrows raise. She lifts up her head, leans on her elbow. "What do you mean, that's what you mean?"

"It's what I was saying this morning." Maggie remembers breakfast, trying to pry open an English muffin while Jeremy berated her. "This is a perfect example," he continues. Maggie remembers continuing to toast the muffin while he talked, and she buttered it thickly and spread it with strawberry jam while his words came at her in a storm. "It's like your grand-mother's funeral." Maggie sits up. Is he going to bring that up again? "You were glad," and the word *glad* comes from somewhere in the back of his throat instead of from his lips, "that I accompanied you, you used the word *accompanied*, to your grandmother's funeral."

"You don't like the way I speak?"

Jeremy takes her hand, turns it over, rubs her skin with his fingers. "You know that's not what I'm saying. It's that I don't want to feel I've done you a favor. I —"

Maggie pulls her hand away, lays her arm over her face so that the flesh of her forearm covers her eyes. "But did you like the show?"

Jeremy pushes her arm from her face. "Would you stop for once? For once, will you just listen to what I'm saying? The words. Will you listen to the words?" His eyes roll skyward when he sees that look on her face, her lips set, her eyes like blue stones.

Maggie stands up, walks out from under the tree. "I really want to have my own show." Her voice gets harder, yet littler. She looks to the river, sees a crew team out from one of the houses. There are three people standing on the float nearby, dressed and ready for rowing, she thinks.

"Maggie, I know you do. And you will. Someday," he adds. "And I shouldn't have brought this up again today. But I hate the way you leave things —"

"And you don't like the way I say 'I appreciate,' or 'I'm glad.' " Her eyes continue watching the rowers. "I understand. I will never use those words again, if that's what you want, if —"

"Okay, let's stop this. We're not getting anywhere." He rises from the blanket, folds it in half, and again in half, and again, until it is small enough to fit back in its case. He approaches Maggie from the side, looks at the hair that falls from the twist down her neck. He touches the hairs, pulls at them. "I like this little grass here at the back of your neck."

Maggie smiles at him, but inside she is jittery. Inside she

feels murky. She cannot understand how they always get to this point. She feels she is trying. Thinks she is sensitive to Jeremy. So why does he always turn on her like this?

"It's been a long week," he says.

"But things went well today, don't you think?" She wants him to talk more about the show. She wants to hear specific things he thinks, things he noticed. Instead, he suggests they go back to the car, go out for dinner.

"Maybe Chinese," he suggests.

He is missing the point, she thinks.

On the way to the car, she suggests they go inside the museum. "I want to see the tapestries. On the walls at the top of the stairs."

"You always want to see those tapestries," as he looks at her, searches for a clue.

They deposit the blanket in the trunk of the car and walk up the long set of steps to the front entrance, under the columns that are as wide around as several hundred-year-old pine trees put together.

Inside Maggie listens to the echo of their steps as they climb the stone stairs to the second floor. As they turn on the landing and head up to the second floor, she pauses, wraps her hands around the railing. Her face smoothes as she looks up.

"What is it you love?" Jeremy whispers behind her. He looks up at the tapestries. "They seem so dark to me. No color."

When Maggie looks at them, however, she is moved to some emotion she can't identify. Yet she knows she must continue to return to them, to stare at the colors, at the weave, at the intricacies, at the totality of each piece, at the magnitude of happenings in each piece. She prefers the one to the right. She likes the focus on nature, the castle on a hill in the distance, and the main figures alive in the woods, a stream rippling over the ruts and rises, and she fancies she can hear the water, can hear the rush of its force as it makes its way through the valley. She likes the birds in the trees.

"See that bird," and she points a finger. "The one there above the tree, the one that is more blue than the other, perhaps because it is in flight."

"It's a pretty faint blue," he responds, watching Maggie. He pulls again at the hairs at her neck.

Maggie notices a road, or perhaps it is a path, that winds behind the trees, through the valley, up to the castle. "Do you see that road?" she asks, pointing.

Jeremy nods.

"I never saw that road before," she tells him.

"Neither did I."

She looks into his eyes. She smiles. "Yeah, but I've studied these tapestries for years." And she turns to look back at the masterpiece on the wall.

"You probably saw it, but didn't think about it," he says.

"I guess not." She is thinking about the drive she will take with her mother, the days she plans to spend with her at the lake, wonders how she will tell Jeremy, knows it will cause a problem.

"You want to sit over there?" he asks, holding his hand in the direction of a stone bench in the upper hall.

From there, Maggie looks up at the tapestries by leaning her head back against the wall. Jeremy looks out across the space over the stairs, up to the ceiling. "Can you imagine the forces it took to construct this building, the engineering, the vision —"

Maggie wants to tell Jeremy about the trip, but she likes the peace of the moment, likes sitting there by his side near the tapestries she has come to love. It reminds her of the times when she was just a girl and her grandfather would take her and her brother into New York to the Metropolitan. It never mattered if there was a new exhibit, or an exhibit he wanted to see, because she and Evan always headed to the second floor to walk along the walls covered with the medieval work. There was something about the way the figures were portrayed, so dramatically, yet their faces plain and unemotional, that fascinated Maggie and gave rise to games for her and Evan about the happenings in the paintings. When she first moved to Philadelphia to go to art school, she began visiting the art museum every week, searching out the areas where the medieval work was shown. She especially liked the tapestries, often sketched here, or set up her work outside along the river.

She remembers the day Jeremy came upon her, how he planted himself next to a tree and watched her sketch from behind. She reminds him of that. "I'd never had anyone watch me paint before."

"I liked to watch your brushstroke. I still do. It's always sure. And I like your subjects. Nature, birds, water."

It is not until a week later that she tells Jeremy about the trip with her mother. She waits until one morning at breakfast, after Jeremy has stayed the night, when she knows the time constraints will not allow much discussion.

"Want some eggs?" she asks as she pulls the bread out and drops two pieces in the toaster. She does not start to toast them, waits to see if Jeremy wants eggs.

"Yeah, sure." He opens the back door, bends down to pick up the newspaper and returns to the table. "I've got one hell of a day ahead. You shouldn't plan on me for dinner." He turns to the second section, flips a couple of pages. Maggie is relieved, knows she will not have to talk to him that evening.

"Jeremy," she says minutes later when she places a plate with two fried eggs in front of him. "I've been meaning to tell you that I'm going to the lake, that I decided to go to Land's End. With Mother."

Jeremy holds the paper firmly in his hands. He lays it down on the table. He brings a hand to his lips, rubs his chin. He shakes his head. "I don't understand." He looks at her face, at her brown eyes, her hair sloping onto one cheek as she cocks her head at him. "I don't understand *you*, I should say."

Maggie turns to the stove, cracks an egg for herself into the pan, hears the crackle of egg in butter, frying. "I know you don't think it's a good idea."

"I don't think it's not a good idea. I know it's not a good idea."

The toast pops up. Maggie pulls it out of the toaster, butters it, knowing that Jeremy's eyes are on her. "Start your eggs," she reminds him. "They'll get cold." She looks over at him, his mouth drawn at the edges. "You hate cold eggs."

Jeremy picks up a fork, stabs the two yolks, watches the yellow ooze over the crispy edges of the egg white. "But it's your life. And I can't tell you —"

Maggie feels something inside her give. It starts in her chest, spreads quickly through her limbs. Her hands tremble. She wants to get control of this, does not want to say what she is thinking, does not know what she is thinking, wonders what that feeling is that keeps working its way to her brain.

"I mean, after all you've told me, after all the crap you've told me, I just can't see why —"

"Don't —" she cries at him suddenly, her eyes widening, some place in her chest paining her. "Don't say that."

Jeremy stops. He is caught by her abruptness. "Don't say what?" He sticks a piece of egg in his mouth, chews.

Maggie hears her egg cooking, frying in the pan. The noise nags at her, but she can't get to it. She is not cooking an egg, she is not about to go to work, she is not about to argue with Jeremy. But where am I? she hears her mind ask. "Don't say anything. About it. About my going. Just don't say it." She thinks she will cry, feels it pull at her throat, behind her eyes.

"It's okay, hey —" he starts.

"I said don't." She is standing with her back to the stove. More toast pops up. She sees it. She sees two pieces of toast. She knows she should take them out and spread them with the butter that is on the plate by the toaster. But she doesn't. She turns her face away so she won't have to look at the toast. "You'll never understand," she tells him slowly.

"I don't expect I will," he agrees.

"I mean, you will never understand what it was like."

Jeremy's fork clatters onto his plate. "So why do you want to go there? I mean —"

Maggie moves to the edge of the table, rests her hands on its edge, leans her face near Jeremy's. She brushes her hair out of her face, but it glides back like silky grass around her face. "I want to go," and she hears her voice waver, holds on to the words until she can speak clearly, "I want to go because I want to try, I want to try one more time, I want to see if she'll —" and she stops. She does not complete the sentence that is in her mind. She does not say the words *forgive me*. She does not say them because she can only feel their rightness, but she does not understand them herself. She feels self-indulgent, or self-pitying, she is not sure why. How can I feel, she wonders, that my mother does not love me?

Later in the day, she returns to the museum, sits by the tapestry, walks from side to side in front of it. She stares up at the blue bird above the tree. She follows the road to the castle with her eye.

And she hopes for something different this time.

❦ TWO ❦

THESE MOUNTAINS, Amanda thinks. These are my mountains.

The black Peugeot wheels through the mountain roads on an early October morning. Amanda narrows her grey eyes, taps her black onyx ring against the rim of the steering wheel, presses her foot firmly against the accelerator.

These are my mountains, she thinks again, but the land is dying, growing ancient. She runs her eyes over the slopes of mountains, colors dusty as dusk in the early morning sun.

"Did you say something, Mother?" Maggie asks, her china blue eyes warm, as she widens them to look at Amanda.

"Did I say something? Oh, just about the mountains, how it's like coming home to be on this road."

"It's been too long, for both of us," Maggie offers. "After all these years —"

"All these years?" Amanda repeats. "It's hardly 'all these years,' dear, just eight, and there are reasons, you know there are reasons."

Maggie closes her eyes, hears her own voice when she told her mother that she wanted to come to Land's End. Inside her pockets her fingers play, making lines through the material against her thighs, tiny circles and perfectly shaped hearts.

"I hope we're doing the right thing, Mother," Maggie says, sitting upright.

"Margaret, I told you I wanted to see my father's grave once more before I see my own, and —"

"Mother, you've got to stop this, you're only fifty-eight, you're in good health." Maggie wonders why her mother insists upon such words.

Amanda hunches further over the wheel. The black onyx ring twirls around her finger, rubs against the steering wheel. From beneath her black beret bits of silver hair curl out like tiny fingers. "Dr. Wescott reminded me only last week that the swelling in these joints will last as long as I do. When I ask him what's wrong, he says it's my old age. Old age, Margaret, that's what is wrong with me. And my heart, it has always been weak."

"I don't think he means 'old age' as in 'about to die,' Mother. He's known you for so long. I'll bet he's teasing." Maggie smiles, to hide her irritation.

Amanda ignores her words. "The land looks lonely this time of year," she muses.

"Lonely?" Maggie looks out the window. "It's anything but lonely, Mother, it's warm and safe, it's —"

"It looks lonely to me, Margaret. And at your age, I probably couldn't see it any better than you." Amanda pauses, slows the car. "But we're here, aren't we, and we shall make the best of it."

Maggie consults the map, follows the route lines with a finger. Getting an early start from Willis was a good idea, she thinks, remembering the early morning coffee steaming in her hands, the patch of blue above the roofline of the motel. She knows they won't reach Casco until late in the morning, so that they can wait until they pass the rapids after Casco to have their sandwiches. She knows also that her mother is nervous about being on time; driving in to Chad by the road and saving time will not help her nerves, she thinks.

"I'm going to pour myself some coffee, Mother," Maggie says, reaching to the back seat for the thermos. "Want some? Or some fruit?"

"Not yet, dear," Amanda answers. "Let's drive awhile before we give in to hunger."

Maggie drops the thermos back onto the seat. Okay, she thinks, we'll wait. She knows her mother cannot give in to things. Big things, she thinks, like feelings at Grandmother's funeral. Little things. Like this morning, not caring about how blue the sky was, when Maggie pointed it out as they walked out to the car. Maybe she does not even hear me, I am never sure. She tells herself, Mother is too preoccupied, she has too much to be concerned about. Other times, her mind fills with angry words, protestations. Why? she sometimes wants to scream at her mother. Her mind goes back and forth, works the moment. After all, I'm not really needing coffee. And then, but I don't know if that's true.

How can I not know what is true in me? The words translate into an image, an abstract painting she had worked on that summer. The shapes and shades of red swirled on the canvas, the crimson base heightening the darker reds, the black shadows. When Jeremy saw it, his eyes kept blinking. Up close, then from afar. He couldn't verbalize his reaction. She couldn't explain where the painting originated in her mind.

"It has something to do with —" and the sentence hung, unfinished. Moments flashed across her mind, something following a day at Land's End when she and her brother, Evan, had canoed along the shore, something about the way her mother looked when they returned to the shore and found her down by the water's edge, about to go into the lake. Her hands kept smoothing her waist and while Maggie sensed some discomfort on her mother's part about going into the water, she listened to her words, "I don't know why you two waste time in a canoe when you could be swimming." The words confused Maggie, she remembers. What am I supposed to want to do? she remembers wondering. It was that sort of sensation that led to the painting, these years later. And the moment, so small in terms of the scheme of her life, seemed too small to put into words. He would think me silly, she thought as he looked to her for some explanation of the painting.

"Why must I explain it?" she asked him.

"It's not that you must explain it," he told her, his hands in his pockets. "It's just that I'm interested."

Maggie found that hard to believe. She felt Jeremy was trying to embarrass her. *After all this time, he doesn't realize I don't like to explain a painting. He knows I don't like to argue. With Jeremy, or anyone.* When he pressed her about marriage in July, she remembers walking around the apartment with him trailing behind her, his voice getting louder, hostile, until she headed for the door and kept going. He was right behind her. "Don't do this," he pleaded, but she kept on going. She wouldn't argue.

Maggie sleeps, her head bent forward. Her chestnut hair falls into her face; with each breath, she pulls a piece of hair into her mouth, and then as she exhales, she pushes it out. Amanda reaches over, pulls the strand back behind her ear. It slides back in front of her face.

Just like silk, Amanda thinks, and she remembers her father saying that about Maggie's hair. He used to rest his hand against the back of her head, she remembers, run a single finger through her bangs, tell her how silky it was. Amanda remembers the last time she touched Maggie's hair. It was before Evan's accident, so Maggie must have been nine years old, she thinks. It was also the time she stopped calling her daughter Maggie. "Margaret suits your plain face better," she once said, and she remembers Henry saying that it was no way to speak to their daughter. "Margaret doesn't feel like my daughter," she used to tell him.

"But Evan feels like your son?" he asked.

"Of course," she said.

He still feels like my son, though he's been dead eight years, she thinks, and she looks at Maggie and feels a sour distaste.

The Peugeot climbs, up through the mountains, the road shadowed with billowing red-leafed branches, the sun still on the other side of the peak. When the car reaches a crest, Amanda pulls off to the right to see the view from a turnoff, stopping the car near a row of grey granite slabs that border the tarred area. Amanda gazes with watery eyes at the string of lakes that lie off to the north and through the valley, small ponds like dots on the landscape, the lakes like shiny pieces of mirror laid flat against the golden autumn land. On the horizon the mountains frame the valley and the morning sun casts its light against their slopes. Patches of red and orange show in the lowlands like flame against the deep forest green, now black in the shadowed places higher up.

In my day, Amanda thinks, it took three days to make this trip to these lakes. She remembers her father describing the journey it was for him as a boy; sometimes his family came by train, switching in Boston, then Portsmouth, and then at Concord. At Willis they followed the river by car, and it took most of a day to get through the mountains to Carter Lake, near the Canadian border. It was a journey to the end of the land, he told her, and she remembers him explaining that was how the house was named Land's End. The trip across the wide expanse of the lake was the final part, and Amanda wonders what he would say if he knew she would drive in through Chad.

Leaving the motor running, Amanda leans back in her seat, realizes this is the place her family often stopped because it gives the first view of the lakes. One time her father got out of the car, she remembers, to stretch and survey the landscape, while her mother waited in the car, claiming she didn't want to waste the time of getting out of the car when she could see perfectly well from where she was. She said it was better to push on, so as not to be late for the boat. Father ignored her. "The boat can wait," he would say, "after all, it's our boat."

As a girl Amanda was not sure whether to wait in the car with her mother or to join her brothers Michael and Will, when they got out of the car with Father. She often waited a few minutes with Mother, listening to her silence, then would leave, saying she would gather the others. Then she would stand out on the edge with them.

Amanda shuts off the car and looks at her sleeping daughter. She pushes open the door on her side, slides her legs out so that her feet rest on the ground. She rubs her knees slowly and in circles, easing the stiffness. She recalls the way her father stood at the edge, one foot raised onto a granite slab, his hands pressed into his hips, his head thrust back.

"See that line of mountains against the sky," Father said, a finger pointing from his outstretched arm, as if he had never said those words before. He turned to see if his children were looking in the direction he pointed. "Stockton is the one all the way to the north, the low flat one, a sleeping bear, some say. Behind Stockton and to the left you can see Mount Speck. It's the one with the crooked line along the south front. I climbed that for the first time when I was about your age, Will, just a boy, I was."

Amanda looked at the spider lines around her father's eyes, lines that blackened when he smiled, his eyes turning blue as the night sky. His hand remained outstretched, unwavering.

"Next to Speck is the two-humped Wisdom Peak, the one we'll hike this summer. We'll follow the river at its base down to the rapids," and with his finger he pointed the route.

Michael and Will stared at the line of mountains. Amanda watched her father. She heard her mother call from the car, her voice ringing, willowy with impatience.

"In a minute, Eleanor, we're looking at the mountains," he called without turning his head, letting the wind carry his words back to the car. "Mount Eden is the tallest one in the range, though. See it?" he asked, looking at the boys, who dangled their legs over the edge of ground and stared with one eye at the horizon. "In the early part of August, the moon rises right out of that mountain, as if the mountain held it there all day, waiting to let it go."

Amanda swallowed, and practiced what she wanted to say in her mind. "Maybe this year I could go with you, Father, when you take Will and Michael up Wisdom Peak," she put the words out loud.

Her father did not answer, and the voice of her mother came from the car.

"Amanda, go back to your mother," he said. "Tell her we're just looking at the mountains."

Amanda looked at her brothers, who sat together on the granite ledge. They were quiet, just staring out at the land. Like they own it, she thought. Like it's more theirs than it is mine. She looked at her father, who had pulled out a pipe and was filling it with tobacco from the pouch he always carried in his jacket pocket. She watched the lines around his eyes tighten as he became aware of her eyes on him, and she waited, feeling his tension, until he said again, "Go back to your mother, Amanda," and he kept his eyes on the pipe, wrapping up the pouch carefully.

Amanda waited, but he did not turn her way.

Amanda looks at the line of mountains, she hears her father's voice, she can see her brothers, but her heart begins to race, the palpitations rising in force, and soon, the beating reaches her head, a throbbing kind of rhythm.

"Mother," calls Maggie from the car, "shall I bring the thermos out, shall we have some coffee?"

When Amanda turns, she feels surprise that it is Maggie and not her mother, calling from the car. She nods her head, yes, and quickly turns her eyes out toward the mountains.

As Maggie sets the thermos on a rock, she feels the wind against her face. It is cool and refreshing, she thinks, and she rises, stretches first one arm and then the other into the air. "I'm stiff," she explains to Amanda, "from sleeping in the car." She pulls up the collar on her coat, turns her face to feel the sun. Then she stares at her mother's face, watches her sip from a mug, the steam swirling away into the wind.

"You must have wonderful memories, Mother, about all your summers here. You stayed all through the summer, didn't you?"

"All through the summer?" she repeats. "Yes, dear, we generally came the end of June and stayed through September. Father liked to hunt birds in the fall." Amanda shivers. She swallows the coffee in her mug, places it on the ground.

"What did you do about school?" Maggie asks.

"About school?" Amanda looks at the ring on her finger, holds her hands together. "What do you mean?"

"Well, if you stayed up here through September, what did you do about school for that month?"

"About school?" She nods her head. "In September, Mother tutored me. In literature and French, anyway. She could speak French beautifully, from those years she lived in France as a child." Amanda smiles.

Maggie studies her mother's profile. The pointed chin gets thinner as she gets older, Maggie thinks. But the lines of her forehead and nose are classic. I should try to sketch her at the lake, she realizes.

"One September," Amanda offers, "Father took the boys and me for a hike up Wisdom Peak. I guess it was the bird hunting he was most interested in. I'd forgotten all about that." Her voice trails off.

"Which one is Wisdom Peak?" Maggie asks.

"Which one? Why, Margaret, it's the two-humped one, there to the north, next to Mount Speck — do you see Mount Speck?" and she points her finger.

"Yes, I see that, so Wisdom Peak is the one to the left, with the two humps?" Maggie asks, and she watches her mother for a reply.

"Yes. That's the one we climbed together. Then we took canoes down the river that winds around its base. And we ended up at the rapids. It was the fall when I was fourteen, just a girl. I was so young, so —" and her eyes focus on Maggie. "Yes, the rapids," she says, "where we can stop for sandwiches." Amanda pulls her eyelids down over her eyes. She twirls the ring on her finger.

"It must have been quite a hike, just you and your father, and Uncle Michael and Uncle Will, it must —"

"It's time to head off, Margaret," Amanda says as she rises, "if we want to get to the rapids by noon." Amanda's grey eyes widen, turn a softer silver as she shifts her gaze out over the view, and her eyes narrow against the wind or in some thought. She points a finger at Mount Eden. "In early August, when the moon rises," her voice lilts, "it comes right up out of Mount Eden, as if the mountain had held it there all day." The fingers of her left hand pass lightly over her lips, reach up to tuck the hair under the rim of the beret. "Let's be off, though. We don't want to be late."

Maggie feels the sun still on her face. Maybe we'll have some good weather, she thinks, as she collects the two cups and stacks them onto the thermos. Maybe we'll have an Indian summer, she thinks, as she looks out at the mountains, tries to remember which one is Mount Speck, and turns to follow Amanda to the car.

Maggie drives now. "What do you think, Mother, might we have Indian summer now? The sun feels so warm, I wasn't expecting this." She backs the car away from the granite slabs, looks over her right shoulder out the back window, feels Amanda's eyes on her face.

"Indian summer? Now?" Amanda says, and she smooths her coat over her legs. "Not if you expect it, dear. Or even hope for it. I can guarantee you that, it won't happen."

Maggie smiles, her mouth settling into a natural grin. "That sounds like New England fatalism to me," and she laughs as she pushes the gear into first and heads the Peugeot back onto the road.

"Margaret," and Amanda's voice is lighter than her words, "that's what this life is all about. You must prepare for tragedy, it's the frequent storm that hits us." Amanda straightens out her legs, crosses her feet.

Maggie pushes her hair behind her right ear, leans forward over the wheel and waits. She continues to be confused by these lines of her mother's, these apocalyptic lines about life. She imagines that as a child these kinds of words caused ripples of fear in her stomach, though she cannot remember exactly; she recalls a sense of danger, yes, it was danger, she thinks, about the world outside her home. Yet she knows she has no answer for these words, knows her mother will use her own life as proof.

"It's not just a simple matter of attitude," she once told Jeremy, who insisted that her mother had the wrong approach to life. "It's just the way she is, she's more vulnerable than the rest of us, feels the hurt more." Maggie remembers a flat feeling after saying these words, a sense of untruth about them that she felt in her heart, yet the words echoed from her mind and made her feel that she was unkind to feel such betrayal of her mother.

"Bullshit," was Jeremy's response, and Maggie remembers leaving the room after that, retreating to her sketch pad.

The road is smooth through the mountains, wider than it was the last time Maggie came to the lake. The dark pine woods are cut back away from the edge of the road as it stretches over the mountains and into the valley. There are no houses in the high lands, just woods. But as the car begins the descent to the valley, Maggie recognizes clusters of farmhouses, and as the road reaches the river that leads to Casco, the land near the road is cut and divided among the farms.

The road follows the river closely through this area. She notices a series of orchards along the water's edge, orchards that must once have been rich with apples and pears, but the trees stand now twisted and bent from years of weathering the north wind. Maggie blinks her eyes, holds the image in her mind, sees the rows of leaning gnarled trunks, the jointed branches, the roots buckling up through the earth. She knows she can sketch from memory, and she works to see as many details as possible in her mind.

Maggie thinks of the painting of the cherry tree that hangs

in her bedroom. She remembers the series of sketches and paintings that she did on the banks of the Schuylkill River when she met Jeremy. She developed the skill of remembering the details that spring. So many people had painted the scenes along that river, she once thought, that their paintings hung between the trees she sketched and her own vision of them. So she had to see the trees with her own eyes, learn to hold the particulars, learn to recreate what she saw through her own skill. Jeremy often sat and watched her paint. "It doesn't make you self-conscious?" he asked. "Not at all," she answered.

Maggie glances at Amanda, notices how small she is, curled stiffly asleep against the window, her shoulders angled. Her hands are folded in her lap, the fingers curled together like claws, and Maggie thinks of the twisted limbs on the trees in the orchards. On an impulse Maggie reaches over to touch her mother's hands. She feels the dryness of her skin. She tries to uncurl the fingers, to ease the tightness, feels frightened by their image.

Amanda's hands clench and she draws them to her chest. "What are you doing?" she snaps, sits up.

Maggie pulls her hand away, directs her attention back to the road. "I'm sorry, Mother, I was just trying to —"

"Well, don't. Don't try to do anything but keep your eyes on the road. And don't touch me like that when I'm sleeping. I don't like it." She crosses her arms, tucks her hands in against her sides, leans her head against the window.

Maggie feels small, instead of insulted, at this reprimand. She is used to this, to feeling small, and she does not realize that she should combat the feeling, that she doesn't need the child in her to take in such rejection, but she is so used to it that it doesn't feel like rejection. It is as if she has done something wrong. She remembers how different it felt to be with her grandfather, to feel important with him. At the lake, he often relied on her to walk with him over to Chad and along the trails to the west arm, where they would rise onto a ridge where blueberries grew thickly in July and August, and to a pond where the trout and bass fishing was always fruitful.

"Take my finger," he used to say as they headed down the steps of Land's End and he extended his littlest finger for her to clasp. Maggie can remember the dry feeling of his hand as her fingers wrapped around his finger, and there was something in that contact that made her trust him, with her life, even, she once told Evan. "It's like he won't let me hurt him," and he nodded, knew just what she meant.

When she complained to Jeremy once that her mother never touched her, he just shook his head, told her it didn't surprise him. "She's cold, Maggie," but Maggie couldn't see it that way, couldn't allow herself to think the word *cold* in terms of her mother. "It's not that," she told him, but she couldn't explain just what it was.

In the distance against the far side of the valley, Maggie sees the white spire of Casco's church above the low tree line. She notices the rooftops of the houses in the town, forming a continuous line from the church. Golden maple trees line the river on this side of the town, leading up to and encircling the church that rests like a fortress to the town.

The brown fields that line the roads have been harvested. Dry cornstalks stand withered, ready to fall with further frosts. Once black cows grazed in these fields, she thinks, and she sees the summer green and the black cow splotches in her mind.

She looks at Amanda's sleeping face, sees the lines around her eyes and the single indentation between her eyebrows. Amanda does not like that line, explains it away by saying it is a family trait, and she often reminds herself that her father had the same line between his brows. Maggie can see Grandfather pressing a finger against that line when he was tired. He would close his eyes, lean his head forward, and press solidly with just one finger against it. Then he would rub it, pushing upward against his forehead. Amanda never touches that line, keeps her hands away from her eyes.

"Where'd you get that crack in your face?" Maggie remembers Evan asking Grandfather once. She can see Evan's wide blue eyes looking out from under his yellow bangs when he asked that of his grandfather, who laughed a little and looked strangely grateful for the question.

The car passes beneath the maples. Ahead Maggie sees the full lines of the church, the windows on its sides arching toward the roof. The grounds around the church are well cared for, and the maples are carefully spaced across the front, their leaves a bright orange and red in the sun. Passing by on the road into the town, Maggie sees a young boy, maybe nine or ten, swinging from one of the maple trees behind the church. He pulls his legs up and holds to the branch with his feet. Then he lets go his arms and hangs there, upside down; his cap falls off onto the ground, and just before the car passes the church, Maggie can see his blond hair hanging free.

Evan used to swing like that from the large beech tree that stood beside the house on Wentworth Street, Maggie thinks. She can see his hair hanging down in just the same way. Once he carved his initials in that tree, on the side facing the road, so people driving by could see them and know that was his tree, he explained to Maggie. Evan had that blond hair that everyone noticed, the blue eyes shaded. He had a wiry frame. Standing still, when he was grown, you couldn't tell his strength. But as soon as he did anything, as soon as he moved a muscle, his body became a tight line of energy, and his eyes steamed with the tension. As a boy, he was always moving. Climbing, running, hanging from trees. He couldn't sit still for long. But later, he slowed down. The tension was still there, but it didn't come out as much.

The sign for Belmont's filling station lies ahead on the road. Same old sign, she thinks. Same old place, Maggie notices, as she pulls the car in and stops by the single pump. A young man with a cigarette hanging from dry lips wipes his hands on a greasy rag as he approaches her. Maggie rolls down the window, feels the cool air, asks him to fill the tank.

Amanda does not move. Her head rests against the window, her hands still tucked around her sides.

Maggie feels the warm afternoon sun on her face. She

leans closer to the open window and closes her eyes, listens to the sound of the pump, the fresh smell of gasoline drifting into the car.

Maybe you were right about the land, Maggie thinks. For you, anyway, it must be lonely. We'll stop on the other side of town, near the rapids. Maybe you'll feel better when you see the water and remember the hike with your brothers. Maybe that's what you need. To be closer to all of them. To this land.

Maggie opens her eyes, glances at her mother, who sits still silent in her seat, her face placid, but for the deep line between her brows. Maggie wishes she could speak those words to her mother. She says them again to herself, practices; but she knows she will say nothing, knows she will be silent.

❧ THREE ❧

AMANDA opens one eye just a crack. Belmont's, she thinks. Casco. She closes the eye and listens to Maggie talk to the attendant. A young fellow, she thinks, from the sound of his voice.

She remembers Willie Belmont, the old man who ran the place when she was a girl. "Willie," Father would call out each year when they stopped for a fill-up, and Willie would wave an arm.

"How are you, sir," he would call back as he approached the car. Willie knew the Elliott children by name, and he would ask, "How are you, Will, and Michael, and little Miss Amanda?"

Mother didn't care for his familiar ways, she would whisper to Father under her breath, words Amanda could not hear from the back seat, but Father would always draw his head back and stare at her, and he would have words like "For God's sake, Eleanor," to say to her. Then he would get out of the car, and Amanda would see the hood go up, and he and Willie would be under the hood, and from inside the car they could hear laughter and Father's even voice.

"Let's not dawdle," Eleanor would call from the car, her voice shiny and clear as glass, shattering the silence in the car. Father would peer from under the hood, his face cloudy, his blue eyes darkening, and he'd wave a hand at his family and return to the motor. Mother's head never moved as she stared forward and hummed non-tunes.

Amanda hears the attendant ask Maggie if she wants the oil checked.

"No, thanks, I think we're all set," and she turns the key, and the Peugeot starts up.

As the car pulls forward, Amanda peers out from a crack once more. She sees the attendant head back into the garage where a light blue car waits, its motor still running, black fumes billowing from the exhaust. She notices a telephone booth beside the building, a new addition, she thinks. A young woman stands in the booth, the phone cradled to her ear, her mouth working with words. She wears a pink parka.

Amanda knows the car will follow the road through the town, then they will turn right and pick up Route 28, the last long stretch through the mountains and around to the lake. Amanda thinks about how they will take the road in to the lake now. She knows it has been there all along, but since her family never used it, it did not really exist for her. Father used to say, "The only way to Land's End is over the lake, it's the only way to get there," and Amanda feels a twist in her heart as she tries to imagine driving in.

"Mother," Maggie says, "we're almost at the rapids; we can stop here and have those sandwiches."

Amanda does not answer.

Maggie feels irritation rising, her shoulders tensing. "Mother," she repeats, "we're almost at the rapids, we can —"

"I heard you," Amanda answers, her eyes closed, and then, "don't you need your glasses to drive, Margaret?"

Maggie turns quickly, sees her mother's closed eyes, looks back at the road. "Well, I do, and I don't. I left them at home, but I don't need them so much for driving, more for —"

"I can drive after we stop," Amanda tells her.

"No, Mother, I think you should just enjoy this scenery."

Amanda opens her eyes, sits upright, looks out the side

window. "It doesn't look much different, I must say. More grown up in places, the woods filling in."

"I guess the land stays pretty much the same."

"This view here," Amanda starts and waves a hand toward the lake that lies at the foot of the mountain they now descend, "these mountains and lakes, I've looked at them many times from right here, right on this road, as we head down to the rapids. And I've seen it in every season, and it doesn't change much."

"You were here in the winter?" Maggie asks. "I didn't know that. When? Was that when you were a girl?" She wants to hear more.

Amanda removes her beret and pats her hair on top of her head, runs her fingers through the sides. She brushes the lint from the beret, rubbing her hand lightly over the wool, picking a few pieces of dust off with her fingers. Replacing the beret, she tucks her curls inside it. "Not when I was a girl, Margaret, no. That was just for the men. Your uncles went up every winter with my father, usually in late February, snowshoed in from the west, over this direction somewhere, they followed a woods road in. But no, as a girl, I was not allowed."

"When was it, then?"

"When was it?" Amanda repeats. "It was the winter after your father and I were married. Father thought Henry should see the place under snow. The lake, that is. And Henry insisted upon my joining them, said he wanted to see the place for the first time with me along."

"Did you snowshoe in from over this way, from the west? Where did you stay?"

"As a girl it wasn't proper for me to go off with my brothers, and Father thought I wouldn't hold up well, and of course, Mother worried about my heart."

Maggie feels a sinking in her chest. She doesn't want to hear about her mother's heart. She has heard about it for too long. And in too many ways. Jeremy has told her she is guilty of complicity, and Maggie remembers how he explained that. "Sure," he told her, "you let her get away with it."

Maggie looks over at her mother, sees her greying eyes as they widen in a girlish twinkle. Is that what I do? Maggie wonders. Comply with her? "You must have been quite an adventurer," she tells Amanda, "wanting to do such things." Already she knows she has skirted the issue.

"Well, I wanted to go where Father went. And Michael and Will."

The road leads down a steep incline. Shadows from the trees lie in patches on the road's surface. The road narrows as it leaves the open high land. Here the foliage is brilliant. The yellow birches catch the sunlight, the red maples glisten.

"Have you ever seen such colors?" Maggie asks. "I've never seen anything like it, the world is brighter here in the mountains, isn't it, the lakes just reflect the light of the sun." She smiles with warmth and satisfaction, turns her smile to her mother. "I'm so glad we're here, Mother."

Amanda looks out of the window. "Yes, it is pleasant, isn't it."

"We'll stop at the foot of the hill, shall we? I'm hungry, we can eat those sandwiches, and walk a little by the rapids. It's beautiful here, just beautiful."

"No, it just wasn't proper for me to leave Mother and go traipsing off in the woods." Amanda puts her hand on the dashboard, leans forward to look out the window at the sky. "Except that once. And never again, after that."

"During the winter?"

"No, no, not during the winter. No, the time I mentioned back there," and she waves a hand, "when Father took us up Wisdom Peak, and we canoed down around the river to the rapids."

"What time of year was it?"

"What time of year?" Amanda rolls the onyx around her finger, presses a thumb against the stone. "It was this time of year. Early autumn. October."

"And you were fourteen?" Maggie tries to imagine Amanda at fourteen. She doesn't remember seeing photos of her as a girl, guesses at her beauty.

"Fourteen?" Amanda sees the bridge that crosses the rapids. "There we are, Margaret. The rapids are there, ahead. Pull over on the other side of the bridge."

Maggie slows the car as she crosses the bridge. It isn't as high a bridge as she remembers, the rapids are less choppy. She remembers her mother saying something about the current, or the river, about the danger, Maggie cannot remember exactly, but she realizes it formed a picture in her mind.

Maggie reaches into the back seat for the basket of sandwiches as Amanda opens the door and climbs out of the car. The early afternoon sun is still warm on Amanda's face. Spray from the river reaches into the air and touches them as they step carefully from the roadside down a slight incline to a smooth surface of rock near the water's edge.

"You can never be too careful on this river," Amanda says, planting her feet together on the rock, gazing down at the moving water.

That's it, Maggie remembers. That's what she used to say, as we passed over this bridge each year. In that thin glassy voice.

Amanda sits down on a rock. She looks back up the river to a calm, smooth piece of water. But here, the water swirls, catching branches, and rising up and over chunks and edges of rocks. Here the water whirls into foams of white, and the sense of speed, the water rushing, pushing, powerful, holds Amanda's attention.

"You can never be too careful on this river," she repeats, and her eyes reflect the current, a swirling silver. The line between her brows deepens and darkens. She watches the river.

And Maggie watches Amanda. She watches her head turn back and forth as her eyes follow the river downstream and then back up to watch it move downstream again. Maggie thinks that Amanda has looked much the same for as long as she has known her, perhaps because her hair has been silver for that long, giving her an older appearance. There were some changes along the way, she thinks, remembering how after Evan's death the skin on Amanda's face became almost transparent, as if she could see through the skin if she got close enough to her mother, and Maggie often imagined seeing grey swirling things there under the skin, in the flesh. Maggie wonders now if it was not so much that her mother changed but that Maggie began to look at her mother with a different eye, an eye that sometimes saw into Amanda with an acute perception and at other times could not see those things at all.

For instance, as she hears Amanda say the words "You can never be too careful on this river," Maggie cannot understand. She cannot see into her mother at all. She can only recall hearing those words frequently, and she can recall the moments with clarity. A sick feeling echoes through her stomach when she remembers the time her grandfather took her for a long ride in the rowboat across the lake to a point of land that was covered with rocks, bereft of trees because of the north wind, he had explained to her. On the south side of the point, they walked along a beach, shoeless, their bare feet squishing into the grainy sand that was cold from a sunless morning. Maggie followed her grandfather into the woods on a trail that led along a narrow stream until he stopped, his hand reaching behind him for her. As he stooped down, and before Maggie could ask him what he was doing, a movement farther up the stream caught her eye. It was in the midst of a reedy, marshy patch that a young moose angled his lanky frame slowly along the water's edge, his enormous head splashing the water, raising, green long stems of grass hanging from his jaw, his brown shoulders ragged and fuzzy as a rug. Maggie squatted behind her grandfather, leaned onto one knee so she could see over his back, and waited for his cue. She kept her eyes firmly on the moose, who was some thirty feet away, and though she knew her grandfather would protect her, she felt her mouth get dry so that her tongue seemed to take up too much space, and she felt her thigh wobble with the tension of leaning on her knee for so long, but there was nothing that would have caused her to move until Grandfather told her to. It was those unspoken requests of his that she always followed to the letter, and though he never said it directly, she could tell he was proud of how she handled these situations. For there were other such situations, where she had to sense from him what it was she should do, and it never failed to work. Later, when they returned to the rowboat and finally spoke about the wonder of coming upon a moose at eleven o'clock in the morning (for he told her that was unusual, that to find a moose feeding so late in the morning was something close to a miracle, and she believed he was right, that she had indeed witnessed a miracle), she listened to him tell her about the life of a moose in these parts, how hard the winters were, how scarce the food, how thin was the population, and he told her they surely had been blessed and Maggie felt the feeling of being blessed until they arrived back at Land's End to an empty house so they could not immediately share their good fortune. There were two bowls of cold tomato soup set at their places on the table. The other place mats had been returned to the drawer in the sideboard, but theirs awaited them with a note written in careful script by Amanda. "Gone to the Barnes' for games. Too bad you missed it. Hope there is no danger." Maggie remembers feeling a stab in her heart at those words. She remembers her grandfather taking the note and folding it in half and then again in half, and again, until it was the size of a small pillbox, and then he tossed it in the coals and it sizzled for several seconds before a ribbon of flame lit up. Her grandfather added more kindling, some small logs, and then he blew gently into the fireplace and watched it grow. They sat together on the bench before the fireplace and Grandfather spoke occasionally, returning to the moose, while Maggie listened. She had trouble paying attention, she remembers, she half-listened to his words while the other half of her wondered what her mother would say when she returned. Would she speak about the danger she referred to? Would it turn out that Grandfather had done something bad? Or that she had? It was not until that night at bedtime, not until Amanda came to the door where she and Evan shared a room, that she told Maggie those words, "You can never be too careful on this lake." And later, when Maggie asked Evan what she meant, he told her it was nothing, that she shouldn't worry, that it was just their mother being queer about stuff, but Maggie did worry, she did wonder, and the feeling of doubt about what she had done with her grandfather stayed with her.

For why would a mother, she would ask herself, why would a mother frighten her own child?

And she still wonders, Why would a mother do that? Jeremy once told her not to wonder, that it was obvious. Her mother would frighten any child. "But why?" she asked him.

"She doesn't know the difference between fear and caution, between justice and integrity."

Maggie hated it when Jeremy talked in those terms. She could not pursue such a discussion, would try to change the subject, or just leave the room, shut him out.

Maggie passes a sandwich to her mother, watches Amanda reach out a hand to take it. Mothers protect their children, she tells herself. They do not frighten their children. She watches Amanda unwrap the wax paper, smooth it out, rest the sandwich on the paper.

Maggie watches her mother's silver eyes watch the river.

And she wonders, What are these dangers?

It was finally morning.

Amanda pulled the window shade aside to see the day's first light graze in the woods, shadows forming in the spaces between the trees. She was awake before the others, as she often was; she did not sleep soundly at the lake, her ears sensitive to the life sounds in the night woods. That night she had dozed off and on between the scurrying of squirrels across the roof, the single hoot of an owl, the scratching of mice in the walls. She lay awake in the dark, watching the line of light from the moon, a line that crept along the floor as the moon fell, replaced by the dim grey of early dawn.

In the time before the sun rose, when the moonlight was gone, she pulled her woolen pants over shivering legs, leaving her pink flannel nightgown on as well. In the dimness she made her way to the kitchen to build up a fire. She watched the cracks in the wood stove brighten as the fire took hold, and she held her hands over the surface to warm them. Then she filled the kettle and placed it at the back of the stove to heat for her father's morning coffee.

It is a perfect morning, Amanda thought as she gazed at the tree line through the window, stared at the trunks of trees that stood singly between the house and the woods.

She noticed the food that had been left out the night before for the men to have for breakfast before their hike up Wisdom Peak. There was a pan of cornbread covered with a linen towel, a bowl of fresh applesauce with dots of nutmeg sprinkled on top, and a tin of sausage, Father's favorite. Lindy is always ready, Amanda thought as she pulled down a pan for the sausage and laid it on the shelf by the stove. On the table by the window the equipment for the hike was piled neatly: foodstuff, carefully wrapped and packed into red containers, cooking utensils, clean pressed scarves, and camping gear. The partially packed canvas backpacks lay on the floor by the table, three of them, for Father, Michael, and Will.

The dusty morning light began to brighten as the first sun hit the land. Looking out at the grey scene, Amanda watched the shadows shrink in the woods. She watched the woodshed take shape before her eyes, and above it, she could distinguish the thick mass of tree limbs and leaves, a clear sky above the trees. She listened to the crackling wood in the stove; the flue was open, creating a good draft, and the crackling became more of a roar. As she moved to the stove to adjust the flue, she heard the front door close sharply.

Father is up, Amanda thought. He always gets up and heads to the lake before he does anything else. Often Amanda watched him in the early mornings, standing down on the shore, binoculars usually in hand and raised to his eyes, and he would stay like that, searching the lake with his binoculars for signs of a loon, or a boat, just watching and waiting.

Walking into the living room, Amanda saw the outline of her father still on the porch. She waited near the woodbox and watched him stand first on one end of the porch and then the other. He pulled the binoculars to his eyes and stood still for a few minutes, looking out at the lake as the new morning sun spread across the water. Amanda tiptoed to the front door on stockinged feet, pressed her face against the glass window, felt the lace curtain against her cheek, and the cold of the glass beneath the lace. Though separated by the front door, Amanda felt her father's shivering, a gentle trembling in his chest. His heavy wool shirt hung untucked over his long stick legs. She heard the beating of her own heart mingled with his, a pounding reverberation in her head. She put her hand to her breast, took a deep breath, waited for the sound to die as she watched her father.

From the front bedroom Amanda heard her mother's voice call, "Thomas," and again louder, "Thomas, will you come here?" Her father could not hear the words, stood on the porch, still looking at the lake. Amanda held her breath, hoping her mother would not come out and find her there by the door. She didn't want to be seen watching her father through the window, and she didn't want to be sent back to bed.

From the upstairs loft Amanda heard her brothers' voices, talking low. Sounds of feet against the floor, things shuffling in the room, the creak of springs on a bed, the sliding of a drawer came to her ears. Sunrise was strengthening the light as it filtered through the pale white curtains onto the floor, the walls, the wide padded chairs clustered by the front windows. Looking through the window Amanda watched the grey and pink sky give over to blue as the sun rose from the east across the lake and into the house. Upstairs the voices grew, and Amanda heard Will laugh, and Michael curse in low tones.

Amanda watched her father leave the porch and head down to the lake, swinging the binoculars in his right hand, his left arm loose by his side. He stood by the water's edge in front of the house and looked to the north and then to the south. He raised one foot, rested it against a rock, as he lifted the binoculars to his eyes. Amanda opened the door and moved out onto the porch, felt the crisp morning air on her skin, shivered.

It is a magical morning, she thought, a morning for a miracle. The words just popped into her mind as she watched the sun cast a long shadow against her father. She stared at the black shiny surface of the water. There was a silence in the air, a silence that spread from the lake into the mist and into the air, and she knew her father felt the same silence in his bones.

Amanda saw a slight movement on the lake near the dock, and she watched her father shift his gaze through the binoculars to the same movement. It was a loon, sitting motionless in the water, its head directed toward the shore. And then she heard its call, a low wail that filled the air slowly like the mist. Again the loon called, moved its black head from side to side, slipped its head beneath the surface, then its body, and it was gone, the water glassy where the loon had been.

Father feels alone, Amanda thought.

It was then that he turned. Binoculars lowered, he looked at the house. Amanda felt his eyes on her, saw his stance change, and she was paralyzed. She lifted her arm and waved her hand at him, turning before she could see if he waved back.

The loon called again, and Amanda turned back to see it out beyond a buoy. This time there was a response from a distant loon across the lake, a loon she could not see, but whose call reached her ears. Amanda listened, watched the mist lift from the black water as her father headed up the path to the house, his head raised, peering at the trees and the mountains beyond. His hand shaded his eyes against the low streams of light from the sun as he turned for a final look at the lake, and he kept his hand there as he reached the porch steps.

"Dawn at Carter Lake," he said, folding the strap around the binoculars, "it's a beautiful thing, but there is no need for you to be up now, Amanda."

"I like to see the sun rise, I like to watch the loons this time of day. Like you, Father," Amanda said as she stared off at the mountains.

"I don't watch the loons, Amanda."

"Oh, I thought you had the binoculars, I thought you were —"

"I was listening to and watching the loons," he said and smiled, but he looked at the pillows that leaned against the wall along the bench, and he straightened them with one hand.

"It's a miracle kind of morning, don't you think?" Amanda asked.

"A miracle?" and he turned in her direction and stared at her hands as they twisted a ring round one finger.

"Yes, a miracle, because it's so —" and she looked into his face.

"Time's moving here, Amanda, I must get the boys up." He started for the front door, and as he turned the knob, added, "We have a hike today, you realize."

Amanda stood alone on the porch. She looked at the lake. The mist was nearly risen, and the early blue sky reflected the water. She watched for the loons again, her eyes straining to catch a sign of one, to see the water break, to hear a long call. But the lake's surface remained still, unbroken.

She waited awhile, then turned and headed into the house. Maybe it isn't a day for a miracle, she thought. Maybe it's just another day, like all the others.

It did not turn out to be just another day, like all the others, Amanda thought on the third day of the trip, as she sat at the bow of a canoe with Michael in the stern.

"Stay steady," he yelled at her through the wind, and she felt an ache in her right shoulder as she pulled another stroke with her paddle. I'm doing my best, she thought to herself, but she had spoken those words so many times in the last few days that she hesitated to say them again.

When Lenny, the hired hand, backed out of the trip at the last minute, her father had thought to postpone it since they needed a fourth person. "You can take me," Amanda said at the breakfast table without thinking. Michael and Will had laughed at the idea, and Father had told her it was a tough trip, not a little walk up a mountain.

"I can do it," she answered. "I know I can do it. I'm fourteen years old, after all."

Maybe it was the tone of her voice, she wasn't sure. But after staring out the window from his place at the head of the table, Father pushed his chair back and commanded a silence, which he filled with the words, "How quickly can you be ready?" And he looked Amanda right in the eye, so that her face burned with red and her heart trembled. "We need a fourth," he reminded her.

"Ten minutes," she shot back, her face frozen in a flush. She replaced the piece of cornbread she had just picked up, and she posed on the edge of the chair ready for his answer.

"Ten minutes, then. I'll tell your mother." And he rose from his chair, his cup of coffee jingling in his hand, and wiped his mouth with the red napkin.

Amanda's heart sank at the thought. Mother, she realized, Mother will never let me go. Father sent her with a wave of his hand to her room to get ready, and she listened, as she opened drawers and pulled out extra socks and her heaviest navy sweater, to the voices in the next room, her mother's shrill with resistance, his calm and low, but she could not hear the words. She could not even imagine her father speaking in her defense. What can he be saying? she thought, knowing exactly what her mother's argument would be. It's my heart, Amanda thought, and she placed both hands together and spoke to her heart in a quiet whisper.

All right, heart, this is it. You must be good. No fuss, now, please. Take care of me. For once, take care of me, heart.

"Amanda," she heard Michael yell again from the stern. "Stay steady with your strokes. What are you doing?"

Amanda turned and looked back at Michael. Take care of me, heart, she repeated to herself, and she steadied herself. Michael's green wool jacket was now wet, and his face glistened with droplets of water that sprayed into his eyes and nose and ears. His cap was pulled down low over his forehead, his blue eyes radiating like sapphires. Again he told her to steady her strokes. "We're off balance," she heard him call, and she realized this was the reason they were taking in so many waves.

She spoke again to her heart. No fuss, now, she said to it. More hard strokes, and she could feel the canoe shift, and then instead of fighting directly with the wind and waves, the boat angled them. Looking up, Amanda could see her father's canoe pulled up farther ahead along the shore. She could see Will hunched low in the bow.

The bones in her knees ached from pressing into the floor of the canoe. She shifted her weight a little, trying to lean back against her seat. Ahead, she saw Father wave his paddle in the air, pointing at something in the water, out where she and Michael were. A loon, she thought, maybe a loon is out here riding the waves, warm in his shell of down and feathers. Still paddling, she kept her eyes on the water ahead of them, looking for what he still pointed at with his paddle.

"Can you see anything?" Michael called. "What's he pointing at?"

Amanda shook her head. "I can't see anything," she called back, but as her paddle sank with another stroke into the water, she noticed a tiny patch or a flicker of white as a wave lifted something up higher. "Wait," she said, and she pointed her paddle to the left and lifted herself higher onto her knees. "There is something," she called, "there, over there," and again she saw the spot of white.

Michael directed the canoe toward the object. "Paddle," he yelled. "Harder. Can you see what it is?"

Facing the wind again, their strokes moved them forward slowly. From the shore Father followed their progress. Why didn't he go after it? Amanda wondered. How did he notice it from such a distance?

"Michael, I see it now," she called, "it's some kind of animal, some kind of bird or something," and she paused, struggling to keep an even pace with her paddle. "It's, I think it's —"

"Just ahead." Michael said. "Yeah. I see it."

And then they were beside it, a loon, as Amanda had first pictured, but not a loon riding the waves as she had hoped. It was a dead loon, waterlogged and floating in the current of the waves.

"Michael, it's a loon," Amanda whispered, quivering as she saw the black holes in its dirty white breast, its black and white collar glistening. Its webbed feet floated back and forth, lifeless, and one shiny red eye gazed up, and Amanda wondered how it could be dead if its eye was still open.

"I'll get him," Michael said, and he used his paddle to pull the loon closer to him. Then he leaned over the side, bracing his knees for balance. With a low grunt he lifted the dead bird out of the water and held it, dripping, above the water. With another grunt, Michael hoisted the loon over the side and onto the floor of the canoe.

"He's so big, Michael, look how big he is, I never knew a loon was so big."

They looked at the bird, at its great black wings speckled with white, the white underside of the wing, the cotton white breast dirty and dark with wet.

"What happened, Michael?"

"Shot," he answered. "Someone must have shot him. Could be a day or so ago. But no more. He's waterlogged. But not decomposed, and that happens pretty quick. Let's get going, though. Let's get over where Father is."

"Why didn't Father get him?" Amanda asked.

Michael shrugged and began paddling, brushed at his pants that were wet where the loon had dripped on him.

"How could anyone do that?" Amanda called to him. "Shoot a loon and just leave it. Maybe it wasn't even dead. Do you think it was dead, Michael?"

Again Michael shrugged, a sigh heaving his broad shoulders. "All I know is, it's dead now. Come on, Amanda, keep paddling."

Amanda kept quiet as they headed for the shore, but her mind kept seeing the floating dead loon, the waves lifting it, carrying it, cradling it.

Maybe it's still alive, Amanda thought. She looked back at Michael, whose face showed he had forgotten the loon. His blue eyes are black and shiny in the wind, she thought. They look empty.

And the loon dripped wetness, seeping across the ribs of the canoe, and Amanda prayed for its life and spoke to her heart as they paddled to shore.

Amanda lay under the night sky. Buried in her sleeping bag, she held her body's warmth. A few feet away, the fire burned low, the embers glowing orange, blueing with a breath of wind. She listened to the night sounds; a light wind rustled the trees, and in the distance she heard the low, soothing roar of the river.

Earlier in the evening, after finishing a supper of stew heated over the open fire and the last of the tinned biscuits, the four of them had walked around to the river, Father striding over to the highest point of land that looked out over the rush of water. Swirling patches of white sprayed into the air, and Father held his hands out, palms down, to feel the wet. Farther down, as the river made a turn to the left, the water was smooth and black.

"River's full," Father told them. "We'll move along tomorrow. No worry about that." His chest puffed out with a deep breath.

Michael and Will scrambled over the embankment, sliding down the slick dirt to the sandy shore. Amanda felt the dark woods behind her, turned to see if something was there, but it was only the feeling of something. She watched her brothers at the water's edge as they squatted down, fingering the rocks and tossing them into the river, talking. Then she watched her father, whose head nodded up and down in some random pace, a habit he had developed when he was tense, her mother once explained.

As she lay under the night sky trying to sleep, Amanda saw Father's nodding head again. She opened her eyes, stared down into the dark of her sleeping bag, pushed the flap of the bag down, away from her face. She saw the soft luminescence of the firelight covering the camp, and around the fire she saw the others, wrapped motionless in their sleeping bags. Now the image of the drowned loon lay in her mind along with her father's nodding head. She remembered how little he had said when she and Michael brought the bird to shore in their canoe. The four of them took the time to bury the loon in the woods, and after they filled the dirt in, her father stood long at the grave, looking at the mound of fresh brown soil, his head nodding, his hands limp by his sides.

Michael and Will went back to the canoes to find something to eat, but Amanda stayed with her father as he collected two rocks to lay on top of the new grave.

"It's better this way," he said to the grave.

"Better this way?" Amanda repeated, unsure. What was better? she wondered. But he didn't respond, didn't answer her question until they were back at the canoes.

"This way," he muttered as he pushed her canoe off from the shore, "this way he won't be hunted. He has known what it's like to be watched, his existence is ageless and he knows it. He knows the infiniteness of his soul. But he knows he has been hunted."

The night closed in on Amanda. She saw again the loon floating in the water, bloated, the fluff of its feathers weighted with wet. She saw the loon resting in its grave, stiff against the curve of ground beneath it. Father had bent the feet back against its body, perverting its form, to make it fit into the space they had carved in the earth. Will had laughed, and in remembering, Amanda felt an emptiness grow in her chest, a painful deepening wedge of emptiness, and try as she might, breathe as she might, she could not fill her lungs with the air she needed to get rid of the emptiness.

And she lay like that, the images dancing in her mind, her heart pressing its beats into her throat until the embers dimmed, and the air grew black all around her, and finally she slept.

When she awoke, the black was still all around her. She felt her wet face, her hair damp, her long underwear sticking with wet to her body. She sat upright. There was no sound of wind. Even the river was silent.

"Where am I?" Amanda said aloud.

She listened for some sound to tell her where she was. Her stomach tightened into her chest. She heard the sound of something pounding, rhythmically darkening the night shadows; it was her own heart. She listened to it, tried to remember where she was. The night shadows lightened, and slowly the sound of the river came to her ears.

It was then that she heard a new sound.

It was a thin sound, a kind of whining, and it struck Amanda's heart and she froze in fear. She pictured a baby, a tiny infant, lying naked on the forest floor. She imagined it was a baby boy with a broad little chest, his arms waving in the air, his feet kicking.

Lifting onto her elbow, she looked over to where her brothers lay, motionless and quiet as they had been hours earlier.

"Father," she called. She lifted up higher to see on the other side of Will to where her father's sleeping bag lay. "Father," she spoke again, a little louder. As she raised herself up onto her knees and gazed through the dark at the forms of the sleeping bags, she could see that her father's was empty. His sleeping bag was flattened out. He was not there at all.

"Michael," she whispered, but he did not stir. "Will?"

Amanda lay back down, pulled the sleeping bag over her head, wrapped her arms around her head. She quieted her breathing and listened again. There it was, a tiny whining, each whine starting low and ending high. Then silence.

Lying quite still, Amanda listened to the silence, wished for some other sound, something to explain what she had heard. There was only quiet. Again she could not hear the river sound, though she knew it had not grown still. She began to think she had imagined the sound of crying, that it was part of the dream she had. But when she heard it again, she knew she was not dreaming, and she listened to the soft low sound, an animal sound, something kin to a groan, and it stirred fear in her chest.

When Amanda opened her eyes, she was relieved to see a glow of dim light in the air, a soft greyness. The first light of dawn sifted down through the trees, lighting the world in layers. The shadows of the woods lightened to shades of grey. Sitting up, Amanda searched the spaces between the trees. Turning, she scanned the riverbank. By some trick of sound, she could not tell the direction of the whining, whether it came from the woods or behind her by the river.

She waited, letting the morning light sharpen the shapes around her. Michael and Will lay as before, lumps in their sleeping bags. A slight breeze eased through the trees and carried the odor of the camp fire to her. The black remains of the fire was a pile of crusty coal.

Then the sound came again, louder, and as she pulled herself out of her sleeping bag, Amanda recognized the sound of laughter. Not laughter that she was accustomed to, but a gruff release of a moan that was not a cry, that was a burst of a moan. The sound clearly came from the water, and as she stood up, she directed her attention through the trees to the silver-black river. Heading back to the woods, she worked her way from the campsite, using the trees to hold to. Later she wondered why she did not call out when she saw him, but the sight of her father, standing knee deep in the water, his upright frame somehow limp and lifeless, brought a frozen silence to her body. Easing behind a tree, she wrapped her arms around its trunk for support, stared out of frozen eyes.

Amanda noticed his boots at the water's edge standing side by side. He had rolled his trousers up to his knees, but the water had seeped up the pant legs, making dark stripes around his thighs. His back was to her so she could not see his face. But it was from him that the whining sound came. His shoulders were hunched over, his arms held out in front of him, and his upper body was trembling. Amanda knew she should call out, and she heard her voice in her head, Father, it said, but no sound came out. Michael, she tried to call, opening her mouth to form a word, but no sound came out, and she could not take her eyes from his back.

Then he turned slightly, enough for Amanda to see that in his hands he held a shiny black gun, his shotgun, she realized, but it looked larger than before, as if it had its own life. As she watched the shininess and bigness of the gun, she saw her father cradle it to his chest, run his hands up and down the barrel, and he was whining all the while, and then he held, or pushed, the barrel to his throat, against his adam's apple, and Amanda thought, He's pushing it so hard against his throat, it must hurt. His teeth bared as he drew his lips back and started to whine, his eyes clenched shut, just tiny little slits in a face she did not know. Then he bent down, still cradling the gun to his chest, and here she heard the sound that reminded her of laughter, gasps of breath let out in quick short exhalations. Then again he straightened, threw his head back, pushed the metal barrel back into his throat with a force, as if someone else had shoved that gun against him, and he could not defend himself.

Amanda waited for the sound of an explosion. She clutched the tree, her fingers pulsing into the bark, her cheek caressing the rough bark, dimly aware of the dampness that ran down the inside of her legs as she wet herself. She knew the explosion would come any second, and she knew what it would sound like, she heard it in her head, a large loud thundering crack through the air, and she saw her father's eyes open in the moment of the explosion, in the moment of his own blood running.

But it did not come.

The explosion did not come, and Amanda watched through squinted eyes as he cradled the gun against him still, as he rocked the gun in his arms as he would a helpless baby, and he rocked his own body with the rocking of the gun, his head tilted to one side, the corners of his mouth pulled toward his ears in his crying, and then he stopped. He stopped rocking, he stopped crying, he opened his eyes, he took several steps over to a rock near the riverbank. He sat down on the rock, leaned his elbows against his thighs, holding the gun with both hands at his knees. One hand let go, and the gun stock slipped down between his knees to splash in the water, and Amanda watched her father rest his cheek against the cold barrel that stared at his eyes.

Minutes later Amanda crawled back into her sleeping bag near her brothers. She lay on her back and closed her eyes, felt the muscles in her face pulling under her eyes, felt her lips tight over her teeth. Her hands lay at her sides, the fingers still. Her heart thumped, high little beats, frightening her with their rapidity. She lay like that until she heard footsteps on the ground near her, and she knew he was back, knew he was sliding down into his sleeping bag, heard the breath from his lungs push out in long slow breaths, heard his breathing slow after he lay still for a few minutes.

Soon the others were awake.

"Amanda," she heard Will's voice. "Sun's up," he said. "We need wood for a fire."

Amanda rolled to one side, listened to the sound of her heart still beating too fast. Like the wings of a bird, she imagined, beating against the walls of some enclosure, beating hard for its very life. When she opened her eyes, she saw her father rolling his sleeping bag. She saw the slope of his shoulders, the way his back rounded. As he stood, she looked at his neck, searching for some trace of the gun's pressure against his throat, but there was nothing. She looked at his eyes, noticed a puffiness around the rims, shadows in the skin beneath the eyes. For a moment she caught his eye. He looked directly at her, and she felt herself squirm under his stare, wondered if he knew that she knew.

"We need some wood here, Amanda," he said and looked away.

Later she wondered just what it was that had happened. In the canoe that morning Amanda fought to hold the image of her father as she had seen him in the early morning dawn, felt she had some secret to carry, felt she must guard his secret as hers. And yet she remembered the way his eyes turned from her, the way his hands pushed her canoe into the water with a certainty of purpose.

So it was decided she knew nothing at all as she pulled her paddle through the water and heard Michael yell at her to pull harder, as her father paddled in the other canoe with Will and offered her no look to tell her it was all right, that what she had seen was all right.

And so it was that she decided, There is nothing to know.

❧ FOUR ❧

MOTHER, are you all right?" Maggie asks.

Amanda sits upright in the seat, her hands working the onyx ring around her fourth finger. "Am I all right?" she repeats and wonders to herself, Am I?

"Mother, seriously, are you okay?" and Maggie puts a foot on the brake to slow the car so she can look more closely at her mother.

"Am I seriously okay, you want to know. Yes, Margaret, of course I am." Amanda watches the curve of the river as the car follows the road that winds through the lowlands. "I've just been thinking," she tells her daughter. "Thinking about this road. And this river." She starts to sigh aloud but catches herself, swallows her breath.

"What about the river, Mother?" and Maggie's eyes jump from the road to her mother's face again. "You said that back at the rapids, about how you can never be too careful, did you —"

"I was just talking about the river, dear, how one must be careful when traveling in a canoe. It's what every woodsman knows." Amanda leans forward to rub her right knee. It always stiffens when I have to sit this long, she thinks, and she rubs with both hands and stretches the leg out as straight as the space allows her.

"But the river, what about the river?" Maggie tries to get her mother talking. She knows something is on Amanda's mind, knows the way her mother stares and thinks, remembering how she held a sandwich out, and how her mother had not seen it there before her eyes, how she sat with that flat stare and those greying eyes and her mouth so tight across her face.

But Amanda does not answer, hardly hears Maggie's questions. She is caught instead in the web of a memory or an image, she cannot tell which. She thinks it must be something she dreamed, maybe when she was just a child. The memory or image is of a distant road that winds through the woods. And there are fragments of memories of the days and nights she spent with her father and her brothers when they hiked Wisdom Peak.

It's better not to think of these things, she reminds herself. Forget them, as they are long gone from me. But the images do not leave her, they cling instead to the intake of her breath, and she feels her heart beating fast and hard in a tight, rapid pace. She holds a hand to her chest, covers the fluttering with her fingers. She feels an increasing pain, a cold spreading through her breast, and then a numbing, and she feels the beat of her heart through her fingers and she hears the rhythmic pumping in her head.

Amanda is familiar with this pain. This is different from the pain in her joints that has come with aging. That pain is hot and grinding, and it comes and goes with a mind of its own. This pain, however, has been with her so long that she hardly recognizes it as pain. It's part of the functioning of my heart, she thinks, and as before, these words return the warmth to her lungs and her heart, and the beating subsides.

"Mother," she hears Maggie's voice. "Mother, what is it?"

Amanda looks Maggie in the eye, notices the clear china blue of her daughter's eyes, the black lashes curling heavily. She hears Maggie's words, but she just stares until she feels tears sting her own eyes, and she squeezes them shut. She feels the tears spill over the lids. She turns her head to face out the window.

Maggie cannot remember ever seeing her mother cry. Not when my father died, she thinks. Not even when Evan died. "What is it, Mother?" she asks, feeling her own eyes water.

"Margaret, you must keep your attention to the road. I'm just an old woman going to see the past."

Maggie knows she has asked too much, has seen too much even. She wants to see more, though. "But I want to go there with you," she tells Amanda.

"You'll never go there with me, my dear," and Amanda straightens her back and tightens her lips.

Maggie sees the ring on her mother's finger move. From the corner of her eye she watches the other fingers on Amanda's hand rotate the onyx round and round. She looks at Amanda's face, can see only the side of it, notices the skin around her jaw trembling. It is something Maggie remembers in her mother's face from years past, from times when she would watch her mother from across the table or across the room or from the back seat of the car, a slight twitching in the jaw that pulled on her ear and shaded her cheek bone as it moved. It was because she had that way of closing her face off to the world, which was successful, but for the trembling around her jaw. There were times when Maggie would go to her mother's room, as she felt all girls should be able to go to their mothers' rooms when they need reassurance, when they need to talk, about the things that plague only a young girl. Or so Maggie figured, perhaps because whenever she was at Betsey's house, they would find themselves on Mrs. Brier's bed at some point, usually when Mrs. Brier was dressing for the evening. Maggie remembers the way Mrs. Brier would pull out one dress after another, would hold it up in front of herself, standing before a full-length mirror, the way she would turn and ask them which one they liked, and Maggie remembers how she and Betsey almost always agreed, they liked the green dress or the chiffon dress, or the navy shawl, or the long pearls. It was like that at the Briers', she realizes. But it was not like that at her house. She and Betsey never sat on the bed in her parents' room. Maggie never sat on the bed in her parents' room either. There were times when she would try, times she remembered wishing that she could push open the door to her mother's room, could flop onto the bed, could speak the thoughts that tortured her in those years. But it was not that way.

Maggie looked at the leaf patterns on the blue hall rug outside her mother's door, rubbed her bare toes against its softness. Near the door the rug was worn thin, tan and blue threads reached out in wisps onto the floor and the doorjamb. Behind her the air felt cold at her back; ripples of goose bumps rose up her spine, so she turned to look behind her, down the long, darkened hall. Evan was at Mark's house, as usual, and her father was on an extended trip to England. Maggie had asked Betsey to come for the night, but she was going to another friend's, and it was at times like this that Maggie wondered if she was too attached to Betsey, for she herself had no other friends. There was only Betsey, and when she was busy with someone else, there was no one. It made Maggie feel an ache inside, and she didn't like that. She wondered why she had no other friend. And that made her wonder why Betsey was her friend, if she only pretended to like her, if perhaps she would forget about Maggie someday.

Maggie rested her hand on the shelf by the door, touched the stack of white towels with her palm, her mother's white slip, the one with the embroidered lace and pink stitching, her brother's blue spotted pajamas and his brown wool socks wrapped neatly in a ball, the toes sticking out from the inside. The light on the wall above the shelf spread a dusty glow, the yellowed shade filtering the light to a soft nighttime grey.

Turning her eyes to the closed white door before her, she felt a familiar wedge of pain inside her frame. Her head began to nod as words from within instructed her. "Go ahead," her voice told her, "knock." Slowly she raised her arm. She noticed that her hand was already clenched into a fist. How had her fingers curled into that shape? she wondered. Had they been like that the whole time she had been standing there? She knew she had not told her fingers to wrap them-selves into the palm of her hand, and she noticed that her other hand was not clenched, but lay, instead, loose, by her side. "Knock," she heard again, and she pulled her hand back through the air and forward again a few times, practicing the motion. "Go ahead," she heard, "knock." Maggie ceased the movement of her hand in the air and rested her knuckles lightly against the door. To knock, she knew she had only to pull back and release her hand. And despite the voice that encouraged her to knock, something else told her not to, something that warned her that her mother would not want to listen to her. That something was wrong with her feelings.

Opening her fingers, she pressed the palm of her hand against the door. "Can you hear me?" said the words in her head. "Can you hear my hand against this door?" And then, "Answer me if you know that I am here." Silence from the room. Maggie leaned her cheek against the doorframe, let it slide soundlessly against the door. Her ear listened, heard some small movement from within. She felt her fingers move back into a fist. Lightly, ever so lightly, she pulled her hand back and let it knock against the door by her face. One small sound, it could almost have been just a sound of the night, but she knew it was a sound of insistence and despair.

Maggie waited, listening.

"What is it?" a voice called. It conjured up a picture of Amanda's face, tight and hard, in Maggie's mind. Then came a picture of Mrs. Brier's face, open with a smile when she heard Betsey's voice, when Betsey picked through the jewelry on her bureau and found the perfect piece for some dress. It was an inviting face, Maggie often thought.

"Mother?" Maggie whispered. Her fingertips touched the doorknob.

"What is it?"

Maggie's hand encircled the doorknob and turned it. The door pushed in. Maggie drew in her breath and took a step forward, saw her mother sitting on the stool at her dressing table, pulling a brush through her long loose hair that crinkled with electricity with each stroke. Maggie could see Amanda's face in the mirror, could see her eyes looking at her from under their lids. Even from across the room Maggie could see that her mother's face was closed to her.

Maggie moved closer. She could smell the lily-of-the-valley fragrance of her mother's room. She walked close enough to notice the silken texture of Amanda's rose-colored robe. Silver hair spread out over her mother's shoulders when she placed the brush on the glass dresser top and shook her head. Then she pulled a tortoise barrette from a drawer, twisted her hair into one tight strand, and wound the strand into a ball which she clipped with the barrette. Maggie noticed the twitching of her jaw, a sign that she took to mean displeasure.

"What are you staring at?" Amanda asked.

It was then Maggie noticed the back of her mother's neck, the hair pulled tight so that the skin was taut, and it looked so unprotected to Maggie, so soft and tender, so exposed, that it made her uncomfortable, as if she had seen into her mother in a way she should not have. In a way that would hurt her mother if she knew. And in a way that made Maggie feel ashamed of her need to talk to someone.

"I just," Maggie started. "I just wondered," and she stopped.

"Time you were off to bed, dear." Amanda began to straighten her dressing table. She replaced the cap of the perfume bottle and moved it next to the mirror in the corner. She picked up several bobby pins and dropped them onto a glass tray that sat in the middle of the table. She opened a drawer and swept some earrings away.

"Sure," Maggie responded. She was trying to cover the moment of feeling something revealed about her mother, trying not to let her mother see what she had seen. She felt uncomfortable about being in the room, as if she was somehow in charge, but she didn't know how. She only knew one way out of this kind of moment. "Be pleasant," a voice told her. "Be pleasant and get out," she heard. "I was just wondering if you wanted anything from downstairs, from the kitchen, I'm —"

"Not for me, dear," and Amanda's head was shaking back and forth.

Maggie knew she had gotten past the moment. There was nothing in her mother's face of disapproval. If she could get out of the room, she knew she could correct what she had done. She took several steps backward, her hand running against the bed frame. "Well, I'll be downstairs, if you need anything," she muttered as she turned and headed to the door.

But later, as she lay in bed reading, her mind kept wandering. To Betsey, to Betsey at her other friend's house, to Evan at Mark's. She knew in the morning her feeling of loneliness, for she knew enough to call it that, would be gone. Evan would come home by early afternoon. She could call Betsey on the phone.

"Everything will be all right tomorrow," she told herself.

And she read on into the night.

"Only an hour of this driving left, Mother," Maggie says to Amanda, wanting to reassure her that they would soon arrive. "You must be stiff from sitting so long —"

"Margaret, you worry about getting us there, I'll worry about whether I am stiff or not." Amanda twists her head to stare out the window, rests it against the glass, watches the woods thicken and thin as the road follows the river. Cattails line the edge of the bank; from the car, she sees only the tops of the tails, fuzzy brown worms on top of stiff green stems. In places the bank is so high that she cannot see the water, only the trees on the distant shore, and a sense of space in between. Her eyes close, the lids lowering almost against her will, covering her eyes until she hears Maggie tell her there is only a half hour left of driving.

Amanda gives no reply. She sits stiffly in her seat, her feet folded together, her hands tightly wound. One eye peers at her hands, stares at them lazily until they assume the look of claws, the fingers curled like sharp talons, the tendons lifted, and she starts to twirl the ring on her finger again. Round and round she twists it, running her thumb over the smooth onyx with each turn.

"The road in to the lake is supposed to be about twenty-three miles beyond this post office," Maggie tells her. "The directions from Martin say there will be several roads leading off to the lake. I guess they're all old logging roads." Maggie wonders what it will be like to drive in to Land's End for the first time, whether the mystery of the place will vanish without the trip across the water in the boat.

"Did Martin tell you when this road was opened up to people?" Maggie asks.

Amanda sighs, lets her breath out slowly. "These roads have always been there, Margaret. They just weren't passable for cars."

"Well, when did that change, do you know?"

Opening her mouth to answer, Amanda pauses. A picture comes to her mind of a time when she came to the lake with her parents and her brothers, a time when she must have been seven or eight. It was late at night, later than they were supposed to arrive, but heavy rains had slowed them down. She remembers how anxious her mother was about being late, and how her father paid no attention to those anxieties. When they arrived, Lenny was there waiting for them, and Amanda recalls the way he lifted her up and into the boat with strong arms, telling her to take the seat behind his. She can hear still the gurgling sound of the water as the propeller splashed in the blackness beneath the boat. The night was still, the water like oil, and the boat slid through it and glided across the lake. She saw the lights from Chad, and when the boat was about halfway there, the lights from the house, like fluorescent eyes in a flat black sky. But they were the welcoming lights, and as the boat pulled up alongside the dock that loomed above the surface of the water, the eyes grew to squares of glowing windows, and the smell of the wood fire drifted in the air as she walked up the dock and followed the path to the front steps of Land's End.

It was a dream world, Amanda thinks, a dream world

where the warmth of the firelit house led us across the black water and through the black night.

"It must have been in the last couple of years, don't you think?" Maggie asks.

"Don't I think what?" Amanda asks.

"The road, that people have been allowed to drive in," Maggie reminds her. "Was it something to do with the lumber company?"

Amanda forgets the night image on the lake and thinks about the road they will follow in to the lake. "I really don't know, dear," she finally answers. "And I don't care to think of it, and I don't see why Martin couldn't have met us, as he used to. In the boat, I mean. As we've always done."

Maggie knows the idea of driving in on the road will disturb her mother. "Well, it's late in the year, and it will be better not to cross the lake. It will be cold, I'm sure."

"Of course it will be cold, but my father always said that the only true entry to the house was the ride across the lake. When I was a child, I believed him. Literally, I mean. That one could not reach the house except by water." Amanda thinks again of the night ride.

"It was fun that way, wasn't it," Maggie agrees. "But just think, we're the first to arrive at Land's End by car. The first in our family. That's kind of exciting. To be the first in the family."

"What's left of it," Amanda mutters, feeling a pinch in her chest.

"I always remember Grandfather standing on the dock, waving to us as the boat drew near. I could never stand waiting those last minutes."

Maggie remembers her grandfather reaching out for her as she placed one foot on a seat and another on the side of the boat, and she can almost feel her hands reach out to him again to curl around his neck as he swung her onto the dock. She remembers her mother's eyes on her when he finally put her down and turned to carry some boxes up to the house. Something in her mother's face bored into her own eyes, so that she had to look away, so that instead of reaching to help with the luggage, she ran after her grandfather, and she stumbled up the path with him to the house, aware of some discomfort about herself, as if she had done something wrong.

Maggie remembers her grandfather taking her up to Lenny's one evening to see the goats. It was late in the summer, she remembers, picturing the corn growing over her head as they passed the field on the other side of Chad and made their way to Lenny's. The goats, two of them, lived in Lenny's barn and spent their days out in the field by his barn, often tethered to a rope that ran between two apple trees. This one time, they arrived as the sun was setting, and the evening light spread across the field, and as they approached the barn, Maggie looked through the window and saw clear out through the window on the other side where the sky was scarlet red with the setting sun, and the pine trees through that far window were silhouetted black against the red sky. "Were the windows built that way on purpose," she asked her grandfather, "so you could stand on one side of the barn and see the sunset on the other side, so you wouldn't have to miss the sight?" and her grandfather had looked at her with wet eyes and lifted her into his arms, held her like that, and together they watched the sky darken as the sun went behind the mountains across the lake. Then they found the goats, and Maggie held her grandfather's hand as they approached one of them whose name was Alfred, and she held tight to the hand because she knew sometimes goats were unpredictable, and that time, as she held a hand out with a piece of bread, Alfred came close and lowered his head, touched her ankle with his wet nose and then nibbled at her pants. She screamed until her grandfather shooed the goat away, and by that time the sun was down, and the sky was a light shade of pink with thin amber streaks along the horizon. "We'd better head back to the house," he told her, and she nodded, "Of course, Grandfather, it's getting dark." So they followed the path back to Land's End, and as they walked up the steps to the house, he said, "It'll be dark soon, good we're back, Maggie." And he held a hand to her shoulder as he opened the door and the light from inside poured out onto the dark front porch.

Amanda was waiting inside for them. She sat on the bench by the fireplace, and Maggie remembers the glow of the owl eyes of the andirons as her own eyes adjusted to the light. "It's past your bedtime," was all her mother told her, and when her grandfather offered to tuck her in, it was Amanda who interceded. "I can do it," she told him in such a way as to prevent him from insisting. Maggie remembers that happening often, knows that she felt herself between the two of them. "You were a pawn," Jeremy told her when she described these instances. "And you still are."

"What do you mean?" Maggie wanted to know. She could not see his point. In her mind, she had somehow wronged her mother.

And she did not know how.

The road starts out nice and wide.

The land on either side is marshy; golden grass grows along the edges of the muddy bogland, and slender trees rise out of the water like slivers of silver tusk, aged and long dead. The road is well packed. A smooth gravel surface has been built up to accommodate the new traffic of cars.

"This is better than I thought it would be," Maggie says.

Amanda does not answer. She squints at the road, looks for some sign of recent traffic. "Do you think we'll meet a truck coming out?" she asks.

"Probably not, Mother, but if we do, it's wide enough here for me to pull to one side."

"You can't pull to one side, dear, you'll be in the bog." Amanda looks at the edge of the road and the wetland that falls off beside it.

"We'll be all right," Maggie says. She leans forward to get a wider view. She rolls down the window a few inches to smell the air. "We're really getting closer. Mother, I can smell it already, the lake and woods smell."

The air that comes in the car is sharp and cold. It hangs

by the windshield against their faces, then starts to mix with the warm air that rises from the heater. Amanda draws her knees up and pulls the bottom of her coat farther down to cover her legs.

"Close that window, Margaret, it's too cold."

"Oh, but the air feels so good, just having it down in my lungs, it's like —"

"I don't care what it's like, Margaret, it's too cold. Close the window."

Maggie closes her eyes for a second longer than a quick blink. She feels the breath of air pull in through her nostrils. "I guess we have to go over this mountain, to come in behind Land's End, don't we," she says. The road heads out of the bog area. The trees thicken and are taller. The road narrows, but the surface of the road is still well packed. In places along the way, there are cutouts in the woods, and stacks of logs lie ready for transfer near piles of fallen trees. The muddy paths that lead into the woods are marked with the imprints of tires from the rigs that cut and pull the trees out to the road. Instead of the thin birch and spindly pine trees that filled the low marshland, here the trees grow firm and strong. The white of the birch glistens in the afternoon sun, the pale yellow leaves startling the otherwise green pine woods.

"I don't like this," Amanda says.

Maggie looks over at her mother, who sits erect in her seat, eyes squinting at the road. Maggie can hear the intake of short, shallow breaths. The collar of her mother's coat is worn, the big black button at the top is nicked.

"I don't like this at all," she repeats.

"What, Mother, you mean the road?"

"Yes, I mean the road. It's getting narrower, and if we meet a logging truck, there won't be any room for the both of us on this road." Amanda looks down at her hands. "We should have never come this way."

The road takes an abrupt turn and heads up a steep section of the mountain. The autumn reds and golds shine like jewels on the trees and the ground, which is not as well packed.

Instead of the finer gravel surface, this section is covered with small pebbles that slide out from under the wheels. Maggie can feel the Peugeot pulling itself up the hill. The trees edge the road, forming a latticework of branches over their heads. The afternoon sun comes through to make small light patches on the hood of the car.

"Margaret, please roll up your window," and her voice pleads the words.

Maggie rolls the window shut and quickly places her hand back on the wheel to steady the car as it reaches the top of the incline. Here the road evens out some, but it is narrower. She realizes that two cars could not pass here. What if a logging truck does come? she wonders.

"Look at that," Maggie says, as she slows the car to a stop and gazes out at the view. "Just look at that — it's incredible." The mountain falls away in front of them, a steeply sloping wave of green and gold woods, the dirt road winding its way diagonally down through the trees. Partway down, the colors of fall mingle with the firs: deep scarlet reds and bright yellows, first in splotches, then in the lower lands, the colors of the maples and birches sweep across the green. The afternoon sun reaches across the valley and onto the lake that lies below, a blue-black patch under a grey-blue sky with clouds on the far horizon. On the far side of the lake the mountains do not get direct sun, and the colors are muted into dusty rose and gold, the green of the higher woods closer to black.

"We can't drive down that road, Margaret," Amanda says, her voice thin, but flat.

"Don't worry, Mother, we'll be fine. I can see there's nothing coming along the road; it'll be okay."

"The road is too steep. I don't like this."

Fearful her mother may insist they turn back, Maggie reminds her to look at the lake. "And the house. Land's End. We can't see it from here, but it's there, at the foot of this mountain. Just close your eyes, Mother, and imagine that we're there, because we are almost there, we really are almost there." Maggie pushes the gear stick into first and eases forward slowly so as not to jolt Amanda.

"I will certainly not close my eyes, and I repeat, I don't like this." Amanda pulls a navy scarf out of her bag and begins unfolding it. She lays it across her lap, runs both hands across it to smooth the wrinkles from its folds, then folds it in half and again smooths the surface.

Maggie keeps one foot on the brake as she shifts into second gear. The woods fold around their car, the trees too tall to let them see much ahead or to let the sun brighten the road. There is only the sound of loose gravel under the wheels of the car.

"What's that?" asks Amanda.

"What's what?" Maggie presses her foot harder against the brake.

"That roaring. Can't you hear it?"

Maggie listens to the Peugeot's sounds. Then she hears another sound, a low rumble.

"It's a logging truck, I knew it, it's come up from the lake, and we won't be able to get by." Amanda fidgets with the scarf, flattening it and folding it smaller and smaller.

Maggie rolls her window down partway. "You're right, Mother, it is a truck, but there's nothing ahead, maybe it's in the woods on a road we can't even see. Besides I'm going slow, there's nothing that can go wrong."

The rumbling grows louder, and Maggie feels the vibrations on the road through the steering wheel. Must be a big one, she thinks, and wonders how they will manage to pass one another. Ahead on the road is a square of sunlight. Maybe there's a clearing, she thinks, some place off to the right where we can pull over. Just at that moment a roar blasts the air around them, but ahead there is nothing. Maggie looks in the rearview mirror in time to see a monstrous rig descending on them.

"Good God," she shrieks, and without thinking, she steers the car off to the right and into the clearing she had hoped for a few seconds before. Her foot presses the brake into the floor, the Peugeot stalls as it jerks to a stop, sending Amanda off her seat toward the dashboard. Maggie's hand shoots out so that her mother pushes against her arm. As the car settles, Amanda leans back into her seat.

The logging truck rattles down beyond them on the road, leaving the rising dust in a swirl. The driver waves a hand and Maggie can swear that he casts a wide grin at them.

"It's not carrying any wood," Amanda states, and rests her hands on her lap.

"I guess that's why it was going so fast," Maggie answers, aware of a trembling in her hands. "You'd think it wouldn't head down the mountain like this, though. It could just fly off the road at any point. All those curves ahead, that's crazy."

"It may be crazy, but it's typical of these people up here. They think they own the roads. I told you it wasn't good. I told you, Margaret." Amanda leans her head back and closes her eyes.

"You're all right, Mother?"

"Let's just get going, Margaret."

Minutes later the lake is in sight.

"There it is, Mother, look!" Maggie tells her.

Amanda opens her eyes. It is daytime. The sky is blue, and waves of sunlight stream through the thinning trees. Land's End stands before them on a rise, the green clapboards and grey shingles blending the building into the woods. Off to the right, the lake shines in the afternoon light.

Maggie edges the car along the grass, around familiar rocks and a stump from an old birch tree, until the house is before them. Maggie stares at the granite foundation, the wide porch that wraps around the front of the house and back around the sides, the rows of windows and grey shutters, the black glass reflecting the waving branches of the woods and the blue sky. A few pine trees stand in front at the corners of the house, their protective limbs pushing now at the porch railing and the roof. Two white birches stand in the clearing outside of the kitchen windows, their branches above the roof that slants down from the red brick chimney.

"Smoke, Mother, do you see the smoke, it's —"

"I asked Martin to ready the place for us, Margaret, and I told him when we'd be arriving." She glances at her watch. "In fact, we're late, as I expected we might be. He probably is not here now."

"Late? We're not late," and Maggie looks into her mother's face for some sign of excitement. She tells herself to ignore the irritating habits her mother has, to try to be herself. Just to be herself. She looks down at the lake. "Look," she says. "Just look at the water."

Amanda blinks, feels disoriented.

"See the lake, Mother, look, the afternoon is beautiful —"

Maggie opens the door to get out. "Come on," she says. She rushes ahead to the front of the house, pauses to run her fingers against the pine bark of a tree, turns the corner, passes the path that leads over to the cabin that is all but hidden by overgrown bushes and young trees.

Amanda can see her race down to the water. She watches her daughter stop at the lake's edge, turn, and wave an arm to her. Amanda feels annoyed at Maggie's girlishness. It has always annoyed her, though it does not often show. She wants to call to Maggie and tell her that she left the car door open. She feels for the handle on the door on her side, but she cannot pull it hard enough to get it open. She closes her eyes, opens them again. The house is still there, the smoke wafting from the chimney. She sees Maggie wave her arm again from the dock. Then Maggie is there, opening the door, and Amanda unfolds her scarf and wraps it around her head, tucking the edges down into the collar of her coat. She pulls the sides of her beret down over her ears.

"You'll catch your death," she reminds Maggie, and she pulls herself from the seat of the car. She looks at the house. "There are no lights in the windows."

Maggie wonders what is in her mother's mind. She wonders if she should say, What are you talking about? But she responds instead out of habit, tells her that it is still daytime, that soon it will be dark and then they will light the lamps, and then there will be light in the windows. Maggie feels light and free as she approaches the house. The lake is cold and deep, she thinks, the pine trees are bowing to the wind, and the house is strong. As it used to be.

"It hasn't changed at all, Mother," she tells her. "Come, you'll see. Everything will be the same. Everything will be all right."

❧ FIVE ❧

MAGGIE wakens with a start. Eyes closed, she listens, hears a scuttling from behind a wall. She thinks she is at home, that the sound is Muffin, scratching from the ledge at her window, meowing to get in. She rolls to one side and pushes up onto an elbow, waits to hear the sound again. She opens her eyes.

A log still burns in the fireplace, a soft glow spreads onto the raised stone hearth. Two sets of lemon eyes gleam in the dark. Maggie realizes where she is.

I used to be afraid of those owl andirons, she thinks. Those yellow eyes spooked me.

She remembers once helping Grandfather clean them. Maggie remembers scrubbing the rusty caked iron with wire brushes late one afternoon down by the lake. The embedded ash fell easily from the owl bodies, but there was little that could be done with the supports. Later he showed her how to clean the glass eyes, rubbing gently on the inside with an old toothbrush, polishing the outside with a flannel cloth.

Maggie hears a cry echo from the lake. A loon, she thinks, and wonders if it has a companion. She hears the call repeated, a lone sound eerie as it billows into the night. Then it shifts, is higher, in shorter tones, and Maggie remembers her grandfather telling her a story of two loons who had come to the lake from another continent, from China, she thinks he told her, in search of a peaceful lake to live on. As a child,

Maggie thought all the loons were the descendants of those first loons from China.

"Why do they cry so at night?" she once asked him. "Because they are afraid of losing each other in the dark," he had told her, "because they don't like to be alone." From then on she always listened for a companion call to each loon cry, hoping they would find each other.

Pretty silly, she thinks as she sits up, drawing her knees up and wrapping her arms around them. She peers out the window that is beside the sofa where she fixed her bed after supper with Amanda by the fire.

"You can't sleep out here," her mother had told her when Maggie carried a pile of blankets out to the living room and laid them on the sofa by the window.

"I can keep the fire going during the night," she told Amanda, and she took the loose pillows from the corners of the deep high-backed sofa and laid them on the floor, then she spread the blankets out and tucked them into the corners.

"Home sweet home," she smiled to Amanda, as she finished the bed. "I'll be happy out here, because I'll be closer to the lake. I like to hear the lake sounds at night."

"True," Amanda had answered, and again, "true, the night sounds are nice. But Alice fixed up the room next to mine for you. I saw those peach quilts laid out in that room."

Maggie didn't answer. She knew they were both thinking the same thing: that had been Evan's room. "I know," Maggie continued, "but I like it out here."

The night is black, Maggie thinks, as she searches the sky for stars. A starless night; I guess tomorrow will be cloudy. She can see the shadows of trees, and a shadow where the dock must be. Maggie remembers how the lake looks when there is a moon to glisten, but now there is nothing to shine and nothing to glisten.

The fire crackles and Maggie turns to see a log break, a chunk falls away, and a bright flame gusts where the air makes the fire grow. Pushing back the covers, she gets up and walks to the hearth where she kneels down, rests her knees against the edge of the stone hearth, and holds her hands toward the warmth of the fire. Lightly she touches the eye of one of the owl andirons with her fingertip. A crack lies across this eye, forming a thin space, shifting the focus of the eye upward instead of straight ahead. As a child she had imagined that the owls had thoughts, that they watched her just as she watched them. The shifted eye gives the owl an appearance of craziness. Maggie shudders and looks instead into the single flame that rises from the broken piece of log. It is blue against the blackened back wall of the fireplace and the glowing orange embers.

Maggie reaches for the poker and pushes at the log, breaking it up into two more pieces. She stirs the embers until they shine with a brighter flame, then she lays two more logs on top. The large birch log crackles with the flame that spreads through its bark. Soon the fire burns more fully, the logs evenly heating the space around her.

Maggie remembers how her mother's face looked when she started to cry in the car, as they drove through the mountains. She was not accustomed to the lines of Amanda's face breaking as tears filled her eyes and her chin quivered. Mother hasn't cried at the times I would have expected, she thinks. Not at her own husband's death, when she made the arrangements with brisk efficiency and sent me off to England for the burial. And the days after I returned, when I helped her sort through all his stuff, before I went back to Philadelphia, I never saw a tear in her eye.

Maggie remembers that time as if in a dream, sorting through her father's shirts, and sorting for what, she asked at the time. There was nothing to be done with any of those old shirts, she realized, they were so old, and the seams were ripped under the arms and frayed at the edges and the collars were worn clean through. She had taken a couple of shirts back to Jeremy. "I wanted you to have something that was his," she told him, "so I could be reminded of him when you wear them." And Jeremy had pulled them out of his bureau on weekend mornings, and Maggie remembers running her hand along the collar at the back of his neck, where the cotton was so worn, when they walked along the river, and she gazed at her father's shirt on Jeremy's back.

Amanda had thrown her husband's things away without remorse. "No one will want this," she had said, "or this," and she had filled several boxes with his clothes and shipped them off to Goodwill.

And his personal possessions, Maggie thinks, had all been thrown into one large box in his study. She had sorted through it, searching for bits and pieces of something, anything to give her a feel of her father. But there was little in that box that reminded her of him, except the old photos, a small packet that he must have kept wrapped in a blue velvet ribbon for years. When she untied the ribbon, it ripped in two places, and she wondered if he had not looked at them since he was a young man. There were pictures of his mother standing beside him, when he was a boy, outside of the house he grew up in, and there was a picture of his sister who died, when she was still a child, of tuberculosis. The third picture showed a young woman with tight curly black hair and large mournful eyes, and her hands were wrapped together around a small bouquet of flowers, wild flowers, Maggie thought, and she stood beneath the branches of a poplar tree. Her skirt billowed to one side, showing it was a windy day, and behind her, in the background, was a sloping valley. The photos were yellowed, soft around the edges, and the one on top, of his mother, had a dark strip across the middle where the ribbon had rested against the paper for some time.

Maggie can see the picture of the young woman in her mind. She has often wondered who it was, for certainly it was not her mother, and the scene looked like it was in England. Her face had floated to Maggie's mind off and on during the months since her father's death; she wished at times that he was still alive. "If only for a moment," she told Jeremy once, "so I could ask him about the woman, because I wonder if he loved her, because she looks like someone he would have loved." Jeremy had asked what made her look like that. "Oh, it's in the way she held her hands around those flowers," Maggie answered, bringing the photo out to show him, "as if she was capable of holding tight to what she loved."

Maggie closes her eyes and recalls a memory of her father, one of the few she has of the years when she was a girl at home. She sees him standing in the doorway to his room, a leather-backed brush in each hand, practicing an unselfconscious and programmed method to his brushing, first one and then the other, sweeping back through his thin hair that showed silver in the light even when she was a young child, and he could not have been more than forty-two years old. She sees him asking her to join him in a trip to England during the summer, to see his home, to see where he was born, and where he went to school. "I don't really think so," she had told him, "not this summer anyway," and his brushing had not missed a beat, his hands had worked their mad brushing steadily without a pause.

Her eyes sting with new tears as she feels the knowledge of her father, a knowledge that has grown during the eight months since his death. "It doesn't make any sense," she had told Jeremy in September, "to find him like this, after he dies, to find him in my heart."

Jeremy said little at the time. He just pressed his face against her hair, told her it smelled good, told her that was the way of things. And later, when he lay beside her in the bed beneath the double windows in their room, as they listened to a misty rain in the dark, he asked her to rub his back, and he told her about his own father, who died when he was a senior in high school. Maggie knew that he had died in a veterans hospital in New Hampshire following a stroke that left his entire body paralyzed, but that was all. Jeremy had kept his feelings to himself about this. "I had trouble going to see him," he told her. "I hated to see him like that. So I avoided him." He told her how it had been four months since he had been to visit his father in the hospital when he died. "Just like that. My mother greets me at the door after a game, and her eyes are all wet and red, and she tells me he's dead, just like that, and then she cries and my brother cries, but I don't cry for two years." Maggie listened to his every word, realized how far away from him she had been without this knowledge, asked him why he took so long to tell her. "That's how I understand why you run from things," he told her, and Maggie felt herself pull in, felt the touch of her hand on his bare back tighten, so that there was some space between her hand that touched him and the fine feel of his flesh. "I just never knew what he meant to me until he was gone," he said.

"Yeah," Maggie answered, thinking it was true, true for her about her father. But not with Evan. She knew what that loss was all about right away. Maybe it was because of the time he was twelve, when he nearly died. Maybe that told me, she thought, that it was coming. That his death was coming. Like some premonition.

Maggie was walking to Betsey's house that day, as she did most days after school, when Evan whisked by her on his new three-speed Schwinn, the one he got for his twelfth birthday in the summer. He had picked it out himself, turning away from the bright red bicycle that his mother pointed to, decided instead upon the black one that was in the window of the store. It had a sleek and racy look, and Evan liked that.

As Maggie and Betsey turned onto her street, Evan came back and turned in beside them. He stopped at the curb and undid the strap that held his books to the back of the bike. "Will you take these?" he asked, handing the books to Maggie, "I'm going over to Mark's, see if he can come over. Maybe we can get a game going; you coming home soon?"

Maggie noticed the way he balanced the bike, leaning one foot on the curb. She wondered if the bike was too big for him but knew she wouldn't say anything. Evan didn't like to be questioned that way and she knew it, even at nine. "I don't know," she answered. She looked over at Betsey, who appeared impatient. "What do you think, Betsey, want to come over?"

Betsey said no, she wanted to clean her hamster's cage and her mother was sewing her a new hoop skirt, and she wanted to be at home for that. "She said she'd make one for you, too, if you want."

Evan wheeled off, somewhat unsteadily, Maggie noticed, but she was thinking about whether she wanted a hoop skirt. "What keeps it out?" she asked Betsey, who explained how a piece of wire was worked into the hem. Maggie thought that it sounded good, but that she'd like to see how Betsey's came out first. So she helped her friend clean out the cage and she watched as Mrs. Brier pinned the skirt together for a first try-on. "Maybe we can shop for some material for you this weekend," she told Maggie, who thanked her before heading home. A light rain was starting, just a drizzle, and she wished she had her own bike so she could hurry home. She took a short-cut, crossing through someone's backyard, and onto another street that was unfamiliar to her.

Maggie was concentrating on the sidewalk at her feet as she walked home. She found a stretch of smooth macadam, thought how perfect it would be for roller skating, wondered when it had been done over. She imagined how uneven it had been before, with pieces of stone chipping out and large cracks forming and pushing wedges of sidewalk at odd angles like the sidewalk in front of her house. She was counting the number of steps she took in each square when she came out on Winslow Street, the street before hers. She looked up to cross to Wentworth, and it was at that moment that she saw Evan heading toward their street from the other direction. He was on the far side, about to cross over, when he saw her. She remembered later how her eye caught his, how his head cocked in recognition, how one arm went up to wave, and it was in the moment that his hand waved that she saw some kind of wobbling in the bike, some sort of imbalance it was, that took him too soon into the lane where a green sedan was passing him.

Years later Maggie would be haunted by that moment.

Years later she would see again the shivering motion of the bike as it hovered next to the car, was almost carried with the car for half a block, until, from where Maggie stood, the car was directly across from her, and Evan was on the far side of the car, and for a moment she thought she could see his mouth move with the formation of words, but she couldn't tell what he was saying, and she couldn't hear him, for the brakes on the car were screeching, and then the car was swerving, and then she couldn't see Evan anymore.

He was down. On the other side of the car, Evan was down, as the car slid with skidding tires and locked brakes into an oncoming car. There was a crash of metal against metal, a sound that was close to a squeal, the chugging of one engine as it stalled, the horn of another. Then the horn quieted, the engine stopped, and one door flew open. It was then that it started to rain harder, as if a curtain of water had landed on the street where the two cars sat crunched together.

Within seconds there was a crowd. Maggie felt herself backed up against a fence to someone's property as she watched the people come from every direction. There were people getting out of other cars, and people running from nearby houses, and a dog was yipping, a little terrier straining on a leash as its owner stood on the curb and watched from under his umbrella as the crowd formed. Maggie kept thinking she should run over to where Evan was, that she should pull her hands away from the fencepost to which she clung, that she should find out what was happening. But she couldn't move. Her knees trembled uneasily under the plaid skirt of her school dress. She couldn't even bend over to pick up Evan's books, which she had dropped on the ground at the moment when she could see Evan's face no longer, and now the books lay on the wet ground, and she could see the covering to one of his books turning a dark brown as the rain stained it through to the pages. She focused on the books, drew her mind away from the scene on the street in front of her, until she heard the whine of a police car, and then the crowd was stepping back, and the drivers of the two cars stood at the rear of the green car, and Maggie wondered what they were doing, why wasn't anyone doing anything about Evan, why were they standing there talking to the policeman as if her brother wasn't lying on the ground on the other side of the car, maybe dead.

When the word *dead* entered her mind, Maggie began to scream.

It was then that all the eyes in the crowd turned to her. Her hand came up to her throat as she screamed, "It's Evan, it's Evan, don't you see," and she was pointing under the green car, and in the rain it was hard to see, so grey and slick was the air, but everyone looked in the direction she pointed, and finally someone walked closer to the open door, bent down, and saw him.

It was Evan, her brother, lying in some contorted shape, under the green car.

That was when things got confusing. That was when everyone started yelling, running in all directions, around the green car, around the other car, a wooden-sided wagon, and the policeman went to his car, spoke into his hand radio.

After that, there were people standing all around Maggie. Someone was wrapping some kind of jacket around her shivering shoulders. A man was down on his knees, he was talking to her, asking her questions, asking her what her name was, and who the boy was, and where he lived, and there were so many questions that Maggie couldn't think. So she pointed to her street, where a neighbor was heading toward them.

The ringing whistle of the ambulance deafened Maggie's ears when it arrived. She tried to peer through the people who stood around her, tried to see where Evan was, caught a glimpse of him being lifted onto a stretcher, and then Amanda was there, Amanda was bending over the stretcher, and she was climbing into the ambulance with Evan, and Maggie watched as it backed onto someone's front yard and pulled away with a skid on the slippery grass. Maggie could see a shape through the back window of the ambulance, figured it was her mother, and though her thinking was now as clear as a crystal, she couldn't find the words to speak, to call to her mother and her brother.

So it was her neighbor, Mrs. Sanford, who led her back to the house, who phoned her grandparents, who waited with her until her grandfather arrived.

And when he came through the door, Maggie's relief was so great that she spoke the first thing that came to her mind. "Evan's books," she told him. "I've left Evan's books —"

Grandfather's blue eyes watered as he knelt by her, as he pressed her head into his shoulder and told her he would help her pack her things and she would come with him to his house.

"And where will Mother stay?" she asked.

"She'll be with Evan at the hospital," he said in a voice that creaked.

And that was how Maggie knew Evan would live.

It was several months before Evan could come home, though, and during that time, Maggie stayed mostly with her grandparents because Amanda spent so much time at the hospital. There were operations that Evan had to undergo. The internal injuries were severe. One leg was broken in three places. But the thing that was most painful for Evan was the injury to the back of his head. The skin was pulled away, burned off almost, the doctor told him, by the scraping along the roadside as his body was pulled along under the car. Had it not been for his bicycle, which got tangled up under the wheel, the tangled thing would have been Evan, and instead of multiple fractures and internal injuries and the problem with the burn on the back of his head, Evan would have been dead. And though the skin grafting was tedious and painful, the family was glad it was no worse.

"There is a lot to be thankful for," Amanda told her after the first month, when Evan's condition stabilized. "Your brother should really be dead," she told Maggie.

Those words burned into Maggie's mind with intensity. She wondered why her mother continued to say that about

Evan, why she seemed so attached to the idea that he should be dead. At the hospital, Amanda was called a saint by one of the nurses who told Amanda and Maggie that her mother was a selfless person. "Well, of course I'm here to help my son," Amanda answered. "It's what any mother would do in such a situation." But Maggie wondered why the nurse made such a point about it, why she continued to tell Amanda that she was so selfless. Something about that struck Maggie as wrong, yet even to think of it made the back of her neck tingle and her shoulders tighten, so that Maggie was tossed back and forth between two sensations, and she could never tell if either one was true. One night she asked her grandfather about it when he came to sit by her bed when she was doing her reading assignment for the next day. "Do you think she would do the same thing for me, if it was me in the hospital?" she asked him, shutting her eyes against seeing his reaction to the question. She felt his hand reach for hers, felt his fingers touch each of her fingers, and felt reassured until she heard his voice, the words coming out like stiff little pieces of cardboard, "Of course she would," and Maggie kept her eyes closed, afraid of what she would see in his eyes if she looked at him, afraid, not of disapproval that she had asked, but of something that would tell her he didn't believe his own words. And she had never known him to speak to her this way, saying words he didn't believe in, so she kept her eyes closed and hoped not to see his face.

Her grandfather took to coming in late at night to see if Maggie was asleep, and most nights she was not. Most nights, she was fighting the image of Evan's face before it sank behind the car, before his body was yanked under the frame of the car that skidded on the slick road and smashed into the other car. Most nights, she was trying to press out of her memory the glimpse of Evan as he was turned onto the stretcher and slid through the door of the ambulance. Her grandfather bought a night-light for her room so that she would not have to face the dark and the images that haunted her. He left the door to her room open so that a large path of light from the hall could come in as she slept. And finally he took to sleeping on the extra bed, the one Evan slept in when she and Evan stayed overnight with their grandparents, until she could trust the night to let her sleep in peace.

Sometimes even that did not help. Sometimes Maggie woke her grandfather up with the touch of her hand on his shoulder. "Grandfather, I'm scared," she would tell him. One night he tucked her back in bed and told her to wait a minute, he would be right back. She lay in the dark feeling the night enclose her with frightening images of Evan under the car until her grandfather returned several minutes later and sat on the edge of her bed. He took one of her hands in his, pulled her fingers away from her palm, and laid something cold against her palm. "What is it?" she asked, turning onto her side, already loving the feel of some metal in her hand, already knowing it was a treasure for her. She looked at it, saw a slim and simply wrought silver pocket watch, and she bent her hand to get a better look at it, to let the night-light show it off to her.

"It's for you, Maggie. A watch that someone gave me."

"Who?" she asked, gazing up into his face that was shadowed by the dim light.

Instead of answering her question, he took the watch from her palm and opened it. Immediately she heard a series of delicate notes, chiming a tune.

"What is it?" she wanted to know.

"It's from a piece of music written by a famous musician. His name was Bach. And whenever you are afraid, his notes will soothe you."

Maggie took the watch in her own hand again, peered at the silver watch cover that shone in the light, listened to the chime of the notes, and when it was silent, she held it against her cheek, felt its silken smoothness. "But who gave it to you?" she wanted to know.

"This came from a woman I loved," and he paused.

"Grandmother? From Grandma?"

Her grandfather shook his head. "Someone from long ago, Maggie, someone I loved long ago, she's gone now, she —"

"Is she dead?"

"Hush, child. Let me tell you," he said gently. "I don't know where she is now. It was too long ago. But I loved her once, and I love you now, so I give it to you."

Maggie swallowed. She closed the watch, held it tightly in her hand. She knew something important had just happened to her. That she had been given something more precious than she could yet understand.

"May God hide you under the shadow of His wings," he said.

Maggie thought about the words, knew they were important, though she could not fully understand them. But she could see them. She could see a pair of wings, black, that caused a great wind as they flapped in the air and pulled her to them. And Maggie knew she would cling to this watch as to life, that it would comfort her whenever she needed it.

"Thank you, Grandfather." And then she added, "I think I can sleep now."

And she drifted into sleep with the image of the wings, and the thoughts of Evan, and the doom she sensed for him faded into the night.

And several months later, when the watch was gone, after she opened the drawer and found the sock with no watch in it, she wondered if she had hidden it in some different place. If she had placed it in another sock in a different drawer. She searched through her bureau and her desk, her closet too, but there was no watch. And she began to think her grandfather should not have given the watch to her. That he should have given it to her mother, his daughter.

That her mother would not have misplaced it.

Or to Evan, who would not have misplaced it.

Then too, she thought, perhaps her mother had found

the watch, had removed it from the bureau. This froze Maggie's mind. The thought was too unpleasant.

So Maggie decided she must have misplaced it, herself. And for a while, she believed it.

"What are you doing, Margaret?"

Maggie opens her eyes. Her mother stands in the doorway to the living room. Maggie notices the hunch of Amanda's shoulders, her arms wrapped tightly around her waist. In the shadow her eyes look like black holes.

"I heard the creaking of that chair. It woke me up," Amanda says with clear irritation. She taps the stone in her ring against the doorframe.

"Oh, I'm sorry, Mother. I didn't realize you could hear it." Maggie pauses and looks at the fire. "I was trying to keep the fire up."

"It's the middle of the night, Margaret. What are you doing in that rocker? You woke me up."

Maggie sees her mother clasp her hands at her waist, sees her knuckles tighten, looks for her eyes in the shadow. She remembers her mother in a sea green bathrobe, the wooly kind, with the fluff all matted in the back from sitting on it. She remembers her mother running a hand up and down the lapel where there was a satin ribbing. Twenty years ago, she thinks. She was angry about something. I can't remember what, Maggie thinks, but I remember the tone. Her voice wound up from deep inside, her teeth held together as she spoke.

"Mother, why did you agree to my coming up here with you?" Such an obvious question. Why hadn't she asked the obvious before? What had she been thinking when she insisted that she come too? Jeremy had warned her, had told her it sounded like a crazy idea. How had she shut off from herself, unable to know what she now knew?

"Why did I agree? To have you come too? To the lake?" Amanda twines her fingers together and pulls them to her chin.

"Yeah. Here. This time. Why did you agree to it?" Maggie straightens out her legs, pushes one foot against the floor and feels the chair begin to rock.

Amanda sighs. Loud enough for Maggie to hear it. "Well, dear, if you want to know the truth, I agreed to this because I thought you needed a break."

Of all the possible answers her mother could have given, Maggie does not expect this one. "Me? What's wrong with my life?"

"I thought you needed a break," she repeats.

"What are you talking about?" Maggie leans forward in her chair.

"I'm talking about that life you lead. With that man."

Maggie bites her lower lip. I won't even answer, she thinks.

"Well, dear, it's true. You needed to get away from the city. And him. He's just not —"

"Mother, why else did you agree to this?"

Amanda does not answer directly. She lowers her head. She twists her hands. "Look at you," she starts. "Here it is, the middle of the night. You're up staring at the fire, rocking back and forth in that chair, having no regard for me, knowing full well you'll keep me up. You haven't changed a bit."

Maggie rises from the chair. She takes a log from the wood-box, kneels down on the hearth, and rests it gently on the fire. With the poker, she pushes at the coals and stirs up new flame. Without looking at her mother, she says, "I came because I thought this was a chance to be together. I thought —"

Amanda puts her hands in her pockets, turns around, goes into the darkness of her room, and closes the door.

"I thought we might have a chance here," Maggie calls at the closed door. There is no sound from the other room. "I thought it was a chance," she calls a little louder. The sound of her voice is flat in the shadowed, empty room. You never answer me, she thinks.

What have I done to you? she wonders, the words forming slowly in her mind.

❧ SIX ❧

AMANDA stands by the window in her room. She holds the sheer curtain to the side and presses her hand against the glass. Cold as death, she thinks, remembering her mother's expression about cold mornings on the lake. Dark as death, she used to say about a starless night, standing on the front porch as she gazed at the night shadows that were the lake and the mountains that surrounded it.

It's dark as death now, she thinks, pulling her hand away from the window. It's a still, dark night.

Amanda thinks of Maggie in the next room. She pictures her on the sofa by the window, blankets piled on top of her. She sees the way her daughter looked as she ran from the lake back up to the car, how she said everything would be all right, how nothing had changed. How little she knows of life, Amanda thinks, and her mouth tightens.

Putting a hand to her breast, Amanda feels the beating, like a machine, she thinks. What if it stops? Here in the woods? Like Father? She feels a lightness in her head as she draws in a breath and hears the sound in the still, dark night. She holds the breath in her chest. Will the beating stop if I hold it long enough?

She sits down on the chair by the window, the one with the cane seat that she remembers her mother bringing up one summer from the house in Connecticut. There were once flowers painted on the wooden slats of the chair back, but now there are only patches of yellow paint, like smudges. She leans her forehead against the glass and thinks of Henry, remembers the first time they came to the lake together after they were married. She had told him about the place often during the months before the wedding, but he didn't like it much from the start, and she never thought he tried much to like it.

He was too bumbling in the woods, too bulky and unsteady in the canoe, she remembers, picturing him grappling with a paddle as he climbed into one for the first time. In his office he was smooth, she thinks, sitting hunched over his desk, his fingers drumming on the desk top when he was thinking. But here, at Land's End, he was a fish out of water. Father tried to interest him in the history of the lake, took him hiking sometimes. But they would come back with some story of what had gone wrong. There was always something Henry didn't like about the lake.

Amanda shivers in the cold, tightens her shoulders, rubs her arms with both hands. The curtain closes. A tiny ray of light pushes under the door, and she knows Maggie is awake, adjusting the fire. She reaches out for the end of the bed, then guides herself along the side. She rests herself onto the bed, leans back, pulling the covers loosely over her legs.

A memory comes of a time when Maggie and her grandfather went down to the west arm of the lake together. They went to fish, she thinks. Amanda can see Maggie waiting on the porch through the morning, waiting for him to finish his errands in Chad, to take her in the boat. She sat on the swing on the side of the porch, her two squat ponytails bobbing on the sides of her head every time the door opened, or every time she thought she heard someone coming through the woods from Chad. He came finally, took her hand as they headed down to the dock, and Amanda watched the boat grow small as it headed across the lake to the west arm. They didn't fish though, Amanda recalls. They collected raspberries for pies.

"Look how much we picked, Mother," she remembers

Maggie calling to her from the dock when they got back, and she saw Maggie's smiling face when the two of them stopped on the porch to show their success. "Enough for pies, don't you think?" Father had said.

"My, you have been busy," Amanda told them. Father laid his hat, filled to the brim with juicy red raspberries that now stained the lining, on the seat beside Amanda, and Maggie showed a quart container, also filled. "Leave the berries here," she told them, and Amanda mouths the words in the dark and her body shivers again under the blankets. She remembers picking over the raspberries carefully, alone on the porch, while she listened to the sounds inside the house. She remembers thinking that she should have been pleased. But she wasn't. Later she carried the hat and the quart container with the berries across the field beside the house where she dumped them on the ground. The hat too. Then she stared at the red glowing mess on the ground, felt a sense of remorse. What is the matter with me? she thought, as she stooped to the ground and began filling the hat and the container back up with the berries. When she stood up, her stained hands clasping the raspberries to her chest, she rubbed the wet red ground with one foot until there was no more trace of spilled berries. And at supper, when she cut the steaming raspberry pies into generous portions, she found herself thinking of what she had done. She watched her father dig his fork into the cream topping on the pie, watched him smile with satisfaction as he tasted the hot raspberries. She heard him praise Maggie for her efforts on picking with him. She watched Evan hand his plate to her for a second piece, and she watched Maggie consume her pie at a painfully slow pace. No one even noticed that she had no pie. Not even a taste. What would she have told them if someone had asked why? I can't eat of their pleasure — Could she have said that? Would she? Would anyone have understood?

Toward dawn Amanda smells smoke. The air on the lake is still, but it is as if a gust of wind pushed the smoke smell in through the cracks around the windows, it was that sudden. Amanda wonders if it is the smoke from the chimney in Land's End, if Maggie is up, building up the fires in the kitchen and the living room. Then she gets up to look out the window, wonders if she might see some sign of a fire. Across the lake she sees a wisp of smoke rise from the front of the mountain, a curling grey thread. It spreads out like a fan and floats flatly against the dark mountain.

It is just the mist, she realizes, rising from the silver lake in the early light. In places where the cottony mist has evaporated into the air, the surface of the water glistens black as mica.

The sky is still pale, while red and orange jump out from the mountains, sharp in definition.

Amanda listens. The house is silent, but she feels its life in her. Outside is far away, though only a pane of glass separates her from the chill. It was after the canoe trip with her father that she remembers feeling more safe inside the house than out in the woods or on the lake. It was after the canoe trip, she thinks, as they sat by the river and waited for Lenny to come get them, that the feeling took shape in her. It was a still morning, like this, she thinks, even the water flowing by us was still. They had come through some deafening white water, but as they sat at the river's edge, she told the others to listen to the quiet as they waited.

Amanda sat on a rock and gazed at the river, watching the steel blue water move slowly along. Michael lay on the ground, leaning back against a piece of silver driftwood, his arms crossed over his chest, his eyes closed into little lines, his black hair sticking on end in places. His foot tapped sideways against a rock, and Amanda wondered if he was impatient for Lenny to come, or if he was humming some tune in his head. His red hat lay on the ground by his side, the top pushed in to form a hole.

Father paced along the road, his arms crossed over his chest like Michael's, his head bent, the brim of his brown hat down low over his eyes. Amanda wondered what he was thinking.

Amanda looked around for Will. He must have headed down the road on foot, she thought. That was like Will. He never sat still for anything.

It was when she looked up the road in the other direction, not from where Lenny would come, but the other way, that she noticed a thin grey trail of smoke above the skyline. Her eyes studied that smoke for several seconds until it billowed into a small black cloud, a thick dense mass of black that hung in the sky for several more seconds before it expanded and cracked apart in the air, so that it became more like black mist rising. Amanda was struck by the fact that this black cloud made no sound as it cracked into black smoke, and yet in her mind, it was as deafening as the roar of the rapids.

"Look," Amanda suddenly said as she scrambled up from the ground and stood firmly on both feet. Again there was a silence as Michael opened his eyes and slowly sat up to look at her, and as Father stopped his pacing and turned to look at her too. By the time they turned to see what she was pointing to, there was only black above the tree line.

"A fire," Michael yelled and leaped up from the ground and started to run up the embankment, all in one moment. Together Michael and Father raced ahead, while Amanda was aware of her knees giving away as she tried to follow them.

The smoke hung over a farm about two hundreds yards down the road. From the river's edge, Amanda had thought it would be several miles away, but within a minute she was there at the house, and behind her she heard Will calling to them, but his words were lost to her because a new sound was echoing into the air, a thin piercing sound, a cry, and she likened the cry to the first wisp of smoke she had seen and then to the cry she had heard during the night, the cry that was her father in the river.

The farmhouse stood back from the road, unlike most country homes that clung to the edge of the road. The front of this house faced the woods, so it was the end of the house that Amanda stared at. The unpainted barn faced the road, perpendicular to the farmhouse, and behind the barn, a hill began, rising steeply into thick woods. A neat stone wall wound along the back of the house, along the road, to a break where there was a narrow drive to the barn door. Amanda noticed the flaming orange of the two maples that stood between the house and the road, at the height of their fall color. The ground was dotted with yellow leaves, and it was hard to distinguish between the maple leaves on the trees and the flames that rose from the barn behind the house.

It was the barn that was a solid wall of flame, a black and orange wall of flame. Through the flame she could see the supporting structure of the building, the large corner beams that held the roof in place like shadows. The sound that seconds before had been a thin cry was now a dense wailing, first long and low, then high and airy, with no common tone or recognizable rhythm. When Amanda realized what the wailing was, that it was the death cries of the animals trapped in the barn, their cries lasting longer in the air than their very beings would, she dropped to her knees. She fought the image in her mind that the cries brought, of horses with flared nostrils and muzzles arching in every direction, of cows swaying with bent heads and bulging eyes. She could feel the heat from where she stood on the road; it billowed in waves and currents of air around the barn. Black ash flew about the trees that waved their limbs above her head in slow motion, and above the flame rose a current of black smoke that reminded Amanda of the moving river, it was that smooth and sure of its purpose. And still the wailing continued, so deeply from the center of the barn that Amanda felt she was in the barn and the cries were her own.

"There's no one home," she heard Michael yell as he emerged from a door on the side of the house and headed round to the front to watch. From one side of the barn Amanda saw her father pulling barrels away, rolling them on their rims, turning some on their sides and pushing them. A wagon piled with sacks rested against a tree some twenty feet from the inferno; Amanda watched as sparks flew at her, as her father tried to move it farther away.

"Get back," Michael continued to yell, his throat heaving the words into the air unanswered. Amanda could only draw her hands together and hold them pressed against her chest, an instinctive plea to forces beyond her. She was aware of the thought that her heart filled her chest, that it was expanding, that there was no room for her breath. And so she prayed to the fire to stop.

It was not the fire that stopped, though. It was the cacophony of crying that one moment filled the air and the next filled it with its absence. From the barn, deep within the barn, almost as if it came from the ground on which the barn had long ago been built, came a groan, the kind of roaring groan of a hurricane wind.

Michael turned his back and put his hands to his face. Amanda noticed that his mouth was open, but she could hear nothing beyond the roaring fire. She felt her hands reach out in front of her, still clasped. It was all she could do.

As the roof caved in, Amanda saw the flame suddenly squashed out for an instant. Later Michael told her that could not have happened, that fire doesn't stop and start that way, but Amanda told him that was exactly how it happened. For a split second there was no flame. There was merely the pile of a collapsed barn, and she swore she could see the corner beams still standing, rising out of the heap of char. Then the next moment there was only flame again, and gusting smoke, and flying ash.

Then there was nothing. It was over. There was only silence and the smell of dead things. Dead charred things.

Lenny appeared then, and soon there were other people and they all stood together, wordless, in the fire's silence. And when they saw a horse-drawn wagon appear at the crest of the hill above where the barn had stood, when they counted heads as it wound its way down the hill, the pace painfully slow to those who watched, they hung their heads and guessed about the lives of the people in the wagon.

The light from the house shone like the north star. Sitting in the bow of the boat, Amanda watched the night sky blend with the water into a sea of black. There was only the sound of the engine and the white light across the lake.

"Not a single star tonight, is there, Amanda."

Amanda shook her head in reply, then realized that Lenny could not see her face. "How do you know where to go," she asked him, "if you can't see anything?"

Lenny coughed lightly and shifted his hands on the wheel to loosen his grip. "Amanda, I know this lake better than anything. Don't you worry. There's nothing to worry about now."

Amanda guessed what he was thinking when he said the word *now* because he emphasized it so. She felt a tingling in her chest that swirled down to her stomach. Her nostrils quivered as she inhaled and smelled the fire still in her nose. And it was the image of the collapsed barn in that one instant when the flame died that stayed with her. It was as if the interior of the barn were a large gaping hole leading deep into the earth. She remembered losing her balance even though she was on her knees, and reaching her hands out to steady herself.

Instinctively she pulled her hands together again and reached them out toward the light of the house. Then she turned to see what the others were doing, but she could distinguish only shapes in the darkness. Behind the boat the world was as black as it was looking out from the bow, only there was no light across the lake to give a sense of perspective. Amanda focused on the shapes of her brothers, who sat together in the stern. Their heads faced forward but she could not see their faces. She raised her hand in a wave and one of them responded. A black shadow of a hand flickered by a head.

Father sat directly behind her, his arm resting against the

back of the seat that separated them. Amanda could see the line of the brim of his hat. It was facing down at an angle. She wondered if he might have fallen asleep, lulled by the sound of the engine. Or was he just thinking?

Leaning over closer to Lenny, Amanda asked, "Do you think Mother is worried?"

"What?" he said, leaning in her direction to get her words.

"Mother," she repeated. "Do you think Mother's worried?"

"We was due back by supper," he answered. "She's prob'ly fussed by now."

Amanda tried to imagine telling her mother about the fire. She practiced the words in her head. But they sounded empty. How can I tell her about it? she wondered. How can she know what that sound was like? And those people, how can she know what their faces looked like as they sat in the wagon on the hillside and stared at what was left?

When Lenny pulled the boat up to the dock, Amanda stared at the lighted windows of the house. She saw the outline of her mother by the front door, like a shadow, the yellow light all around her form, and suddenly she thought of the burning barn again and the outline of the beams and she thought she remembered the shape, maybe just a shadow, of an animal trapped in the burning flames.

Then the others were out of the boat. Will hitched the ropes to the cleats on the dock. Father walked up the gangplank, and Michael just stood on the edge of the dock, his shape looming and swaying, as he held a light for Will. Lenny shut off the engine and began loading gear onto the dock. Will carried it up the gangplank.

Amanda watched her father make his way up the path. She saw the door open and the shape of her mother came out onto the porch with the light from inside the house. She watched them talk, but only for a couple of seconds. Then he went inside and her mother stood by the steps and waited.

As Michael helped Will carry a load up to the house, Amanda stood up and stepped out onto the dock. Lenny took her arm and led her toward the gangplank in the dark. "Lenny," she said as she lifted a bundle from the dock. "How long does it take before you're just bones?"

She couldn't see his face, but he stopped in his steps and held her arm tighter. "Amanda," he said, and she knew by the tone of his soft voice that he knew what she had asked. "I don't know, Amanda, but you mustn't think on it."

Amanda wanted to know exactly. She wanted to hear the truth. "But what do you think, I mean, what's a guess?"

"Don't think on it, Amanda."

"Lenny. Do you think you can feel anything after you die?" she asked.

"I don't 'spect so, Amanda. But I don't think on it much. You shouldn't neither. Tomorrow you can go swimming and if the weather's good, you and your brothers can get some berries for pies. Lindy'll make pies for you."

But Amanda kept wondering. She walked up the path, saw her mother's arms around her brothers' shoulders as she followed them into the house. Amanda reached the porch and heard the sounds of their voices telling the story. She sat down on the swing at the end of the porch and listened. She listened to them tell the story, but she kept thinking, They're getting it wrong, it wasn't just like that. But she didn't say anything. She sat on the porch and watched the light from the windows and waited and wondered in the darkness, the voices drifting away, her thoughts making the sounds in her head.

"What are you doing, Amanda?"

Amanda looked up to see her mother's shape in the doorway. "What am I doing?" she repeated. "I'm —"

"Come into the house, dear. Lindy has some food for you. It's cold out here."

Amanda watched her mother lean against the doorframe;

her face was in shadow, but Amanda thought she was looking out at the lake. "I'm waiting for the loons," she told her mother.

"You won't hear them by waiting, you know that never works."

"If I wait long enough, it will."

"Well, dinner's coming now, Amanda. Do come in. Don't sit out here and mope all by yourself. I know you had an unpleasant day, but it's no reason to mope."

Left alone on the porch Amanda listened to the sounds inside and out. She heard Will's voice telling about the fire still. No one answered him, though; he could have been talking in an empty room. Outside she heard the silence of the night.

"Eleanor," she heard her father say to her mother, "have you told Lenny when we're leaving?" Amanda listened for an answer, but there was none. She could tell that Lindy was bringing in the food.

"Amanda," her mother called. "There's hot cornbread here. And Lindy prepared chowder."

Amanda left the swing, lingered by the door to watch the lake again. Then she joined the others at the table inside. Will was busily eating his chowder and had piled several pieces of cornbread on his plate. Michael had changed into a fresh shirt, white cotton with no collar. Father sat at the head of the table, motionless, his shoulders slumped, his eyes staring at the bowl of chowder before him.

"Father," she asked. "Do you think all those people will be all right? I mean, with everything that happened today —"

Without taking his eyes from his bowl, he answered her. "No, I don't suppose they will be all right."

"Well, Thomas," her mother interjected, "not for now, but they will be later. After the place gets cleaned up."

"No, I don't suppose they will," he repeated.

"Could we do something for them?" Amanda asked. "Maybe take them some food or something."

"Oh, Amanda," Michael threw in. "For God's sake, drop it."

Will looked at Michael. "Drop it? You think that's an answer?"

"In this case, yes," Michael returned.

As her brothers argued, Amanda studied her father's face. Pale, some trace of the smoke and ash still on his face, his blue eyes darkening with moisture as they stared ahead. What does he see? she wondered. She noticed the line between his brows, how deep it had become. She had a vague memory of his face like this, a memory from several years ago, was it in Paris? though she couldn't quite place it. But she saw him at a small round table, slumped forward as he was then, his arms hanging down at his sides.

Eleanor sat stiffly at the other end of the table, her posture erect. She watched her sons argue, her left eyebrow raised in attention, ignoring her husband with determination.

Looking back at her father, Amanda remembered another person at that table with him, in the memory that formed and dissolved and formed again in her mind. A woman with red lips, she suddenly could see the red lips against the crisp white teeth, and thick brown hair that hung in waves around her shoulders. The woman was holding something in her hands, holding it out to her father, cupped in both palms, and it was something that flashed silver, she thought. Amanda remembered her father's countenance changing, so that a light appeared in his face, so that his features almost lifted out of themselves, and then the woman placed the silver object — was it a watch? she could not tell — in his hand and turned the fingers back over it so that it was his, in his hand, and he was touching it with his fingers. Amanda remembered standing at some distance, across the street, it may have been. But why was she standing there all alone? And how could she know his eyes were wet with moisture if he wasn't looking straight at her?

Amanda shook her head. She put her spoon into the thick milky chowder and stirred it around, watched the steam rise, watched the chowder coat the handle of her spoon. It tasted rich and sweet. Bits of corn floated down her throat, and she kept her eyes on the spoon as it dipped and swirled, dipped and swirled. The memory of her father's wet eyes stayed with her, but then she wasn't sure if it had been a painting she had seen somewhere, or a photograph from an album, and maybe it wasn't Father she was remembering. When she looked at him again, when her chowder was all gone, as she reached for the plate of cornbread, she thought she smelled the fire again. The moisture was gone from his eyes. He was taking a large bite of cornbread, and the blue of his eyes was like the blue paint on the china bowl. Have I just been dreaming again? she wondered.

Michael and Will argued through the meal. The cornbread was eaten up and a second plate was brought in by Lindy, and they finished that off too. Father sat by the fire afterward and Mother went to her room. Michael and Will played canasta at the table. Amanda sat in the kitchen and listened to the fire crackle in the wood stove. Later she fell asleep. She wondered again how long it takes to become bones as she drifted in and out of sleep.

And when Amanda awoke during the night, it was to the beating of her heart, and she listened to that pounding in her head and her chest, and she couldn't remember which of her memories were true, and which were dreams.

❧ SEVEN ❧

At DAWN Maggie watches the new light come into the sitting room, feels it spread slowly across the floor to where she lies on the sofa. The fire burns in red embers and grey ash in the early morning light. A thread of smoke hisses in a pocket of air.

Knowing she will not fall back to sleep, Maggie pushes back the blankets and walks to the windows at the front of the house, where she stands and views the lake, curling her toes against the cold wood floor. It is a grey morning, an October grey morning. The autumn reds are softened by the silver sky. Across the lake the colors linger near the shoreline, but in the mountains beyond, fall is ending. The rich yet somber winter green covers the land. Maggie notices the grey roof of the cabin down by the water; it is nearly hidden by the thickening pines.

Shivering, Maggie returns to the hearth. She pulls an orange blanket from the sofa and wraps it around her shoulders as she pokes at the embers and watches the smoke thicken. A tiny blade of flame grows from a pine log.

Maggie closes her eyes and remembers the night, then she wonders about the day ahead.

How will it be, she thinks, walking to the west arm to see the grave? She remembers what Jeremy said, that she would have to wash her feelings away if she was going to learn anything. "There have to be things you don't know," he had told her. "If you're going to go up there," he had said, "you've got to find out what you don't know."

What I don't know, what I don't know, how can I find out what I don't know? she wonders. Jeremy says it's in my paintings. "What, what do you see?" she asked, but he could not explain.

Maggie places the screen in front of the fire as she stands up. She goes into the kitchen to start up the wood stove, to heat water for breakfast. She reaches for the box of Wheatena and readies a small pot of water to boil for the cereal. Then she lays out two bowls. She finds a box of brown sugar stuffed into the cookie jar and begins working at it with a spoon, trying to loosen it to put on top of the cereal. She senses someone behind her and turns.

"Mother, what are you —"

"I couldn't get back to sleep. The sounds from the lake, the loons just . . ." Her voice trails off as she gazes out the window over the sink. "What sort of a day do we have? For a walk, I mean."

"Well, it's grey, so I don't suppose it'll be too warm." Maggie turns to look at Amanda who still watches out the window. "But there's no wind, so it might be just perfect for us."

"What are you fixing here for us?" Amanda adjusts the bowls, moving them closer together by the stove. Silver hair spills out around her face. The long waves are pulled back and wound around into a knot at the back, above her neck, so that the darker hair underneath shows in contrast to the grey. Maggie looks at the wrinkled flesh on the backs of Amanda's hands, near the knuckles. The skin on her face is dry, tight, with wedges of lines around her eyes, the corners of her mouth, and her brow. From a distance her skin looks youthful, but in the morning light Maggie studies her face and realizes she looks older than her fifty-eight years.

"I'm just heating the water for the cereal we brought, and thought I'd make some coffee, and how about some of those sticky buns I found at the store —"

"You have it all planned out, don't you. Organized as

usual. I guess you don't need my help here —" Amanda holds her hands over the stove's surface, feels the warmth rise to her palms, moves the kettle from one side to another. Then she adjusts the flue.

"Well, why don't you get the coffee ready and I'll wrap some of those buns; how many do you want, two?"

"One is enough for me, Margaret, I can get by nicely with one. Especially if you're fixing cereal too." She reaches for the coffee and begins to spoon it into the filter. "I eat simply, dear, nothing fancy."

Maggie hears a crackle from the fireplace in the other room. "I'll just check the fire now," she tells Amanda.

In the living room she pulls the last two logs from the woodbox and lays them on the hearth. She pulls the screen away and puts one log onto the embered pieces. She lifts the blanket off the floor, folds it, and straightens the covers on the sofa. Kneeling by the fire she spreads her clothes to warm on the hearth. She pulls off her yellow flannel nightgown and folds it on her lap, smoothing out the wrinkles, touching the once-pink roses that dotted the bodice on either side of the buttons. She feels the goose bumps across her bare back, exposed to the air, but her chest faces the fire and is warm. She leans closer and shuts her eyes, feels the heat against her eyelids, her mouth, her hands on her knees, and she draws her hands up to her breasts.

Feeling her skin prickle, Maggie pulls back and reaches for a white cotton undershirt and pulls it over her head. Standing up, she pulls on a pair of brown corduroy slacks. She pushes her arms into the sleeves of a sweater, one that her father had brought her from Ireland, and pulls it down onto her hips. The high neck reaches up under her chin and she turns it down, like a turtleneck.

"Mother," she calls, "how's that water? Is it hot yet?"

Amanda's voice answers right behind her. "Yes, it's hot," and she holds her hands in her pockets.

"Oh, I didn't —" and Maggie smiles at Amanda. "I didn't realize you were there. What are you —"

"I think I'll dress now," Amanda answers. "The water's boiling. You can pour the coffee while I dress." She tightens the belt around the waist of her robe and crosses to her room.

Maggie feels embarrassment, but says, "Good. You dress, and I'll get things ready. Shall we sit in here by the fire?"

"Whatever you say, Margaret. You're in charge." Amanda closes the door to her room.

Maggie looks at the doorknob and waits for it to turn. She knows her mother's hand is still on the knob. She waits several seconds, holding her breath. Maggie sweeps off the hearth with the hand brush and replaces the screen in front of the fire. She goes into the kitchen and pours the water into the pot, listens to the trickle of the freshly brewed coffee, recalls her mother's eyes on her. Still she holds her breath and feels embarrassed.

It has always been that way, Maggie realizes, and wonders now at how she has forgotten such moments from the past, at how they embedded themselves in her so deeply that they were lost to her. But now they return, now they come at her like the wind at night, and she realizes they bring a feeling that is more than embarrassment, though she knows that is part of it. It is more like — and she halts. It is more like humiliation, she thinks. Her eyes water and she feels the humiliation again and anew. And she knows that somehow she has been shut away from the girl in her who could not bear that feeling, who could not be kind to herself, who only knew about herself through what her mother knew of her rather than through her own sense of herself.

There was the first dance that Maggie went to, in eighth grade. Betsey had come to her house after school that day so they could get ready together, so they could wind their hair in pink rollers and hold the hair dryer to each other's head, so they could listen to records together as they bathed and powdered and perfumed themselves before they donned their dresses. Maggie's aqua blue chiffon dress hung on the door of her closet, and her shoes, dyed to match the dress, rested on the floor below. Betsey's red chiffon dress and red dyed shoes lay on the extra bed, and Betsey lay sprawled across Maggie's bed, her feet pressing the wall above the bed. It was when Maggie was pulling out the curlers in her hair that Amanda came in. That was something that annoyed Maggie, the way her mother would enter her room without knocking, so there was no single moment to prepare for her. One second she was not in the room and the next second she was, just like that. She came in to the center of the room and stopped. Then she walked over to Maggie's desk and turned to stare at her daughter. Betsey sat up and began to straighten the covers on the bed while Maggie went on with the business of combing out her hair, seemingly unaware of her mother's presence. That was the way she had learned to be around her mother. It was better that way. She had watched what happened to Evan when he fought Amanda, at how he got so worked up, stomping around the house, slamming doors, yelling angry words, smashing his fist against a wall or a door. Maggie knew that didn't get a person anywhere with Amanda. Not that her way got her anywhere with Amanda either, but Maggie felt she held on to herself better than Evan did, by trying to numb herself to her mother, by trying to continue to please her. That was how she figured it when she was a girl, anyway.

So when Amanda stood there and stared at her, Maggie waited. She kept her eyes in the mirror in front of her, straining to watch her hand brush through her thick brown hair, seeing nothing. Finally Amanda spoke. And the words burned into Maggie.

She can feel them again as she remembers them.

"My, but you are vain, Margaret. And for one so plain —" Amanda did not finish the sentence.

Maggie remembers how her arms came in at her sides as she brushed her hair. She continued to pull the brush through the curls, stroke after stroke, and she said not a word in her own defense. For her mother had spoken the truth. And what defense is there when there is truth?

Later, after Amanda had left the room, Betsey zipped up

the aqua gown and told Maggie she looked beautiful. She remembers noticing Betsey's black hair against her rose red dress, her white skin like the petals of a lily. She remembers looking at her own plain brown hair, impossible to control for its thickness and bulk, at her sallow complexion and the two pink dots painted onto her cheekbones, which she rubbed at with the palm of one hand in an effort to remove, at the aqua dress that hung on her straight and lanky frame. She knew she would be as tall if not taller than all the boys at the dance. And she knew her eyes betrayed her, that they showed the shame she felt, the humiliation that her mother made her feel when she ridiculed her.

Maggie realizes that she could not have known and could not have told herself that she was just a girl. That she would come into her beauty with time. In her own way. She could not have known then that her girlish plainness was not the problem. The problem was that she had believed in her mother's words.

That was the problem.

Maggie wonders where Betsey is now. She has not seen her friend since they finished high school. She wonders how Betsey would remember that moment, if Betsey had known at the time what was happening to her. How could they have talked about it then, though? she wonders.

We were too close to it.

I was too close to it.

Maggie grits her teeth, feels the anger swallowed. Her neck prickles as she recalls her mother's eyes on her. Though she understands it, the shame is still there. It still exists. The words still burn.

Maggie adds a log to the wood stove. She pours herself a cup of coffee. She sips at the coffee and feels the pain. But she holds the girl she was closer to her. And she knows there is some advantage in that. There is some advantage.

"I'm going down to look at the lake, Mother," Maggie calls from the porch. Amanda is in the kitchen washing the dishes and does not answer. "I want to see what the weather looks like," she calls again.

Maggie heads down the path toward the water. She looks up and notices the dark mountains, how soft their lines are against the quiet grey morning sky. She stops and listens to the call of a bird, one she cannot identify, yet is familiar. Noticing the roof of the cabin, she heads in that direction along the lake's edge.

"This cabin has everything you could ever need," she remembers Evan telling her the first time they slept here, away from the house. And it's true, she thinks, as she steps through the thick ferns that have grown over the path in recent years. "Everything you need for comfort is right here," he had said; "beds for sleeping, a sink for washing, a table to put things on, and a stove for warmth."

"What about a bathroom?" she remembers asking him.

"Don't need a bathroom," he told her. "The woods are all around and they're good enough." It was true, Maggie thinks, that for them, at ten and thirteen, everything was right there.

The cabin rests on a foundation of rocks by the water. It does not fit with the style of the other buildings. It is plainer, a more simple structure, no more than a log cabin. The special part is the porch, built out over the water. She remembers lying on the porch swing, rocking back and forth. All I could see was the roof, the cabin wall, the water, and a thin line of sky. "It's like hanging on the edge of the earth," she once told Evan.

The cabin is now nearly lost to sight in the branches of the pine trees that cradle it. The roof shows through in a couple of spots, but the walls and windows cannot be seen. "Once," her grandfather had told her, "the cabin stood in a clearing all of its own." That was when he was a boy and the place was built by his father.

"What did they build the cabin for?" she had asked, and he had answered that it was a retreat, a place to spend the night and believe that you were in the wilderness, closer to

God's arms. It worked, too, Maggie remembers, as she makes her way through the ferns to the door that she opens with the lift of an iron latch.

The door falls open and a patch of light makes a triangle on the floor where Maggie steps. She peers uneasily around the room at the two sets of bunk beds that line the walls, at the zinc-lined sink on the wall to her right, a wooden stool beneath it. The mattresses are gone, the china bowl that once rested in the sink is gone, the white china mugs from the shelf above the sink are gone, the hurricane lamp with the tall, narrow glass is gone.

Maggie walks around the room, running her hand against the wooden bed frames, the sink, the wooden clothes tree that stands in one corner. The roof over the porch cuts off the light into the cabin, making it dark in early morning. Maggie remembers lying on the bottom bunk, being able to see the line where the mountains meet the sky. She tries it out, and yes, she can see the same line, the same sky. When she and Evan stayed in the cabin, they slept in the bottom bunks so they could see that line. "It makes me feel safe," she remembers Evan telling her at dawn once.

One thing about the cabin, Maggie recalls, is that it brings the darkest dark that can be found at night. The moonlight cannot reach into the two windows on the front. On a starless, moonless night, it is black in here, she thinks, remembering waking to the thick night air and not knowing where she was until Evan spoke to her.

The first time they slept here, she left her flashlight on through the night. They talked until Evan fell asleep, and Maggie remembers making shadows on the walls with her light. Evan slept with his head under the covers most nights, but that night he faced her and said that even if his eyes were closed, he could still see her. She remembers it was the summer after his accident on the bicycle, and she could not see the patch of skin where his hair was gone from the back of his head. She did not like to see his skin there or on his neck where the skin grafting was done. It made her stomach turn because it brought back the memory of him falling from her sight under the green car.

Maggie gets up and walks to the door of the porch. This one opens stiffly; the porch is not level, and the door cannot open too far, but she squeezes through the space and breathes in the air from the lake as she leans against the railing.

Evan sat in a rocker over there, she thinks, that last day before I went back home, the last day I ever saw him, when he stayed up for the fall with Mother. I was envious, wanted to stay, too, but there was work and school and — Maggie remembers waking that morning in the cabin, looking out the window at him as he rocked. When the rocker pushed back, she could see his profile, and from her place on the bed, she could see his jaw muscle working, bulging in and out. His hand tapped the arm of the rocker.

"Evan," she said lightly as she slid open the door and stepped out onto the porch. She noticed the bristly growth of a day's beard.

He turned to face her, the chair still pushing back and forth, and her eyes followed him. His blue eyes had a transparent look, but the edges of his mouth pulled into a grin. "Did I wake you up?" he asked, his eyes taking shape and depth.

Maggie sat down on the swing, shook her head. "You couldn't sleep?" she asked him and noticed how he pushed his jaw to one side.

"I have trouble sleeping these days." His blue eyes looked beyond her to the water, to the mountains on the horizon. "I wake up early. At first light." He reached his hand to rub the back of his head.

Maggie slung her arms over the railing as she leaned back, resting her head against a corner post. She heard the water slap against the rocks under the porch. "You remember the plans we used to make out here?"

Evan nodded, yes, and a grin spread across his face. "About

how we'd always come here, to this cabin, when we were old?"

"Yeah. You said you wanted to die here and I said that was awful, I just wanted to stay here when I got old."

Evan leaned way back in the rocker. "Did I say that? That I wanted to die here?"

"Don't you remember? It was the summer before Ivy came up here. You said you felt more alive here at Land's End than you were anywhere, that you wanted to be here even if you were too sick and too old to get out of bed —" Maggie stopped.

"Oh, yeah," Evan remembered. "And you said you'd help me out to the porch every day so I could look at the lake and hear the water under the porch and all that —" Evan smiled again, and Maggie laughed.

"Can't you just picture us," she said, "too old to walk, lying on this porch day after day." She paused and stared out at the water. "I guess we never thought about the winter, did we?"

"The winter? The winter never came to this lake, as far as I was concerned."

Evan leaned back in the rocker and stretched his bare feet out straight until they touched Maggie's knees. She touched them lightly with her fingers, covered his toes with her hands. "Your toes are blue. Are you cold?"

"No. They just get blue sometimes. It's a circulation thing. I haven't been getting much exercise."

"You're still pining for Sarah?" Maggie asked softly.

Evan's lips tightened as he raised a hand to cover his eyes.

Maggie leaned forward, put her hand on his knee.

Evan rocked forward and pushed his feet to the ground, stood up from the chair and walked to the other corner of the porch. "I haven't thought of her for a while," he said, leaning over the railing. "I don't know. I thought I was over it."

"You mean losing her?"

Evan shook his head from side to side. "It was more the other thing."

"What other thing?"

"About the other guy. That she'd been lying to me all that time, that she was planning to work with him in London after school."

"It's only been a couple of months, though, Evan. It'll get better. It always does."

"I don't know."

"When you get started at school this winter, it'll get better," she added. "Is this why you decided to wait until January to go back?"

Evan nodded, yes, and Maggie remembered the way her mother had described it to her on the phone, something about using the time to do some of his own work before he started the program. She hadn't said anything about Sarah. "Mother didn't like Sarah, did she?"

"Mag, she's never liked anyone I do. Haven't you noticed that yet? Don't you remember Ivy?"

"Ivy was my friend, though. She didn't like Ivy because she was my friend. She didn't think Ivy was a good friend for me to have, she thought Ivy —"

"Stop." Evan leaned forward, got up from the rocker. "I mean it, Maggie, you got to stop this shit." He walked to the cabin door, turned to her. "I mean, it was okay when you were little. But you can't keep doing this. You can't keep defending her. You can't let her do this to you."

Maggie's hands went in her pockets. She lowered her eyes, studied the floorboards. She waited for Evan to go inside, to slam the door as he usually did when he was angry.

"Don't you see what you're doing?" His voice had softened.

Maggie looked up at him. His blue eyes radiated like a night sky. "I just meant, it's not you who's the problem, it's —"

Evan was shaking his head. "That's what I mean. Don't do this. Don't say this stuff." He waited for her to speak, then opened the door to the cabin and went inside.

"I don't know why you're staying here with her then," she called to him. "If that's how you feel," she added.

There was no response from Evan. Just the sound of the other door opening and closing. And that was all.

Maggie stands up. She listens to the chattering of a squirrel overhead. She wonders if Amanda is ready for the walk to the west arm. She wonders how she can go to her grandfather's grave with her mother. She is afraid she will say something. About Evan. And she knows this is not the time.

She remembers when she got the call from Amanda about Evan. It was early in the evening. She was making chocolate chip cookies. Jeremy was at the library, researching the history of an area of the city where he had been commissioned to do a study of architectural style. He had said he would stop by later.

"Margaret," her mother's voice sounded flat against the buzzing of the long-distance wires.

Maggie waited, listening to the buzzing.

"Margaret, I have bad news."

Maggie looked at the cookie dough, at the wooden spoon that she had laid on the table when the phone rang. She remembered a dream, a dream from long ago, or was it just last night. She saw a flash of an image and lost it, could not hold on to it long enough to know what it was.

"It's bad news, dear. Worse than anything you could guess, anything you could imagine."

Maggie heard the words, repeated them in her head. The words were whirling around in her head, not making sense, but there. She couldn't focus on her mother's voice. Couldn't connect the words to meanings.

"It's Evan," Maggie stated as if she were the one calling Amanda to give her the news, and already she knew the news.

"My son, my Evan Rhoades," and Amanda's voice cracked. "Evan Rhoades has died, he is dead, Margaret," and again her voice cracked and Maggie heard silence.

Maggie waited, refused to fill in the silence with her own voice.

"It was an accident. A hunting accident."

"What?" Maggie spun back, feeling something large and scratchy in her chest, and she was thinking, Where is Jeremy, how can I find Jeremy?

"I said it was an accident."

Maggie heard the questions form in her mind, but she did not speak them, held them in, made no response to the news.

"Are you there?" Amanda asked, and her voice cracked with the distance in the lines again.

"I'm here," Maggie replied.

Amanda explained that she would be returning to Connecticut the next day with the body.

"What body?" Maggie asked and clapped her hand over her mouth.

Amanda ignored the question and asked Maggie if she would be at the funeral.

"Of course I'll be at the funeral," Maggie answered, offended.

"Will you bring that man with you?"

"You mean Jeremy?"

"Yes, will you bring him with you?"

When Jeremy arrived, Maggie was still in the kitchen, the bowl of cookie dough on the table. Before he had a chance to say hello, she flung the wooden spoon against the window over the sink, where it made a loud crack and fell into an African violet.

"Evan's dead," she announced, as Jeremy took off his jacket by the door.

Jeremy looked at the spoon, then back at Maggie.

"Your brother? What do you —"

"I'm saying Evan's dead. He's dead."

"Your brother, Evan? What do you mean? Why?" and Maggie noticed fast tears in his eyes.

"Why is he dead?" Maggie's throat ached. "He's dead because he's dead. And don't ask how. Because I can't remember."

Driving back to Philadelphia from the funeral, Maggie asked Jeremy the question in her mind.

"Maybe if I'd stayed, he wouldn't have died."

"Do you think you're God or something?" he answered.

"No," she whispered and then louder, "No," and then she repeated the word over and over.

Jeremy reached a hand over, laid it on her thigh.

"Maggie, everyone has to ask that question. But you know there is no answer."

"But maybe I could've made a difference. Maybe I could've kept him at the house that day."

"That's what I mean. Do you think you're God?"

"I can't cry yet." Maggie bent her head, ran her hands through her hair.

They drove in silence the rest of the way. Jeremy went to his office for a few hours and when he stopped by her apartment later, he found her stretched out on the floor of the living room, her feet resting on the seat of a rocker, her hands under her head, asleep. He lay down on the floor beside her, touched her hair with her fingers, leaned close to her face to look at her closed eyelids.

Maggie shifted, pulled her feet onto the floor. When she opened her eyes, Jeremy's face was there before her, his dark eyes searching her face.

"Jeremy," she whispered, closed her eyes again, and turned her body toward his.

He undid the buttons to her blue blouse, ran his fingers down her neck, under the soft fabric of her slip, laid his hand against a breast.

Maggie repeated his name, always liking the sound of it. "Should we do this now?" she asked him, burrowing her head into the crook of his arm, sliding a hand around his chest.

"Now?" he questioned. "You mean, because of Evan?"

Maggie nodded.

"Evan's dead, Maggie," he said. "He'll be dead forever. I'm alive, here with you." Suddenly his own tears sprang, as he pressed his face against her chest.

"You loved him too," she said, and he nodded.

"I'm sorry. You're the one who should be crying."

"I am crying. Inside. It helps, though. To see you."

Jeremy sat up, pulled a pillow from the sofa, placed it under her head. He looked her directly in the eye.

"Mother doesn't approve of you, you know," she whispered.

"I know. I've noticed."

A thin smile passed across Maggie's face. "Evan did, though, he told me you'd be good for me."

"I know. He told me that too. And that you'd be good for me."

"Yeah," she sighed, "I think he was right, I —" and she stopped, feeling the bramble of pain in her chest rise up through her throat and into her face, feeling a stinging in her eyes as tears came. "Jeremy, I want to tell him —" She closed her mouth.

"It's all right, Maggie. Say it, if you want to. Or don't." He ran his hands over her arms, pulled the blouse off her shoulders, rubbed her arms.

Voices from the street below echoed in the night. An argument, two men yelling loudly, their voices distracting. When they were gone, Maggie turned to Jeremy. "He didn't have a chance," she said. "Ever since the accident." She paused and listened for the sounds of the street. "I watched that ambulance go around the corner at the end of the street. I watched him go, Jeremy, and I did nothing."

"That was years ago. You were just a child."

"I know. But somehow it's like yesterday. This whole thing feels like yesterday. I keep thinking I'm going to go to the hospital, like then, and I'll see him, and I'll know, it's all right, that he's okay. But he's not okay this time. And I can't tell him I'm sorry."

"Maggie, what do you have to be sorry for, there's nothing —"

"I should have run after that ambulance, Jeremy. I should have done something. I should have stayed at the lake. I shouldn't have come home."

Jeremy took her hands in his. He squeezed them together and held them. "You did what was right, Maggie, all along, you did what was right."

"No. No, I did what I wanted. Always, what I wanted. I never should have left him there with her."

Jeremy pulled his shirt off, his trousers, and lay beside her, his long legs wrapping around hers.

"It doesn't matter, your mother not approving of me."

"I know."

"And you did what was right. You know you did."

Later, as they slept, Maggie dreamed about Evan. She dreamed about the accident, when he was struck on his bicycle by the car as Maggie stood and watched. In the dream, Maggie ran to him, found him there beneath the car, but he was already dead, his limbs limp as she pulled on them. "Don't do this," she cried in the dream to her brother. "Get up, Evan, please get up." His eyes were open, blue crystals that stared unseeing at her. "Get up, please," she pleaded, but the eyes were stones and he did not get up.

Maggie's cries awakened Jeremy and herself. "Make him get up," she told Jeremy. "Or close his eyes. Don't let him look like that."

"You're dreaming, Maggie," he told her, his mouth close to her ear. "It's just a dream."

Maggie twisted in the dark, the dream image pulling at her. She thought of things she loved, things that were gone, people she would never see again.

"Grandfather should have given him the watch and not me."

"What watch?" he asked, his eyes opened to the dark room, following the slices of light from the street across the floor.

"The watch Grandfather gave me. You know, the one I told you about, the silver watch with the chime, that he gave me when I stayed there, after Evan was hurt. The one I lost. Or at least that disappeared —"

"What do you mean, disappeared?" he asked. "Are you saying you think someone took it?"

"Well, I don't know, it's just, it was gone one time when I went to look at it. I kept it hidden in my drawer, in a sock."

"In a sock?"

"Well, it was a secret. Sort of," she tried to explain. "Well, it wasn't that he said it was a secret. It was just that I understood it was."

"Why should he have given it to Evan?"

"I don't know." Maggie raised onto one elbow, felt her breast press against Jeremy's upper arm, felt his hand reach over to touch her. "What do you think?" she asked him.

"I don't know. I wasn't there, remember?"

Maggie knew she was lost in old memories, things she couldn't sort out, things that didn't make sense, things that just made her want to cry.

"He died at the lake too, right?" Jeremy asked.

"Grandfather?"

Jeremy nodded, turned to face Maggie, but her eyes were shadowed in the dark.

"He drowned. In the lake. God, that was awful too. But I don't remember much about it."

"Was he up there alone?"

"No, it's not a good idea to be up there alone. We were all there. Well, except me."

"Where were you?"

"I was with my friend, Betsey, and her family. But I went right away, before he was found, because they thought maybe he was lost in the woods, and I knew his favorite places. I guess they thought I might be able to help."

"And did you?"

Maggie paused after opening her mouth, felt the moment of arriving at the lake and hearing the news. "No, he was found by the time I got there. He was dead." She felt a dull ache in her chest, knew it was the ache of losing him, knew she had not felt it in years, and yet knew it had never left her. She had an image of herself, small and complete within herself, her hands raised to the skies, screaming at the world with the ache in her heart, while her big self lay there talking without emotion to Jeremy. She saw it as a painting, with a scene in full color placed within her chest, while her serene outer self gazed at a world of black.

"What do you suppose happened to the watch?" she asked.

"God, Maggie, I don't know."

"But what do you think. Really."

"I don't think anything," he said. "It's the middle of the night. Let's move into the bedroom."

Maggie said no, she wanted to stay there. She pressed her fingers lightly against his eyes, closing them to the dim shadows. "You sleep," she said, and she rested her head against his chest, ran her hand over the fine covering of hair on his chest and stomach, listened to him return to sleep, and heard the sound of her own voice, pleading with Evan to get up, knowing that he never would.

Maggie remembers her plans with Evan to grow old at the lake.

"It's no good, Evan," she speaks to the emptiness around her. She sweeps an arm out toward the lake. "This lake, this lake we love, is not going to see you get old." Maggie turns to where the rocker had once stood, to where Evan had sat rocking that morning. "You didn't live up to your part of the bargain," she says to the empty air, gesturing with her hands.

Maggie sinks onto the railing behind her, leans her head back against the post that supports the roof. How can I feel angry at him for dying? she wonders. But I do, and her hand forms a fist as the anger rises again and she slams it against the palm of her other hand. She remembers Evan's frequent displays of anger, forgets her own for a moment.

She remembers the first day Evan went to school after

he came home from the hospital. When their father asked Evan about his day, how it had gone, Evan looked bleak, answered that he didn't know how his day was.

"What do you mean?" she remembered her father saying, laying his fork and knife on the plate to give Evan his attention.

Amanda interrupted, explained that it was impossible to know how a day had gone. How can that be impossible, Maggie wondered, to know how your day is? Evan had responded by staring off at the painting on the wall over Amanda's head, a painting of a great-aunt who wore a black veil on her head and had steely black eyes that followed one around the room.

"Did great-aunt what's-her-name ever have any children?" Evan asked in that sarcastic tone he had developed.

Amanda turned in her chair to gaze at the portrait. Maggie remembers thinking that Amanda's hands looked like claws as they clutched the arms of her chair.

"Aunt Eloise?" she questioned, raising her eyebrows in imitation of the great-aunt. "Did Eloise ever have any children?"

"She doesn't look like the mother type," Maggie added.

"The mother type?" Amanda repeated. "And just what do you see as the mother type?"

"Drop it, you guys," Evan interrupted. "Sometimes it's just not worth it." He pushed back his chair until it bumped into the highboy. Then he ran from the room.

"Sometimes it's better to hold your tongue," Amanda retorted to Maggie.

From the stairs, Evan yelled again. "Drop it, I said." The sound of his footsteps racing up the stairs and the snap of a slammed door brought tears to Maggie's eyes.

"You should be more thoughtful of your brother, dear."

In the spring after the accident, Maggie noticed that Evan was growing more distant from her. Amanda told her to leave him alone, that he was merely maturing, that he didn't want his younger sister trailing along wherever he went.

"I'm not trailing along wherever he goes," she had responded. "He just seems different, that's all."

"Well, of course he seems different. He's growing older." Amanda leaned forward to rearrange the pillows behind her, to fluff them up more.

"Here, Mother, let me help you," Maggie said, approaching the settee.

"I'm not that old, Margaret, that I can't puff my own pillows. Now run along. But leave Evan alone."

Maggie walked up the street to her grandfather's house. "Can we go feed the ducks?" she asked him, feeling a little old for feeding the ducks with her grandfather, but knowing he would take it as an opportunity to be with her. They walked together down the hill and along Parker Avenue to where the duck pond was.

"Did you used to bring Mother to feed the ducks?" she asked.

"Not so much, Maggie, she stayed off on her own, with her mother. She was closer to her mother."

Maggie always had trouble seeing her grandmother as a young woman. Or as a mother to her own mother.

"Do you think Evan is different?" she asked him.

He let go of her hand, let his eyes run along the road to where it twisted away between the trees. "Everyone is different. All the time."

"Are you different?" she asked him.

His blue eyes folded in on themselves. "I hope so."

"Am I different?"

"Is this why you wanted to feed the ducks?" he asked.

Later that day, an early spring day, when the ground felt cold under the sun's warmth, she found Evan in the cemetery that ran behind their house. She was walking to Betsey's house, taking a shortcut through the cemetery. She noticed two freshly dug graves off to the right and paused. She had never seen the inside of a grave before. She thought the dirt looked like ordinary dirt, but she couldn't see the graves.

Keeping her eyes respectfully on the ground, she followed a smaller path that led to the mounds of dirt. Above her, tall pine trees shaded the ground. Orange needles made a covering on the ground. Before she got too close, she turned to see if she could still distinguish her house behind the trees. She noticed the slate grey of the roof and felt reassured.

On the other side of the dirt lay the two graves. She walked slowly around the piles of rich brown earth, peering ahead into the holes.

"Evan." The word tumbled from the back of her mouth and instinctively she drew her hands to cover her eyes.

Evan lay stretched out in the grave closest to Maggie, spread eagle in the hole. His arms lay out to the sides, bent at the elbow, his wrists resting against the walls of the grave. His two feet pointed to the far corners, too short to reach all the way.

At the sound of his name, his eyes opened. From between her fingers Maggie could see the white all around the blue of his eyes. His head did not turn, but stayed fixed in a stiff position, yet his eyes moved to look directly at her.

"Hey, hello," he said, a grin spreading across his face like a wave. "Come on in." Still his head remained facing forward, while his eyes had to twist in their sockets to meet hers.

Maggie drew closer to the grave, fell down onto her knees, felt her hands reach out in a gesture of prayer.

"Evan, what are you doing?"

Suddenly he sat up and brushed the dirt from the backs of his arms. "Hey, it's okay, Maggie. But what are you doing, praying or something?"

Maggie's arms fell to her sides. She felt embarrassed. "Evan, what are you doing?"

"What am I doing?" he repeated. Again he smiled a wide open smile. Maggie noticed the muscles of his jaw working. "I'm seeing what it's like." He moved quickly to one side, sweeping his hand in the air in invitation to her.

"You're seeing what it's like?"

The smile fell from his face. "It," he said. "You know, in here." He waited for her expression to change. "It's just a game, Maggie."

"It's a dumb game, Evan. I wouldn't climb in there for anything." She backed off her knees and stood up as he reached a hand in her direction. Then he stood up, hoisted himself to the edge, where he sat, his legs dangling, the back of his feet hitting the loose earth on the side.

Maggie felt her head swim. She couldn't watch his feet swinging in the grave like that. She thought she would be sick, as the odor of the grave reached her nostrils.

Evan stood up. "Hey, will you brush the dirt off my back?"

Maggie did as he asked. She looked at the patch of grafted skin on the back of his head and neck. "Does it hurt, Evan?" she asked without thinking.

"What? My head?"

Gently, with one finger, she touched the smooth skin. "It's soft," she murmured.

"What does it look like?" he asked.

"The skin?"

"Yeah, the new skin. I can't get a good look at it."

Maggie tried to imagine not being able to get a good look at it for herself. "It doesn't look bad," she assured him.

"Yeah, sure."

Maggie felt the urge to fill in the holes behind them, to run home and find a shovel, to get those mounds of dirt back in the ground where they belonged.

"Why are there two?" she asked.

"There must be two people needing eternal rest."

"Oh, come on, Evan. It's not funny."

He didn't answer.

"You seem different," she told him.

"Hey, well, I am," he answered. "I got hurt, remember?" and he smiled.

Maggie's stomach heaved. "I didn't mean it that way —"

*   *   *

Maggie feels an ache in her stomach now. She looks out at the water, notices a pair of black ducks off shore beyond the dock. She smells the autumn air, earthy and humid. She wishes she could cry, could let out the feeling that lies within her.

Her eyes twitch as she remembers the sight of Evan in the grave, playing at death. She remembers the feel of her grandfather's watch in her palm. She remembers how she felt when she discovered it was gone. Like some part of her had been lost. She misses the watch, still. She wonders where it could be, still.

She feels the shadow of Evan, still.

When her grandfather died, Amanda told Maggie not to forget the days of darkness, for there are many. How could I forget them? she now wonders. They live on. I live on, she thinks, under the shadow of God's wings, as Grandfather told me I would.

But whose shadow does Maggie feel?

❧ EIGHT ❧

AMANDA dips her hands into the steaming water in the basin, pulls the water up to her face, rubs her hands up and down, presses against her eyes. She feels the steam from the water rise to her face. It soothes her skin. Opening her eyes, she watches her fingers undo the ties to her nightgown. She plunges a washcloth into the water, soaps it, opens the bodice of her nightgown, rubs her neck, her chest. Rinsing the cloth, she looks at herself in the mirror. Heavily, she rubs the soap from her skin.

There was a time when she felt alarmed by the sight of her own nakedness, her young breasts, as they filled and softened. Amanda's mother was a stickler for cleanliness, told her daughter that she should wash frequently. Amanda remembers once when Eleanor came into the bathroom just after Amanda had stepped from the porcelain tub that filled the far end of the room. "Did you wash well?" Eleanor asked her, and Amanda remembers wondering, Did I? Did I wash well enough? She pulled a towel from the rack on the closet door, wrapped it around herself, held it to her chest. "There's no need for modesty," Eleanor had told her. "You are what you are. Neither shame nor pride will do you any good." Eleanor took a second towel from the rack. "I'm all right, Mother, I don't need any help," she told her mother, but Eleanor opened another towel and approached her, began to rub against Amanda's shoulders. When Amanda felt the scratchy towel against her skin, she dropped her own towel and stood naked before her mother, feeling helpless. She imagined her hands moving to cover herself, but they hung like false friends at her sides.

Amanda's skin prickles at the memory of her mother's darkened eyes on her breasts. She remembers her mother's words, "You must never take pride in your bosom," and her breath pulls into her chest at the sound of the words in her mind. "Large or small," her mother said, "they are merely functional." Her mother then reached a hand out and squeezed one of Amanda's young-girl breasts. "It's just fatty tissue," she told Amanda.

Instinctively Amanda tightens her arms, covers her breasts with her hands. She presses her palms against the nipples, feels an accompanying stab of sensation between her legs. Her breath pulls in again, and she quickly drains the water from the basin, reaches for an undershirt, and holds it to her chest. She slips her arms into its sleeves. She fingers the embroidered edging along the bodice, remembers when her mother gave her several of these undershirts after Maggie was born. "To keep you warm," Eleanor had said.

Amanda remembers with sharp details the first time that Henry saw her body uncovered. It was their wedding night, which they spent in New York City before leaving the next day by boat for London where Amanda would meet his family. He had made quick love to her that first time, pulling at her white stockings, unbuttoning her silk blouse so clumsily that two buttons ripped away from the silk. He apologized and waited while she took the time to change into one of the nightgowns her mother had given her for the honeymoon. She remembers the look on his face as he opened the front of the smocked gown and looked at her, a kind of shivering running through his shoulders.

"You're beautiful," he had told her, and the memory of his words freshened the sensation in her body again.

"It's just fatty tissue," she had told him, knowing the moment died between them with those words because it dried her own desire, a desire she did not understand or wish to have.

She had seldom felt that desire in her life with Henry, least of all when he could see her body, could trace the line of her bare shoulder with his eye. The feel of his eyes on her skin sent a cold wind through her limbs. Once she confided her feelings of disdain and discomfort with her husband's admiration to her mother. "It's functional, dear," her mother told her. "A necessary part of marriage, but you needn't enjoy it. Let him admire you, it's part of the function. But don't expect that kind of affection to mean love. It won't happen."

Amanda steps into her navy wool slacks, tucks her shirt in, and wraps a maroon sweater around her shoulders, conscious of the rapid pull of her heart in her head. Glancing in the mirror, she watches her hand pull a brush through her long silver hair. She remembers her first Christmas with Henry when he gave her a set of silver brushes, and hand mirror to match. When she placed them on her bureau that night, he took one of the brushes and tried to brush her soft brown hair.

"Let me brush your hair tonight," he had asked, pulling the pins from the tight knot of hair at the back of her neck. Ripples of disquiet ran down her spine. Stiffly she sat on the stool by her dresser and let him brush her hair. With his other hand, he cupped her shoulder, as he pulled the brush, stroking her hair in gentle rhythm.

Amanda remembers watching his hand in the mirror above the dresser. Her eyes glazed as it moved down her arm and slid underneath to touch her side, to move around her waist. She rested on the stool as he removed her clothes and pressed his face against her back. His own desire ignored or did not notice her stiffness as he made love to her. "Lie here on the floor with me," he coaxed her, and when he pushed inside of her, for a moment she felt something. But it was followed by the irregular beat of her heart.

Later, she knew their first child was formed on that night, for in the morning, she knew something in her was different;

the sign was the patch of silver hair that streaked from her brow, and the way, within the following months, all of her hair turned grey. Was this love? she often asked herself with bitterness.

Amanda had given up on the idea of love long before her mother expressed her views on the subject. Love, to Amanda, was a moment of watching her father at the lake when she was a girl. Sitting on the porch, with her mother, she read the books that had been selected for her at the beginning of the summer, and she watched her brothers busying themselves with the boats, with their fishing rods, with rowing competitions, and canoe ventures. Her mother always sat on the bench that faced the woods so that she could not see the lake and the activities of her children and husband. "I don't like to be distracted," Eleanor would explain to her daughter, "and the light is better for needlework over here." Amanda could not understand that; she could not have turned her back to the lake and missed seeing the life that flowed there. And she was aware that in the house she felt confined, unliving. On the porch she was teased by life, and though she had to remain there, especially after the canoe trip with her father, she felt some pleasure in observing.

"Not with that heart," her mother told her sometimes, when she asked if she couldn't go out in a canoe. Amanda often wondered if those were the doctor's orders or if they were her mother's, but she accepted the decision with grace. Amanda was never quite sure what the problem was because she had seen the doctor only once about it, and after he left the room, she heard the murmur of her mother's voice with the doctor's, and Eleanor later told her that the doctor had said the canoe trip had been too much for her, that it had strained her heart. "What exactly did he say?" Amanda asked, and her mother answered, "I just told you what he said, he said you have a weak heart. And if your father hadn't taken you on that foolish trip, your condition would not have been strained." And when Amanda told her about the loon they had found in the water, Eleanor just shook her head, her mouth tight until she said the words, "Such a sight was just too much for you." Eleanor told her this so many times that Amanda realized that must have been it. "It couldn't have been the paddling," she once told her mother, "because I loved that." Eleanor explained that the physical exertion had just added to her problem.

Amanda remembers waking in the night after watching the barn burn, after canoeing down the river with her father and brothers. She remembers that night when she realized her life might end, might stop if the frantic pounding of her heart did not cease. Her mother kept her in bed for several days after the doctor came, and Lindy brought her hot soup every day and sat in the chair by the window while she sipped the soup and watched the steam twirl in the air.

After that Amanda used the phrase "weak heart" to explain why she couldn't do a lot of the things that her brothers did, or that her friends in Connecticut did. After that she would say, "I can't, I have a weak heart," and soon people stopped asking her to do things because they knew about her problem. She figured that no one wanted to have the responsibility of her weak heart.

But when she was first married, Henry suggested several times that she see a doctor and get a new diagnosis. "It's not necessary," she would tell him, and after a while, he stopped mentioning it, and just accepted it as fact. "Amanda has a weak heart," he would tell others when he had to turn down an invitation. "She's fine," he would say, "as long as she doesn't overdo."

Amanda suddenly feels a squirming in her stomach as she remembers the feel of the paddle in the water, remembers looking ahead to her father's large frame in the other canoe. She remembers feeling her heart stab with love for him. She remembers watching him at the table when they told Eleanor about the trip, about the fire that Amanda saw first. She remembers trying to imagine getting up from her chair and putting her arms around her father's neck, instead of just standing by his chair with tears in her eyes. "Sit down, Amanda," her mother had told her; so she did. Later Eleanor explained that it was not right for a girl to be so attached to her father.

Amanda remembers the first time her parents came to see Maggie after she was born. Evan was taking a nap and Henry was at the office when they arrived with a basket of food and a wish to see their new granddaughter. Amanda remembers the way her mother watched Maggie asleep in the crib. Eleanor stood with her arms folded, her lips thin, and she reached out a hand to pat Maggie's round bottom twice. When her mother left the room to see to things in the kitchen, Amanda watched her father turn Maggie gently to her side, then lift her in his arms to hold her to his breast.

"Don't wake her," she told him, as she saw him cradle the baby's head in his palm.

"She won't wake," he answered. And then, "We'll have to call her Maggie, though, won't we? Margaret is too stiff for a soft little girl."

Amanda's eyes sprang tears as she saw the softness in his touch, and when he bent his head to kiss Maggie's brow, Amanda drew her breath in with pain. "Don't wake her," she repeated, but he held her so, and she remained sleeping even as he returned her to the crib, covering her carefully with a pale pink blanket.

Later that afternoon they found him in the library, lying on a settee, with Maggie stretched out asleep on his breast. One large hand wrapped itself around the baby's tiny frame, the other lay beneath his head. When Eleanor saw her husband like that, her voice shrilly reprimanded him. "You mustn't," she cried, "you'll wake her, Thomas, and it won't be time to feed her again until later."

Sheepishly, Amanda's father carried the baby back to her crib. After he left the room, Amanda heard her mother tell him that it was not right to hold a baby that way. She wondered what "that way" was, and it was then that she wondered if her mother had spoken to him this way when she was a child. Instantly her heart began its fluttering, and this time it was accompanied by a headache. Amanda wondered again if she would die as she lay in pain through the evening, and her mind wrestled with her pain rather than thought on the situation. She gave her energy to calming her heart.

Two days later when she was up and around again, able to care for the baby herself, Amanda found a certain distaste for her child. Some connection had been broken. Maggie was not a child to be discovered over the years, as Evan was for her. Maggie's clear blue eyes were not windows of an unformed self. Her tight grasp was not the tender search for roots.

She was, instead, a reminder, however dim and unrecognized, of a love submerged.

And when Henry asked her why she did not tend to Maggie as she had to Evan, when he noticed the stiffness with which she handled their daughter, Amanda could only sigh and reply, "It's my heart, I don't want to overdo."

Amanda takes her brush and pulls it through her thin silver hair. She watches in the mirror as her hands twist and tie her hair in a knot at the back of her neck, and she holds it in place with the hairpins she removed the night before. Threads of hair spill into her face, and she wets her finger and pushes them back, smoothing them into her hair.

She gets closer to the mirror and examines her face. The skin falls away from the bone in places; she sees her skull emerge through the skin and shuts her eyes at the image. Her closed lids flicker.

"I hope my heart can take this walk today," she says to her reflection.

There is no one to answer, no one to reply, and she smiles in embarrassment.

She looks out the window, checking the weather. The grey morning hangs over the lake. There is no wind, no light ripple on the lake to suggest a sudden change in temperature or wind. Just a grey day, she thinks.

She glimpses the roof of the cabin down by the water. Then she sees Maggie head along the path from the cabin; Maggie's arm raises and she waves a hand. Amanda looks in the other direction, sees someone, a man, heading toward the house. It's Martin, she thinks, though she can't be sure.

It's been years, she thinks, since I saw him.

❧ NINE ❧

MAGGIE looks up from the path and sees someone heading her way at the moment she hears him call her name. She waves and calls hello, glad to see someone else on the lake.

Maggie can tell from a distance that it is Martin. He hasn't changed a bit, she thinks, since the last time she saw him, eight years ago. He's probably wearing the same green and black wool jacket. And the same red cap, she thinks, pulled down low over his forehead.

"Martin," she says as he gets closer, "how good of you to come over and see us —"

Martin shows a slight smile, reaches out his hand to take hold of hers. "Why, you look just fine," he comments, some surprise in his voice. "I didn't know how it'd be for you here. And your mother?" he asks, nodding toward the house. "She doing fine too?"

Maggie smiles at Martin's soft brown eyes, deep set under a leathery brow.

"Oh, it's good to see you, Martin. You haven't changed a bit."

"Me? Hell, no. I stay the same. But you?" and his eyebrows raise together as he lifts his head, "you've changed for sure. Grown up tall, you could say." He glances at her hands, and Maggie wonders if he is looking for a ring on her left hand.

She turns to face the water. "What kind of day do you think we'll be having? We're planning a walk down to the clearing at, you know, at the west arm, where Grandfather is —"

Martin studies her face, his eyes shaded under his brow again. "I thought we was going to get rain. But now I'm not so sure. The wind hasn't come up. That's a good sign. Prob'ly a good day for a walk. Not too cold neither." He coughs, pulls a hand from a pocket and holds a kerchief to his mouth. "She planning on the walk down there too?" he questions, looking up to the house.

Maggie looks at the house too, sees a shadow behind the curtain in her mother's room. She must be watching, she thinks.

"Everything all right in the house?" he inquires.

"Oh, just fine, Martin, you fixed everything up for us. You swept up too, didn't you?"

"Well, Alice done the sweeping and dusting, I got the water hooked up —" He pauses, as if listening for something, then breaks into another cough. "No leaks, I take it," he adds.

"No, Martin, everything is perfect." She watches him shade his eyes and look skyward, and he points a finger in the direction of the west arm.

"What'd I just say about the rain? See that patch of cloud? Could mean rain. Then again," and he sucks his breath in fast, "it might not."

"How's your business been?" Maggie asks, wanting to prolong the conversation.

"The mill?" he questions, nodding his head up and down. "Work's been good the last couple of years. People always need wood, now don't they?" Martin looks to the sky over the house and back to the lake. "I was sorry to hear about your father last spring," and he looks in Maggie's eyes. "And Mrs. Elliott too. She loved it here, I guess."

"Grandmother was old though. It was time for her. It was a blessing really, because she'd had a stroke, and half of her body was paralyzed. It would have been awful for her. To live like that, I mean." Maggie shoves her hands in her pockets, pulls her shoulders up. "But Father," and she shakes her head lightly from side to side. "That was a shock. Well, to me, anyway. I never guessed he was sick like that. Mother had no idea —" She feels her eyes water, is startled by the feeling she has.

"That cancer can come on pretty quick, I guess," he says.

Maggie likes his honest brown eyes, knows he doesn't need to say the words. "They're written in his eyes," Evan used to say, and he was right, she thinks, as she realizes his question was meant for an honest answer.

"Actually, Martin, you know, she didn't seem too shaken by it. Or by Grandmother's death either. She's pretty philosophical about these things. It's not like it was after Evan. Life just sort of —"

Maggie wonders if she can ask Martin the questions that have lingered in her mind since Evan's death. Questions that have sunk below her conscious thought, but which have been always there, just at the edge of her mind. She wonders now if he saw Evan after he died, if he saw the hunter who shot him, what her mother was like. She wonders if he knows who the hunter was, if he would tell her, if she could talk to him. Once Jeremy had asked her about this. She had so little information, she didn't know much. "Ask your mother," he had told her, his voice impatient. "I can't," she replied, and she didn't know why. I just can't, she thought at the time.

"Did you see him, Martin, after —" The words spill out, unplanned.

Martin's eyes widen, as he waits for her to finish the question. "After?" he repeats.

"Did you talk to the hunter?" Maggie feels the urgency of her questions, knows there are more, knows Martin can't answer them here, now.

"The hunter?" Martin repeats. His eyes narrow, hide under the brow again.

"The — who shot him, the the —"

Martin's eyes sink farther in shadow. Then he hears his

name called out from the house and he sees Amanda come round the side of the building from the back, her black beret pulled down over her hair, her coat balanced on her shoulders. "Martin," she calls, and he looks at Maggie, then at Amanda, whose arm is still waving.

"Mrs. Rhoades," he calls, leaning back into his hips, a cough emerging from his chest. "Good to see you, Mrs. Rhoades, and you're looking well."

Maggie's heart is pounding. She wants to ask Martin more about Evan. Her mind is working, letting words rise to the surface, words that have been hidden. She watches Martin with her mother, hears him express his sympathy about the two deaths. Martin looks back at Maggie, stealing glimpses into her face, then returning to his words with Amanda.

Can I talk to Martin? she wonders.

Amanda has a gracious expression, the smile settled easily on her mouth, the tilt of her head indicating attention. She asks about Alice, Martin's wife, and their three children, now grown and living elsewhere. Maggie watches her fidget with a strand of silver hair that brushes her eye. And yes, she is grateful for all the work they did to prepare the house for her, she tells him.

"Maggie told me you're going to walk round to the west arm today," he says.

Amanda looks down at the ground; her eyelids flutter to cover her feelings, and when she looks up, it is with an open smile. "Yes, yes," she repeats, "we're going to walk down to the west arm today. To see my father's grave. It's been years since I was there," and her voice loosens, the sound of it barely audible.

"You take care on that walk, now, Mrs. Rhoades. Maggie," and he looks Maggie square in the eye, "you make sure to rest a couple times along the way. No need to rush, now."

Maggie nods in agreement. "No need to rush." And to Amanda, "Right, Mother?"

Amanda's smile sweeps across her face again. "You heard the man. We won't rush."

Martin follows Amanda up the front steps to the porch. "Let me see how your wood supply is, I can bring in another load," he says, and they disappear in the front door.

Maggie turns and heads down to the water. She sticks her hands into her pockets and picks at the ground with her shoe as she looks out over the lake. She thinks of Evan, remembers the last time she saw his grave. Over four years ago, she realizes. And she thinks of her father, alone in his grave in England.

Amanda didn't go to her husband's funeral. The transatlantic flight was too much for her, she said, and her doctor confirmed that she should stay in Connecticut and not make the long trip. She was suffering from pain in her joints, a pain that increased daily, she told Maggie. And there was her heart. There was always her heart, she reminded her daughter.

"You go with him," Amanda told her. "Take him home to Devises and see to the burial."

Maggie had not realized that she and her mother were his only living relatives. "What about his brother," she asked Amanda, "and that cousin that visited the year after Evan died?"

"They're all dead," Amanda told her.

"So there's just you and me and Grandmother," she told her mother.

"That's why you must go, dear."

Maggie took Amanda to see her husband one last time at the funeral parlor in Hartford. The funeral director, a short, thin man with a whining voice, led them through a long corridor, past two viewing rooms where Maggie glimpsed rows of chairs, to a door at the end of the hall.

"Your husband is in here, Mrs. Rhoades," and he slid his arm between the two women to turn the knob and push the door open.

Maggie saw a blue covering over a lanky form that lay on a grey metal table. Amanda hung back, and Mr. Carleton reassured her, "It's all right, Mrs. Rhoades, he's all ready for you."

"Why is he like that?" she asked.

"You mean, what is the blue covering for?"

"Well, I thought he would be in a box."

The two of them went on talking, and Maggie thought about the word *box*, wondered why her mother wouldn't say "coffin."

"Since there was to be no formal viewing," Mr. Carleton left the sentence unfinished, his arm sweeping the air as if in explanation.

Maggie stopped listening. She looked at her father. He lay like a stone, but his flesh was real flesh, the folds and wrinkles in places where there had always been folds and wrinkles. But they looked carved by a sculptor's knife rather than by the passage of years. The blue plastic covered his body, came right up under his chin, and as Mr. Carleton fiddled with the edge of the covering, Maggie realized the skin of her father's neck would not give to the pressure of the plastic. He folded under the edge, patted it neatly against the stone neck, gazed momentarily at the dead man's face, frowned a brief moment at something, and then left the room without a word.

"He looks so —" and Amanda paused, and Maggie thought she was going to say the word *dead,* but she didn't, she said, "Peaceful." Maggie looked for the peace in his face, but she didn't see it. Instead she saw great lines carved around his mouth, the edges of which sloped downward in a bitter angle, and she saw in his nostrils the grey hairs that used to move with the intake of breath, and she saw the large earlobes protruding stiffly, and she saw the gentle curve of his forehead, his bushy eyebrows resting like caterpillars above his two closed eyes.

"For once he doesn't need a shave," Amanda murmured, remembering his heavy beard, his trips to the bathroom to reduce a few hours' growth.

"He would have looked handsome with a beard, I used to tell him so," Maggie whispered.

"Not on your father, Margaret. He despised facial hair,"

and her lips set in a line. She reached her hand out, touched the plastic where she thought his hand was, and held her hand there, leaving a thin layer of air beneath her hand. She then laid it against his.

Maggie watched her mother's face for some sign of emotion. She saw Amanda's nose wrinkle as she ran her finger along each of her husband's fingers. "I wish I could see his hands," she said, "they were beautiful hands, always so calm."

Maggie didn't remember her father's hands as calm. She remembered them always tapping, tapping lightly against the arm of a chair or his own knee. But Amanda talked on about his hands, remembering her own memories out loud, while Maggie kept hers to herself and wished that her mother's voice would stop. Amanda talked on about his gentle hands, his gentle ways with her and his love for his two children. Maggie had never heard her mother use such words.

Maggie continued to shift her gaze from her father's stone face to her mother's. She sat on a straight-backed chair by his right shoulder and wondered if she and her mother were acting out parts in a play, and this seemed more real than the scene that lay before her eyes. She closed her eyes and gave herself to a dream.

She went back to summers at Land's End, imagined that she had hiked up Mount Stockton. She saw the lake before her, its rounded bulging surface opalescent as a moonstone, the edge tucked into the shore. Then she sank to her knees and opened her arms as she saw a black bird rise from the lake straight up into the sky, its beak pointing to the heavens, its wings tucked in by its sides.

"Black bird," she called, and without a noticeable shift, the bird altered its heavenly course and headed her way. She watched its silken form come her way, the wings spreading wide to the sides to slow it down. Maggie saw its black moonstone eyes shine with lacquered depth, and a few flutters of its wings created an air current that pulled her up to meet it in a channel of wind. Then they were face to face, eye to eye. Maggie slid upon its back, and together they began to soar.

With her arms wrapped around the bird's neck, she felt herself carried at exhilarating speed toward the sky, which darkened with the oncoming night. The moon lay ahead, growing larger as they approached it, filling their sight with its creamy white softness. Then the bird leveled its flight, and the moon lay above them, and Maggie felt its light on her back. Looking down at the earth, she could see the patch of moonstone below that was Carter Lake. The bird slackened its beating wings so that they dropped to the tree line above the lake. Then the bird flew around the edge of the lake, and Maggie saw its history, the building of its buildings, the tearing down of others, and she saw her father standing alone on the shore while her mother and Evan remained in the house.

"Daddy," she cried, in a girl voice, and she let go of the bird's neck with one hand to reach it down toward him. "Daddy," she cried again, but he did not hear her until the bird dropped even lower so they were skimming the surface of the water, rising over the points of rock that jutted upward from the lake. "Daddy, Daddy, Daddy," she screamed.

This time he heard her and he looked up and smiled, it was a smile as wide as the sky, and his hand tapped the air between them as she flew by him, her fingers touching his hair that was as silky and silver as moonlight. "Wait," she cried, but the bird did not wait. It carried her on toward the top of the mountain again, and she felt its strong muscles beneath her body working to pull them up. And then she was on her knees on top of Mount Stockton looking down at the figure of her father.

When Maggie opened her eyes, she knew that her father was dead. But she now knew that she once had loved him, long ago, in the early history of her own life.

Amanda still talked. She reminisced about times that Maggie didn't remember, her mouth opening with a flood of words between her painted lips, her eyes staring at the far wall where a painting of a castle on a river hovered over her husband's head.

"I think we should go now, Mother." Maggie rose from the chair.

"That would be nice, Margaret."

Maggie wiped her wet cheeks with the backs of her hands. Amanda's face remained dry. Her incessant chattering continued until Maggie left that night on an Eastern flight to London, the body of her father lying in the bowels of the plane beneath her.

The weather was mild and dry when Maggie buried her father in Devises. She had left New York on a blustery March evening following five days of rain. Jeremy had suggested that he accompany her.

"We could travel a little, after the funeral," he had said. "It's a good time for me. I could take a week and we could explore the Cottswolds."

"Jeremy," she told him. "I'm going to my father's funeral. I can't take a vacation and do my father's funeral at the same time."

"What's this 'do your father's funeral' business?"

Maggie didn't answer. Tears hung on her lids.

"You're not going to 'do' a funeral, Maggie. Let me come, since you're going alone, since your mother won't go —"

"Won't?" Maggie interrupted. "What do you mean, won't? She can't go. Not with that heart, not with her condition, and —"

"Maggie, I can't believe you're swallowing that. You never take that seriously when she starts with that."

"This is different." Maggie ran her hand over the surface of the table, brushed the dust lightly into the air. "My father's dead. She couldn't do that."

Later, on the plane, she realized he was right. She wondered why her mother had refused to go to the burial. She didn't want to be understanding any more. She telegrammed Jeremy from London: "Wrong again. Please come," hoping he would make the effort, knowing she was too late. And too late she was. Sometimes her stubbornness made her contradict herself, made her act in a way that wasn't hers. But if it wasn't hers, she wondered, whose was it?

When she arrived in London, she was met at the airport by a representative from the London undertaker who was to drive her and her father to Devises, as had been arranged by the funeral director in Connecticut. She was glided swiftly out to the hearse by a nondescript fellow dressed in a shiny black suit while another man directed the moving of the coffin.

Henry Rhoades was buried in the family plot in a church cemetery. Maggie imagined Devises in Victorian times as she followed the slate stone path from the street up a low rise to the church that must once have commanded a view of green valleys but was now a thriving town. She followed four men in their black suits to the steps of the church; she ascended the stairs, pulled open a heavy oaken door, and entered the church that her father had attended as a boy. Maggie paused in the entryway, smelled the stale air, noticed the dim-colored light that created a foggy sense. She peered out through the one clear glass window, saw the generous beech trees that shaded the path that wound through the gravestones. From inside she could feel the early March sun on the dark wet ground.

Following a brief ceremony conducted by a young minister who had never met Maggie's father, she followed the procession into the graveyard and watched the black coffin disappear into the damp ground. She then made her way back into the church and found the dark stale air a comfort. She felt completely anonymous as she sat in one of the walnut pews and stared at the cobbled aisle that her father had once walked on as a boy. The tall stained-glass windows that bordered the upper walls along the two sides of the church cast a ruby red and sapphire blue light all around her head. Rich colors to watch over my father, she thought.

Pulling a red velvet kneeler with her feet, she sank onto her knees and held her hands in prayer. She looked up at the metal latticework that separated the altar from the pews, and through the spaces she saw a golden cross that rose from the altar and stretched up in front of a rose window. Maggie pulled her breath up into her lungs as she saw the rose light filter down through the air to touch her face.

It was then that she remembered the look on her father's face at Evan's funeral, and she wondered how she could have forgotten it. She remembered how Amanda had alternated between stony silences and tearful weepings, how whatever she did, there were people hovering around her, tending to her needs. Maggie remembered how she felt at loose ends during those days and it wasn't until after the funeral, at the gathering at her parents' house, that she even noticed her father who had flown home just in time for the service.

She found him in a corner sitting by himself in the dining room, resting stiffly on a straight-backed chair so that he could face the door to the living room and watch the people coming and going. Only he wasn't watching the people, Maggie remembered, he was staring with intent black eyes into nothing. Maggie went over to him, tapped his shoulder lightly, held her hand against his back. She looked at his grey hair that curled down long over his neck, and she gently ran a finger through the waves of hair and remembered how often her mother was at him to get it trimmed up in the back.

When he turned his face to look at hers, Maggie was struck by the watery film over his eyes, the red rims, and his damp brow.

"You have the most beautiful eyes," he told her, and Maggie opened her mouth to respond, but there were no words. He has never looked at me like this, she thought, never looked at me directly in the eyes before. And she wondered if he was seeing her for the first time.

Maggie touched the curls on his neck again, noticed how soft his hair was, how silky and smooth.

"You don't think it's too long, do you?" he asked her, and she shook her head, no, and he told her again that she had beautiful eyes. Still she could not respond. So many things in her mind, but no words to say them.

"It's just us now," he said, and she opened her eyes in wonder at his words, having never heard him speak in this way before. Later she told Jeremy what he had said. "He must love you," Jeremy told her. "My dad?" she questioned, and when she told Jeremy that she had said nothing back, had instead stood up straight, patted his shoulder, and headed for the living room and the crowd of people, Jeremy told her he wasn't surprised. "Typical," is what he said.

And as Maggie sat in the church, she felt the impact of Jeremy's words. Typical. Not surprised. That I walked away from the one chance I'd had with my father as an adult.

Maggie bent her head onto the back of the pew in front of her, felt her shoulders tremble. Tears pushed out of her eyes as she raised her face to the cross.

Later she told Jeremy about the church, about the rose light, about the gold cross, and about her words. "I spoke to God," she told him. "I told Him I was afraid. I told Him all of my sorrows. And He told me these things are shadows of things to come. He told me to be strong and of a good courage."

"Of good courage," Jeremy corrected her. "There's no 'a' in there." Then he added, "And besides, I think you were speaking to me."

"No, it was 'of a good courage,' " she insisted.

And Maggie knew. She had spoken to God.

✣ TEN ✣

MARTIN sips at a mug of coffee in the kitchen. He feels the steam curl into his nostrils and he breathes in the warmth. Resting the mug on the counter, he looks behind the wood stove at the pipe that runs to the hot water tank. He touches the tank with his hand.

"Water keeping hot enough for you?" he asks Amanda.

"Oh, yes, it's been just fine, Martin, I do appreciate all the work you've done for me this time." Amanda dries the breakfast plates with a damp dish towel. "Do you have a bill for me with you?"

"I thought I'd wait till you was done here," he answers. "There might be more things you need doing."

"Well, there probably won't be anything more, Martin," Amanda says as she lays the dishes on the shelf by the sink. "We'll only be here the three days. I'm sure we won't need anything else."

"I thought your letter said you'd be here a week," Martin says, "that's why I got so much wood in."

"No, you must be mistaken. Three days is what I have planned all along."

Martin nods his head, remembers it's always this way with Mrs. Rhoades. She has it one way, he has it another. No use in arguing.

"This will be my last visit, Martin," Amanda says as she leans over the sink and looks out the window to see what kind of sky it is. "I haven't told Margaret yet. But it's our last time here."

"You planning to sell the place?" Martin asks, looking at Amanda's back.

"No, no, this place will not be sold," and she wheels around to face him. "Don't get any ideas, Martin, about this place being for sale."

Martin wonders what she is trying to tell him. Is she saying that she won't be back but her daughter will? He decides not to ask, knowing he'll find out sooner or later.

"There's only Margaret and me now, Martin. And we just won't be returning. I'm not saying the place will be for sale."

"I understand," Martin answers, understanding nothing.

"What's that box behind the stove?" she asks suddenly.

Martin moves to the space between the stove and the wall. He pulls the box out. "It's birds," he says. "Two birds. I meant to take 'em with me when I finished the water system." He runs a thick finger along the back of one bird while he holds the box with the other.

"Birds?" Amanda asks. "What on earth are you doing with them?" Her grey eyes widen as she gazes into the box and watches Martin stroke the feathers. Blue-black feathers, once sleek and shiny, they are now grimy with soot.

Martin lifts one by the wing feathers. The wing does not open out, but remains stiff. "Light as a feather," and he smiles.

"But what are you doing with them?"

"I can use some of these feathers for my flies."

"You're going to use those feathers to tie flies?" she asks, a feeling of horror growing in her chest. "But why are they so dirty?"

"You mean all the soot?"

Amanda nods, yes.

"Oh, they got trapped when they come down the chimney in here," and he points to the living room.

"Trapped?" Amanda asks, feeling her heart start to shift its rhythm.

"These swallows get down a chimney sometimes, looking for a place to build a nest. They can fly down the chimney. But they're not smart enough to swim back up." Martin's eyes narrow as he tells this.

"So, you mean to say, they fly around in the fireplace. Until they die?"

Martin says, "Yup," with a grin.

"But that's horrible," and Amanda is imagining the birds flying frantically around the small space of the fireplace, seeing through the screen, unable to get out of their prison.

"Maybe. But it's what happens. When humans change the world of nature."

Amanda places her hand on her chest. "Martin, that's just horrible."

"It wouldn't have happened, 'cept I left the cover off the chimney last month, when I first come over to get things set here. And there've been no fires." He shrugs. "It happens, is all."

Amanda feels heavy all over. Her eyelids droop with the image of the birds. She looks at the two pairs of dusty beady eyes. One black beak remains open. She reaches over to pick that one up, looks at its twig claws. Closing her eyes, she holds it on her flat palm. I can hardly tell it is here, she thinks, it is so slight.

"I'll take 'em home today, get 'em out of your way," he says, wondering what Amanda is doing. He watches her hold the bird, flat on her palm, away from herself. She steps around him and uses her left hand to lift the cover off the wood stove.

"What're you doing?" he asks.

Amanda does not answer. She merely holds her hand over the heat of the open space, then she turns her hand abruptly, and the bird disappears into the flame. She watches its weightless form flame into nothingness.

"That's better," she says.

Martin looks at her face, her eyes still staring into the flame. "Let me close that now," he says, "before a spark jumps." He places the round cover back on the stove.

"What about the other one?" she asks.

"Oh, I'll just be taking this one with me," he says.

"No, Martin, we must put the other one to rest," and she reaches for the box in his hands. Martin surrenders it, knowing he cannot take it from her. Amanda turns, uncovers the stove again, takes the bird in both hands, and drops it in. Then she lets out her breath in a long slow sigh.

"That's better, Martin. Don't you think?"

Martin nods. He feels a cough coming on, but holds it.

Amanda holds her hands together at her waist. "You send me a bill then, if that's how you'd like to handle it."

Martin nods at her, feels the cough coming.

"And Martin, don't ever let this happen again," she says, pointing to the box. "It's careless."

At that, she again uncovers the stove, crushes the box, and throws it into the fire.

It was Martin who brought the news about Mr. Elliott to Amanda. Martin had not been there at the dock when Tom Elliott was discovered, but Fred Mason found him repairing a lawn mower for the Brewsters.

"Martin, you got to come quick. It's Tom Elliott. Down by the water. He's been — well, you got to come and see for yourself. Since you know the family, we thought to find you first."

He'd been missing for three days. Amanda was beside herself during that time with worry, while her mother remained in the chair by the front window, rocking the minutes away, her eyes looking to the south. He and Evan had gone on an all-day hike, but Evan returned midmorning saying that Grandfather was edgy, that he'd wanted to walk alone.

"So you left him?" Amanda asked her son, her eyes wide.

"He told me to go, Mother. He said he wanted to be alone." Evan looked nervously from his mother to his father, put his hand to the back of his head. He had developed a habit of rubbing there, on the place where the skin was grafted. "It hurts," he told Amanda when she asked him to stop fiddling

with it. "How can it hurt," she would question, "it's all healed."
"It hurts," he would say.

"How far had you gotten?" Henry asked his son. Henry
rarely came to the lake with his family, usually took the summer to return home to England where he furthered his real
estate dollars. This summer he had come back in late August
to join them all for the last two weeks of the season before
they would return to Connecticut and the new school year.
Maggie had spent the month with her friend, Betsey, in the
Catskills, and Amanda, freed of the tension she felt in her
daughter's presence, had been enjoying her time at the lake
more than she had in years.

"We were most of the way to the west arm," he answered.
"We'd passed Chad, we were maybe halfway there." Evan
balanced on one foot then the other, conscious of his parents'
eyes on him.

"And he said he wanted to be alone?" Amanda asked.

"Yeah. That's what I said he said. He wanted to be
alone."

"There's nothing wrong with that," piped in Eleanor.
"When you get to be as old as your father and I," she directed
at Amanda, "you're allowed a little orneriness." She continued her embroidery work, leaning over to get closer to the
stitching.

"It's just not like him," Amanda continued. "He always
likes one of the children to walk with him."

Amanda fussed over everyone throughout the day. Evan
annoyed her with his constant comings and goings through
the front door. Henry sat at his desk in the living room and
annoyed her with the rattling of his papers. Her mother squeaked
the rocking chair back and forth until finally Amanda left her
book and retreated to her room for the rest of the afternoon.

Gloria had supper ready promptly at six-thirty. Since it
was a Saturday, she had prepared a glazed ham and a steaming
bowl of macaroni and cheese. She set the food out on the
table and waited for the family to come to the table, but the
adults remained in their places. Evan, however, sat at the empty

table and drank a glass of milk while he waited for the others.

"Mrs. Rhoades," Gloria called through the closed door. "Your supper's ready. Evan's at the table. Waiting."

Evan's father joined him first, dished up the macaroni and cheese and heaped some ham onto Evan's plate. The two of them sat in silence for several minutes.

"Where is everyone?" Evan asked, nodding his head toward the door to his mother's room.

"They're not ready to eat, Evan."

"Is it because Grandfather isn't home yet?" Evan reached for the pitcher of milk, poured a second glass for himself.

Before Henry could respond, Gloria was behind him. "Mr. Elliott won't be eating with you tonight?" she asked.

The door to Amanda's room opened as Eleanor rose from the chair by the front window. "He'll be along before dark," Eleanor announced. "Amanda, come to the table and eat your supper."

Henry looked up from his place, caught Amanda's eye, quickly looked down. "The ham is cooked to perfection, Gloria," he said, cutting the meat on his plate.

"Are you worried about Grandfather?" Evan asked Amanda as she pulled her chair to meet the table. "Shouldn't he be home by now? I mean, from the walk?"

Amanda turned her red eyes to her mother. "So you think he'll be along?"

"That's what I said, Amanda. He'll be along before dark."

"Grandma," Evan said, "what if he isn't home by dark?"

Amanda's chair slid back and her hands held the arms to her chair. "Evan, I'm tired of your chattering." She smoothed her napkin on her lap as she glared at him. "Now let your grandmother eat her food."

Eleanor finished chewing what was in her mouth, in a way that drew all eyes to her face. She rested her fork against her plate, laid the knife beside it as the ticking of the clock rang out from the mantel in the silence. "Henry, after dinner, take Evan and see if you can find him."

"Evan's too young, Mother —" Amanda started.

Henry spoke up. "I won't let him stay out late. We'll come back before the sun goes down."

Amanda and her mother spent the evening by the fire. Amanda lay on the sofa by the window, a patchwork blanket pulled up over her legs. She held a book in her hands, turned the pages occasionally, until the licks of flame in the fireplace would catch her eye and she would close the book, stare into the fire, her eyelids wide. Eleanor remained in her rocker, gazing off into the black night, listening to the ticking of the clock and the crackling of the fire.

"Henry promised that Evan would be back by dark. It's nearly ten-thirty. What can be keeping them?" Amanda asked.

Eleanor did not answer, kept on rocking and staring. "He'll be along now. You must have faith." Then she added, "The earth abides forever."

At nearly eleven, Henry and Evan returned. Eleanor saw their beams of flashlight through the black woods, the lights wobbling in the dark as they made their way.

"Nothing," Henry stated as he opened the front door and switched off his flashlight. Evan flopped down into a chair by the table, pointed his flashlight at the ceiling until he noticed the plate of brownies on the lazy Susan. He reached for one, then another.

"Nothing?" Amanda repeated, disbelieving. She rose from the sofa. "Where did you look?" she asked as she began to walk around the dining room table.

"Down past the arm," Henry answered. "And up that trail that leads to the old Clayton place. Evan knew the way, said Thomas often went up there to poke around. There's an apple orchard, and we looked up there, and followed a trail to where Pin Mountain begins."

Eleanor continued her rocking, her eyes gazing.

Amanda continued pacing around the table. She slapped Evan's hand when he reached for another brownie. "You mustn't eat at a time like this, Evan."

Evan's hand shot out, knocking the brownies onto the floor. He stared her in the eye, combatively.

"Leave the boy alone," Henry said, rising from his chair.

"I think you're all crazy," Amanda threw back. "My father's out there. Why are we pretending he's late from a walk? Don't you know something's happened? We've got to do something." She put her hand to her heart. "We can't leave him out there, in the dark. He could be —"

"We'll have to wait until morning, Amanda," Eleanor said, still staring out the window. Henry nodded in agreement.

Evan began picking up the brownies from the floor. He took a bite of one and sat back in his chair, leaned it back until it rested against the sideboard and Amanda could not get through. He watched his mother, who began sitting down and standing up again, her hand held close to her heart. He watched his grandmother, who kept rocking. He lifted the plate and held it toward his father. "These are good," he added.

"Where can he possibly be?" Amanda cried, her voice shrill. "I mean, he has to be somewhere, doesn't he?" and she emphasized the word *be* with the force of her voice. "Well?" she continued. "Doesn't he?"

No one answered.

"Put those brownies down, Evan, how can you possibly eat now?" Amanda sputtered at her son. Henry watched her roam around the room. Finally she opened the front door and stepped outside, leaving the door wide open. The night air slid in, and the fire sizzled in response.

Henry joined her on the porch, closing the door behind him. He listened to her words, the edge of frantic fear in her voice. He knew he could not reassure her, that words would be empty to her. He sat beside her, put an arm around her, held her shoulder with his hand.

"That won't do me any good," Amanda murmured.

"It might do me some good. I don't know what else to do. I'm worried about your father too. I —"

"Oh, you're worried, are you?" and she looked at him with shining angry eyes.

"Of course I'm worried. So's Evan. And your mother."

"You call that worry," she snapped. "None of you knows what worry is. I know what worry is." She stood up, walked to the other end of the porch. Henry glanced in the window, saw Eleanor's head moving back and forth in the rocker. "I've lived a life of worry on this lake. There has always been danger here. Days of darkness. I gave my heart to it long ago. But there is no easing of it."

"Amanda, try to calm down."

"Henry," Amanda said, as she stared into the night, her heart pulling a prison around her. "You don't know the danger here."

"What danger?" he asked, pulling a cigarette out of his shirt pocket.

"Danger. No particular danger. Just danger." Amanda peered into the night. "You just can't be too careful here."

During the next two days a search was made. The people from Chad joined in, some running boats in and out of the coves, others on foot. Evan spent a couple of hours with Dan Donahue, the ranger, telling him about the place that his grandfather liked to walk. "Beyond the Clayton place," Evan told him, "he also likes the trail to the McDermotts' 'cause from there, it's just a stroll to Little Knee Pond. And he loves Little Knee Pond," Evan explained.

"He also takes me up on the ridge," Evan continued, "where the blueberries are wild and thick, and the pond, I can't remember the name just right, that lies over the ridge, he loves that too."

"If Maggie was here," Evan told everyone who asked him anything, "she could find him, because she knows every place he goes, even his secret places, she goes with him."

Amanda just turned the other way when she heard that. But by the third day, when there was still no trace of him, she finally wondered aloud, "Should we get Margaret up here now?", feeling that she had betrayed her own soul in making the suggestion. But if it could find her father, she was willing to be betrayed.

"He's lost, isn't he?" Evan said at supper on the second night. Thomas's place at the table remained set and ready for his return.

"He's not lost," Amanda insisted. "And don't say such words again. That could never happen to your grandfather. Not here anyway."

"Amanda," Henry started.

"You neither," she cut in. "He's not lost. Not here. Not on this lake. He knows this lake better than anyone." She held a glass of water in her hand, noticed the slight trembling in her arm, the slight movement of the water in the glass back and forth. She lowered her hand to the table, set the glass down firmly. "This is where he is most at home, isn't it?"

For the first time all that day, Eleanor spoke. "If he's not lost, what is he?"

Silence settled on the table. From the kitchen came sounds of Gloria washing dishes, the clash of china against china. The pink light of the setting sun filled the window that faced west, cast a violet light across the floor and onto Eleanor's knees as they rocked forward and back.

Evan rested his spoon in the bowl of chowder before him, let it slide into the bowl.

"You mustn't play with your food, Evan," Amanda perked up. "And here, Henry, pass the rolls down this way."

"If he's not lost, I said, then what is he?" Eleanor repeated.

"You're so morbid, Mother," Amanda commented. "You've always been so morbid. It defies me how morbid you can be."

The lake remained still as glass that next day, flat and black as mica. The sounds of the woods echoed across the water, the thrush singing through the thin air, loons calling. The motor boats whirred on the lake, slowly searching the inlets and coves. The mountains enclosed the lake and the boats and the people in a secret world.

In the morning Henry walked over to Chad and telephoned the Briers in the Catskills. "Can you bring Maggie up here?" he asked. "We've got ourselves an emergency." He explained that Mr. Elliott had disappeared, that the family thought Maggie might have some insight as to where he might have gone. Henry told them he would meet them later that day with the boat.

Late in the afternoon Henry returned to Land's End to see how Amanda was doing. He half expected her to venture over to the town, to be closer to the activity, yet he was not surprised to find her still submerged in the bed when he arrived.

"I think you'd better call the doctor," she told him as he sat on the chair by the window. "I'm having trouble breathing."

In the living room Eleanor continued her rocking, her shoulders sloped forward over her needlework, her toes controlling the gentle but squeaking movement of the chair. "I'm going to fetch a doctor," Henry called to her as he took his hat from a hook near the door and slipped it on.

Evan sat on an old stone wall near the water at Chad and waited. From there he could watch the boats, and people could stop and talk to him. He was a favorite of the residents of Chad because he was a natural in the surroundings. He had curiosity, spent hours watching Martin repair the motors to people's boats, asking questions, watching and taking in what he saw.

It was Fred Mason who discovered Mr. Elliott as Evan stared out at the lake. He had been out for the afternoon hours with several others, running his mail boat along the shore, looking for some sign of the man, but the afternoon was ending and he was returning to some work in the post office. Evan watched him edge the boat smoothly into the dock, the blue-black water stirring in circles. Fred put the engine into reverse, and Evan listened to the whine of the engine as the Lyman eased back toward the side of the dock, the prop of the inboard gurgling the water into a frothy white mixture.

Suddenly the slow whine of the engine shifted to a harsh

rattle, a scraping sound as if the prop had hit rock, but there was no rock where Fred always kept his boat. The engine halted and died, and one of the men who was sitting in the stern took the stern line in his hand, ready to wrap it round the post on the dock.

"What was that?" Fred called back, his head twisted at an angle.

The words that the man in the stern yelled back exploded into the air: "Je-sus Christ!" he yelled. "My God, Fred, it's him, it's Tom Elliott, we got him with the prop."

Evan sat on the stone wall, a small stone sculpture of a boy, as people rushed here and there, as the bell on the dock rang to call people down to the water and in from the lake, as the mutilated body of his grandfather was hauled up out of the water and dragged over the side of the dock where it made a *thunk* sound as his upper body and arms dropped onto the wooden planks that quickly turned black as water flowed from the body, forming a pool, or a lake, of black. Fred and the other men took off their shirts; Fred wrapped his shirt over Mr. Elliott's head, and he cradled it in his arms as he spread his shirt under the head while the other man laid his shirt beneath Mr. Elliott's shoulders, so when the body was laid back down, he could pull the sleeves of the shirt around the chest, and he tied the sleeves together.

And Evan sat on the wall, at a distance from it all.

And then there were people from the town on the dock and standing on the shore. Two men lifted Tom Elliott, and the crowd followed along to the shore where they laid the body on the ground. There were bits and pieces of words and phrases: his right arm's nearly gone, the back of his head what? the prop must've — he's good and dead, the prop is all bent out of shape. Someone sent for Martin then because he'd worked for the Elliotts nearly six years, so Fred ran up the hill and disappeared through the houses, returning only minutes later with Martin, and the crowd cleared, and Martin looked, saying, "Oh my God, my God, my God," and he turned away and bent on his knees like he was going to vomit, and then

Alice came running along the shore, and Martin got up, and was saying to her, "No, Alice, don't look, no," and then Alice looked right at the stone wall where Evan was sitting all alone, and she rushed to him, "Evan," she yelled, and "Evan," she moaned, and when she reached him, he lifted his arms to her, and she took him in her arms, held him against her heavy bosom, swayed him left and right, saying, "Oh you poor boy, you poor, dear boy," and it was then Evan started to cry, to wail even, and finally he asked, "Is he dead, really dead?" and Alice just answered, "Oh you poor, dear boy."

Henry was pulling on his hat as he headed out the back door and toward the trail that led to Chad. "Gloria," he said, before he pulled the door shut behind him, "look in on Mrs. Rhoades if I'm not back in half an hour," and she nodded, and for an instant they exchanged a look of knowing, and then it was gone.

He was on the last step when he saw Martin appear from the woods. Martin's face was white and drawn, his eyes popping out of their sockets as he saw Henry and called to him, "Mr. Rhoades, we found him." If Henry hoped for good news, it was dismissed when he saw the way Martin ran his hand back through his hair, and when he saw the wet streaks along Martin's pant leg.

"We found him, Mr. Rhoades," Martin repeated. "But it's not good, not good at all." He wiped his hand across his mouth, drew in a breath and coughed. "He's dead." And Martin went on to explain how Fred's boat had run into him, how that was how they found him.

"What was he doing in the water by the dock?" Henry asked.

Martin returned a blank stare.

"Mr. Elliott," Henry repeated to Martin. "What was he doing in the water?"

Martin blinked several times, paused as he drew his hand to his chin. "Fred says he must 'a been dead already."

"Dead?" Henry asked. "But what was he doing in the water by the dock?"

The pine trees rose up into the blue sky all around them. The trees formed a blanket over the sound of their voices, as if they talked in an airtight container, the top of which was the sky.

"He's all bloated, like he's been in the water several days. His flesh is all, like he's starting to de —"

"Bloated?" Henry repeated, giving the word more meaning by saying it aloud.

"He must 'a been in the water several days," Martin explained. "Fred says it's been several days, and he knows about how a body looks, how fast it goes, when it's been in the water all these —"

"What does the boat have to do with it?" Henry wanted to know.

At that moment he heard his name spoken behind him in a shrill voice, cracking the airtight conversation that Martin and Henry were having. They both turned to see Amanda heading toward them, down the back porch steps, one at a time she took them, one hand held to her chest, the other clutching the railing. Silver hair stood wild about her head, and her mouth held a crooked line, the skin over her face grey with discomfort.

"Henry, wait, Henry —" and then she saw Martin, and she saw Martin's face, and Henry's face, the two faces long and slack with what they knew. She stopped in her steps, pulling her sweater closer around her chest, wrapping her arms around her waist. "What is it, Henry?" she asked, but he didn't answer, and "Martin?" she questioned, and he walked toward her.

"Mrs. Rhoades, I'm awful sorry, I hate to be the one —"

Amanda raised her hands to her face, covered her eyes with her two palms. "He's dead, isn't he," and she did not look for a response as she lowered her hands and peered into the dark green woods.

"I'm awful sorry, Mrs. Rhoades, I know it's terrible news, and I hate to be the one to tell you —"

"Shut up, Martin," Amanda directed at him, the words squeezing between clenched lips. "Don't talk on and on. There's no need for on and on."

Martin stopped near a birch tree, put his hand against the smooth white bark, leaned into his arm. He shifted his eyes from Amanda to Henry, waited. "Should I go?" he asked.

"Not yet, Martin," Henry answered; he approached Amanda. "Amanda, it's awful, God knows, but it's over, it's over at last, this waiting is —"

"How," she stated, rather than asked Martin, and Henry lifted his eyebrows in question. "How?" she repeated, this time in a questioning tone. "How did he die, you idiot —"

"Now, Amanda, there's no need to —"

"Answer me, Martin, how did he die?" she screamed now, her face immobile.

"We're not sure, Mrs. Rhoades, but when Fred's boat run into him, it kind 'a . . . well, Fred says he must 'a drowned." Martin pulled at the white bark, and the crackling sound as it peeled split the air around them.

Amanda stared at Martin, her eyes narrow. "Fred's boat?" she questioned. Weaving her hands together, she repeated, louder, "Fred's boat?"

"Yes, Mrs. Rhoades, the mail boat backed into Mr. Elliott right there at the dock, but his body's all bloated, and it's sure as hell that Mr. Elliott —"

"That fool, Fred Mason, ran his mail boat into —" and her voice stopped. "And now he's saying my father drowned? This is rather peculiar reasoning, I must tell you, Martin."

"Amanda," Henry interjected. "I'll go over and see what's happened. Will you come?"

Amanda held one hand to her heart. "Yes, I'll come. I'll —" and her eyes closed tightly, shut out the sight of Martin before her and woods behind him. She saw instead a scene, for a slice of a second, of her father standing in water, his shoulders shivering. Her eyes opened sharply, the image gone.

"If my heart can get me there, I'd best see what there is to see."

"Shall I tell your mother?" Henry suggested.

"We'll wait till we return," she answered, her voice firm, "until we have something more to tell her than what Martin says Fred thinks has happened."

Martin looked down at the ground, pushed at an exposed root with the toe of one boot.

"Come along, Martin, you come too, of course," she told him, and she trailed behind Henry into the woods, the skirt of her nightgown brushing the moss on the side of the trail.

When Amanda looked with open eyes at her dead father, she drew in her breath.

"Someone's shot him," she said to Henry and Martin, pointing at the hole in his chest that oozed black liquid.

The crowd had stepped back when she arrived, making a path for her to follow to Tom Elliott's body. Henry followed behind, a hand on Amanda's shoulder. "There's no need to get too close," he told her, but she walked right up and fell to her knees, her finger pointing at his chest.

"No, Mrs. Rhoades, one of the blades from the prop did that, when Fred backed up," Martin said. "You can see for yourself that he's waterlogged, the skin all grey and starting to de —"

Amanda gritted her teeth together, decided to hold her tongue. It's not worth it, she thought, trying to speak to these people. He knows nothing, nothing about this man, my father. I know a bullet hole when I see one.

Later the coroner's report showed that he had died by drowning, that his lungs were filled with water. But Amanda stuck to her version. "They just want to protect Fred," she argued with Henry, "wouldn't you protect your friend?" she asked him. "No," he said, "not in a case like this, not if I knew he had done something wrong —" "That's exactly it, though," she argued, "they're protecting him from prosecution."

"It was careless," she told her lawyer, "nothing more than careless behavior. These locals think they own this lake."

"Mrs. Rhoades, the facts are here in the report, he drowned," the lawyer told her.

"You too," she said. "You're all in this together."

Amanda never said a word about the condition of her father's face, the features already lost to decomposition. The fact that his face was unrecognizable, that it looked to have been eaten away by the life of the lake, she ignored.

"She only saw the hole in his chest," Henry told Martin later. "And maybe it's better, that she didn't see his face."

"It was an awful sight," Martin agreed. "The man in him was gone."

Amanda stuck to what she saw. "It was terrible," she told people. "A hole, right there in his chest, from a bullet," she said. It was as if she believed it, about the bullet. "It was gruesome," she told people. "Just gruesome."

When Amanda and Henry returned to the house, Alice was there with Evan.

"You can go now," Amanda told Alice, and to Evan, she turned and said, "Let's go together to tell your grandmother."

Evan followed his mother into the living room where Eleanor sat, still rocking.

"He's dead, isn't he," she stated before Amanda had a chance to speak.

"How'd you know, Grandma?" Evan asked, his eyes already swollen with crying, the rims of the lids lined with red.

"I knew the first day, when you came back without him from the walk." She continued with her needlepoint, even as she spoke.

"How'd you know?" he asked her, and Amanda drew back, felt the pounding in her heart begin again.

"I've been expecting this," she announced. "And I don't care to hear the details."

"He was shot," Amanda cried, "by some careless hunter."

Henry interrupted her story. "Amanda, you can't say that until we get the facts. They don't think he was shot, they think he —"

"And I repeat, I don't care to hear about it," Eleanor pronounced, and with a flare of emotion, she added, "he's gone, and that's that."

Evan stared at his grandmother, watched the needle move through the canvas on her lap, looked at the sorry slope of her shoulders, the wrinkles that formed around the corners of her mouth as she drew her lips together and sucked air in slowly with each breath.

Amanda went to her room and slammed the door hard.

"She always has had a temper," Eleanor added minutes later, her fingers working.

"What about Maggie?" Evan asked Henry as they sat on the bench on the front porch.

Henry's eyes widened. "I'd forgotten all about her," he said. He checked his watch. "The Briers'll be there soon."

Though not handy with a boat, he knew enough to make a run with the Elliott's Lyman, and Evan accompanied his father, helped him make a clear landing at the south dock, leaping from the bow with a line to tie up. The Briers were already there, sitting with Maggie on the shore.

Evan ran ahead of his father, racing to meet Maggie who was starting up the dock.

"Have you found him yet?" Maggie called, and when she saw Evan nod his head up and down, yes, he's been found, she knew, and she turned to call to her friend, Betsey. "It's okay," she said, "he's been found, it's okay."

The Briers followed Maggie onto the dock, and when Evan reached her, saw her wide grin, he nodded again, and told her, "We found him, Mag, but it's not okay, not at all." He turned to watch his father approach them, his hands digging into the pockets of his trousers.

"Henry," Rob Brier asked, "What's happened? Has Mr. Elliott been found or what?"

Maggie looked at her father, breathless, waiting to hear the news, and then she looked back at Evan, at his twisted face and his open mouth, knowing it was bad, what she was going to hear.

"It's been terrible these last days," Henry answered. "But it's over now, at least. We've found him. He's dead, but we found him."

Maggie looked at Evan for confirmation, knowing she would see the truth in his face. His eyes pleaded with her, the pain reaching out. He continued to nod his head up and down, up and down.

"Grandfather is —" she started, but the Briers were asking for details, and her father was explaining what little he knew, thanking them for bringing his daughter such a long way at short notice. Maggie meanwhile was trying to think the word *dead* in her mind. Grandfather is — and then she would stop, the word fleeing from her mind as quickly as the wind.

After the Briers left, and as Henry started up the engine of the inboard, Evan untied the boat and jumped into the stern beside Maggie, who leaned against the engine. Three days he was gone, her mind spoke, and no one called me. She tried to remember everything she had done during the last three days, tried to reconstruct it in her mind so that she could accompany each thought with the knowledge that Grandfather was missing, so that maybe she could think the word that he was now, in her mind. But it didn't work. She couldn't remember anything about the last three days.

Evan reached out and took her hand, and they stared in silence at one another as they headed up the lake. "I told them to call you," he told her, imagining her thoughts, hearing her thinking. "But Mother wanted to wait." Of course she wanted to wait, Maggie thought, but I can't figure out why, I just know in my heart it is true. She didn't want to tell me.

Later in bed, after listening to Amanda tell her that Grandfather had been shot, after hearing Henry's words that Grandfather had drowned, and after hearing Eleanor demand silence, she lay in bed in the loft and remembered the watch that her grandfather had given her the summer before. She turned on her side and whispered Evan's name.

"I wish we were in the cabin," she told him, and he said, "Me, too, but I don't think they want us to talk too much about Grandfather."

"That's why I wish we were in the cabin," she continued.

"You have to just not think about it too much," Evan decided.

Evan's breathing grew even.

"Evan," she whispered again.

"Hmmmm," he murmured.

"Did you see Grandfather?"

"No," he lied. And then, "Well, yeah, but it was — you don't want to hear it. You really don't."

Maggie pushed her head under the covers, making the dark night darker around her, so she could sleep.

The next morning at breakfast Evan and Maggie piled their plates with buttermilk pancakes, while Amanda and Eleanor discussed plans for the funeral. Decisions had to be made that morning.

"You're going to have Father cremated, aren't you?" Amanda demanded.

Eleanor shook her head, no, in response.

"I thought he wanted to be cremated," Amanda continued.

"That's what you want for him," Eleanor answered, stirring the coffee in her cup with care not to touch the spoon to the side. "Not your father, though. He'll be buried here, at the west arm, in a plain wooden box." Eleanor pushed back her chair, rose, and walked to the sideboard to get the plate of butter.

"A plain box?" Amanda asked, her lip curling slightly. "That's nearly barbaric, Mother."

"It may be barbaric, but that is how it will be."

"This is the discussion you said you thought we should

have?" Amanda responded. "This is no discussion. This is you telling me what you have decided."

Eleanor sipped at her coffee and looked out the window.

"When was all this decided?" Amanda wanted to know.

"During the night. It's best this way."

Henry leaned toward his wife. "It's obviously settled, Amanda, your father must have told her what he wanted, let's leave it alone."

Maggie and Evan finished breakfast, went down to the cabin, leaving the adults to make the plans. They sat on the porch swing and rocked. They watched the wind shift to the south, watched the clouds come in, felt the new dampness. By afternoon it began to rain, a light glaze of water spreading across the lake from the west, spilling onto the roof of the porch where they rocked through the afternoon. The rain made a gentle sound, a light pattering on the surface of the lake and on the roof, and they closed their eyes.

"Do you think Grandfather knows it's raining?" Maggie asked.

"I don't think so, Mag," he answered, rubbing his chin with the sleeve of his blue sweater.

"Do you think he knows we still love him?"

Evan hedged. He stared out at the lake, rubbing the back of his neck.

"Well, does he?" she asked again.

"Prob'ly." Evan pushed against the floor with his foot, felt the swing lean into his leg, then back.

"Where do you think Mother's hiding that watch?"

"That's dumb, Maggie. She wouldn't do that." He looked over to see her face, her eyes. "That's dumb," he repeated.

By evening the rain was heavy. A solid sheet of water crossed the lake, and when it hit the roof of the porch, it drowned out their voices. Later, at supper, the deluge of rain continued, and the following morning it started in again, heavily.

The rain poured two more days, and Tom Elliott's funeral was postponed a day. There was some question of flash flooding, and it was decided that an extra day would be more sensible.

The day of the funeral dawned wet and dim, but by late morning, there was hope of clearing. It took some doing, but the coffin was carried along the edge of the lake following the narrow trail to the west arm of the lake. There, near the old cemetery which had received no newcomers for over a century, Eleanor had instructed the hole to be dug right in the apple orchard. Maggie and Evan had not known that their grandmother had ever seen this favorite spot of their grandfather's; that she would think of burying him there was magical in their minds.

"She's never been magical before," Maggie told Evan.

"I'm old," Eleanor later told them, "but I was young once and used to traipse around this lake, much as you two do, when I first came here. Before your mother was born, that is. Before we lived that year in Paris."

The family members followed solemnly behind the coffin which was carried by Martin and Henry and four other men from Chad. They had to stop several times along the way to rest, to shift the weight of the box on their uneven shoulders. The ground was slippery from the rain, the footing unsteady in places where water covered the low ground. Amanda fussed for two days about Martin being a pallbearer, arguing with Eleanor that he had no right to the honor, but on the morning of the burial, she announced that she was glad Martin was taking some responsibility, that he had some unsound thinking, but after all, Father had appreciated his labors for several years.

"It was more than that," Henry added. "Martin was a friend of your father's. He'd be honored to think that Martin would do this for him."

"What do any of you know about honor," she sputtered. "What's honorable about shooting someone and not standing up with the truth."

"Truth be told, Amanda —"

"I don't want to hear it, Mother." Amanda left the room,

bumped into the door jamb as she passed into her own room and slammed the door.

"She's more and more like the girl she once was," Eleanor mused, her head shaking from left to right. "Truth be told, there's no honor in death."

Maggie wondered, if Grandfather had drowned, how it had happened. She wanted to ask her father, but she could not get him alone. The night before the funeral, she asked Evan up in their sleeping loft. He turned his back and muttered something about how he must have fallen in the water, and Maggie told him she had figured that much out, but how had he managed to fall in the water?

That's what she didn't understand.

Evan didn't answer. He just breathed evenly.

At the gravesite, the ceremony was short. A minister came from Casco and he read dutifully from the Common Prayer, and Maggie remembered later that he used the word *sinful* several times, and she thought to ask Evan what the word meant, and why he used it about Grandfather.

Maggie watched the men lower the coffin into the hole on some ropes, and she felt her stomach cave in at the thought of Grandfather in the ground. Amanda often said later that she should never have allowed Maggie to go to the burial, but Eleanor said flatly, "She might as well learn the truth now." Henry stood between his two children, a hand on the shoulder of each, his head bowed, while Evan stared wide-eyed at the hole as it was filled in with dirt, and Maggie fixed her eyes on the branches of the apple trees.

Eleanor stood alone by her husband's feet and pointed her cane at the coffin as it slid away into the earth. She bit her lip and muttered under her breath, "You broke the web," and the others looked at her, watched a single tear fall from her left eye, wondered at her strength.

Amanda fidgeted with the buttons on her brown sweater throughout the burial. As the minister began his words, after the dirt filled in around the sides and on top of the coffin, her eyes rolled back in her head, the lids fluttering the lashes against her cheeks, and she threw her head back. Maggie thought her mother was about to scream. She put her hands to her ears in case Amanda should start such a thing, but then she saw her grandmother rap her cane against the calf of Amanda's leg. "Get hold of yourself," she whispered to her daughter, and Amanda stood firm through the remaining minutes.

Amanda saw in her mind's eye the creamy white pine cover to the coffin, and then her eyes closed, and she saw an image in her mind, a vision of a mangled loon, its white breast dotted with fresh blood that beaded from a small black hole. In the vision she lifted the bird to her breast, the blood running freely onto her white silken blouse to form a pattern, shapes of red birds in flight on the white background of her blouse. She dropped the loon and it flew to a branch in an apple tree where it settled down, its red eyes searing her own grey eyes. When she opened her eyes, there was no loon in an apple tree, but there was the black hole of the grave filling with fresh wet earth, and there were the white hands as people threw the black soil into the hole. She reached her hands to the mounds of black earth, took some in her fists, clods of wet, clinging earth that broke into pieces as she squeezed her fingers and watched black ooze from her hands. Her gold wedding ring glistened against the black earth, shone like the sun from her hand, though the sky was still grey with the vanishing storm.

The dirt was thrown onto the coffin, each piece landing with a thud, and Amanda wondered suddenly if the loon was trapped in the coffin with her father, whether the sounds of thudding were really the beating of the loon's wings against the inside of the box, something she thought Eleanor might have done out of a sense of irony. She looked at the faces of the others, knew they suspected nothing, so she wiped her hands together, rubbing the dirt off of her skin, and she held her hands together at her waist and closed her eyes while the others completed the burial of Tom Elliott and a beating loon together in a plain pine coffin.

Later, as they walked back the long path around the lake to the house, Amanda checked her blouse several times, looking for the blood pattern of flying birds, but she saw only the crisp white of the silk blouse that Gloria had ironed so meticulously for her early that morning. Her hands fidgeted with the buttons on the sweater, twirling them between her fingers, looping them through the holes, then pulling them back out.

There was no blood on her blouse that she could see, but when she returned to Land's End she asked Gloria to wash her blouse that night, and it was not until she lay in her bed that she wondered if the loon in the grave was herself, and if she would ever be free of the beating of her heart against the lid of her life.

❧ ELEVEN ❧

THE GREY SKY brightens, takes on a silver hue, the dark mountains showing darker, the golds of the birches and reds of the maples along the shore glowing like gems on a dark green velvet land. Maggie sits on the dock, watches the smooth surface of the water, the grey sky reflecting silver and black. She breathes in the lake smell, listens to the sound of the water rubbing against the cribs of the dock.

"Maggie," Martin calls, his footsteps soundless on the path.

Maggie waves and Martin heads onto the dock. Maggie remembers Martin hauling lumber when she was a child, watching him split and chop the hunks of trees, letting her help by stacking the logs in the woodshed. She helped him replace boards on the dock too after they had grown rotten and soft. She held one end of the measuring tape, called out numbers to him. She liked his easy manner, his open and generous face.

Glancing at the house, she searches for a shadow at the window, wonders if her mother is watching, but she sees nothing. She watches Martin walk to the edge of the dock, drop onto one knee, and peer into the still water. He turns slowly to scan the lake, points a finger at the south shore, says, "A pair of blacks," and follows his finger to mark their path.

Maggie wants to ask Martin about Evan. She wants to

know what he knows about the accident. She asks instead if he hunts ducks.

"Some," he answers. "But not much."

"Did you ever take Evan duck hunting?" she asks.

Martin looks her in the eye, pulls his lips together tightly, says, "No, I don't believe I ever did."

"Did you see much of Evan that fall, that last time he was here?" she asks, holding her breath high in her shoulders.

Martin looks across the lake. He stands up, moves to the other side of the dock, leans against an empty drum. He nods his head up and down, then sideways. "Well," he says, "at first I did. He did some good cutting with me. In the woods up behind your house." Martin points to the woods. "Near where you drove in. Near where —" and he stops.

Maggie says nothing, waits for him to continue, lifts her brow in anticipation.

"Well," he continues, "near where the accident occurred, up there," and he turns again and points in the direction of the road that Maggie and Amanda drove in on, "near an old orchard."

"It was up there, where we came in, that he died?" Maggie feels a sinking in her belly, draws her hands around her waist.

Martin nods his head, yes. "We worked up there a couple of weeks, I guess. When I started hauling, after he was sick, he got busy at the house, there was some job your mother had him doing, she liked him near the house, you know, it being fall, and so —"

"So . . . what?"

"So, quiet like, on the lake. First of October, the bird season starts, people like your mother don't walk much then, it's quiet, like I say."

The pair of black ducks come back across the lake. Martin looks up, follows their flight, pushes his hat back on his head. "You remember that time you and Evan got caught at the Parker place, in that squall that come up so sudden . . ."

Maggie smiles. "Yeah, I remember." She and Evan had

gone across the lake in the canoe. They had taken no life cushions, had paddled close to shore, then had decided to cross the lake and head for the cover where Maggie told Evan she had once seen a moose. They knew their mother would not want them to go so far, but the mystery of the moment pulled them on.

"Oh, I recall that fact, I do indeed. I remember that was the first thing you told me when I found you down there, the canoe broken up further down on the shore. You looked like two drowned mice, and you was afraid I'd give you the dickens."

Maggie laughs. "Yeah, but you didn't, Martin. You pulled up and I could see in your face you weren't mad."

"Hell, no. I was glad to see you. I thought you was gone for good." He thinks of Evan, lowers his head, folds his arms. His dark eyes look up at Maggie. "You was both so young, I thought you was gone," and he shakes his head.

"I thought we were going to be gone too," and she smiles. "That was the longest half hour, hanging onto that float, pieces of it flying off, the waves turning it nearly on its side."

"I've only seen one storm on this lake as bad as that. Two years ago. The spray from the waves hit ten feet, like that one you and Evan got caught in. Hell, no, I wasn't mad. I was glad to find you."

Maggie's face darkens. "It was Mother who was mad."

Martin draws his breath in, whistles it out. "I'll say. She wasn't mad when she sent me out after the squall died down. She was scared. But after, when she knew you was okay, then she was madder'n hell."

Maggie remembers the look on Amanda's face as she walked up the path from the dock. Evan was already on the porch, and Amanda had her arms around him, so he was pressed close against her, her chin resting against the top of his blond head. But her eyes on Maggie were cold and hard. She even let Evan go when Maggie reached the steps so she could stand in front of him, so she could glare at Maggie. Yet she addressed Martin who followed behind her.

"I can remember these words exactly, she said to you, 'Martin, explain to these children about the cardinal rule of this lake.' And I looked back at you, and you looked back at me and repeated her words, 'the cardinal rule,' in a kind of question." Maggie is laughing as she tells the story, and a smile comes across Martin's face. "Then she said, 'Yes, the cardinal rule,' and she paused to take in a gulp of air, and then she said, 'You must always be prepared for death on this lake.' "

Maggie's smile freezes on her face with her words.

"Yeah, it was just like that, wasn't it," says Martin, as he loses his smile and they stare with knowing at each other.

"I haven't thought of that for years, Martin, how she said that, how awful, what did she mean by those words?"

Martin shakes his head left to right. "I seen it all, Maggie, here on this lake with your family. But then, so has she. You got me with those words, though."

"Would you walk up there with me some time, Martin, would you show me the place?"

"You want to see it?" he questions, tugging at the brim of his hat.

Maggie nods again.

"After all these years, though?"

Maggie realizes how far she has been from Evan's death, how unreal it still seems. "I think if I could see the place, just once, just see the place," and Maggie sees her mother come around the side of the house, and she waves an arm. "Would you, Martin?" and she turns her round blue eyes to him.

"What'll your mother say?" he asks, as Amanda heads down the path.

"I won't say anything to her, I'll, I'll let you know."

Maggie feels her face flush, and she stands and looks across the lake, suddenly aware of how much she wants to know, and how little she wants her mother to know, but how she feels Amanda can see into her soul. "Like it's not my own soul," she once told Jeremy, and she remembers his words: "Only if you let her take it from you." And Maggie remembers her response: "She's already taken it, Jeremy, it happened long ago."

"Where'd you find Grandmother's cane?" Maggie asks.

"It was in the closet. It's just what I need today, for the walk," Amanda answers. She taps the cane on the ground. She lifts the cane and runs her hand over the handle, her fingers lingering on the carved initials. Her black beret is pulled down low on her forehead, nearly touching her grey eyebrows, and her eyes shine from their sockets as she lifts her brows and peers at the heavy grey sky.

"I don't know if the rain's going to hold off," Martin says, pulling on his chin. He looks at Maggie.

"You still want to go, Mother?" Maggie asks.

"I can feel the rain in my bones, but it's going to be later in the day." She nods her head in agreement with herself. "Martin, I want to ask you something about the stove in the kitchen." She looks at Maggie. "Margaret, dear, you wait here, and I'll show Martin this one thing and then we'll be off."

Martin looks at Maggie. "I know Alice'd like to see you —"

"Thank you, Martin, I'll try to get over for a visit."

Amanda looks at Maggie and tightens her lips, then she heads up the path, her cane ticking against the ground ahead of her. Maggie knows her mother will not want her to visit Alice. She turns and walks back down to the lake to wait.

She looks back up at the house. The dark grey roof slants long and low over the house and forms the roof over the porch. Shadows from the pine trees at the front corner dance on the roof as a light wind rises from the lake. The front windows reflect the red of the maples from the woods.

Why do I feel more alive here than anywhere else? Maggie wonders. Why does this sight make my heart ache? The sway of the branches, the black glass of the windows, the slant of the porch floor, the green trim around the foundation. These pull on me, on my heart.

Above the trees over the house, Maggie hears a crackling, cackling sound, followed by the appearance of four ducks, who swoop low over the treetops and glide in uniform motion above the pine trees. Their crackling conversation fills the air. Then they are off, soundlessly.

Maggie thinks of Ivy. Ivy, her friend, who came first, and Ivy, her canary, who came second. She met Ivy, her friend, in the spring of her thirteenth year, when they won first and second prizes in a poster competition that a local theater put on for the coming of a new film. Ivy was a year older than Maggie, but Maggie remembers thinking that Ivy's poster showed more than just one more year's experience. But Ivy didn't gloat over her success, and she didn't show any feeling that Maggie's second prize poster was any less than her own first prize piece.

Ivy was home from boarding school that spring because she had come down with mononucleosis, an illness that Maggie thought was glamorous and slightly shocking, not an illness for a fourteen-year-old girl, her mother said several times that spring. But they became friends because Ivy was home alone and looked to Maggie for companionship, and because Maggie loved everything about Ivy. She loved Ivy's laugh, a clear, shrieking kind of giggle, and she loved Ivy's gold hair that remained in its perfect page boy even in the wind, and she loved the way Ivy talked about herself and her life in an open, honest way. Maggie remembers telling Evan later that Ivy was not afraid of herself.

"What do you mean?" he had asked, wanting to know everything about Ivy.

"I mean," she said, "she can boast about herself without bragging, and she can talk about the bad things without apologizing for them."

"What bad things?" Evan wanted to know, but Maggie told him he'd have to find out for himself.

The second Ivy was the canary that Henry gave Maggie for winning second prize in the poster competition. He arrived at the house the day after she received the award, carrying a rectangular bird cage with a rounded roof, and inside was a plump yellow canary.

"I'll call her Ivy," she told him, "after my new friend, because they both have yellow hair." Amanda told her that was a bad idea, that it might bring bad luck, but her father only laughed and said there's no such thing as bad luck, and besides, Ivy is a great name for a canary.

Maggie liked having a canary to care for. She liked waking up in the morning to Ivy chirping and singing at the new blue sky. She liked putting water in the white porcelain dish that fit into a space at one end of the cage, and she liked watching Ivy balance on the ledge and dip her beak into the clear liquid. She liked the sound of the bell that she attached to the swing that hung down from the center of the cage's roof; the bell tinkled every time Ivy landed on the swing. It was a way of knowing what Ivy was doing without watching her directly.

Maggie took both Ivys to the lake with her that summer. She kept Ivy, the bird, in the cabin where she and Ivy, her friend, slept, because her mother hated the sound of the chirping, and because Maggie thought that the canary would feel closer to the outdoors in the cabin. "There are fellow birds all around," she whispered to Ivy as she placed the cage on a table by the window that opened onto the porch, "and you can sing to them here." Maggie was certain that Ivy was blossoming at the lake, because her singing grew more persistent and her golden feathers began to glow.

Ivy and Maggie got into the habit of skinny-dipping in the lake each evening before bed. Maggie worried that Amanda would find out, and she knew that her mother would forbid such display, but when, on the first night in the cabin, Ivy said, "Hey, let's swim without our suits," Maggie felt a thrill at the idea, so it became a nightly ritual. They climbed over the porch railing, stepping carefully onto the rocks to make their way out to deeper water. There was one large rock that rose out of the water like a sleeping hippo and the girls climbed onto its back and lay with their bare backs against the smooth surface, their faces to the night sky, their young breasts pointing up into the dark. From the rock they could easily slide into the water and swim out to deeper water. Maggie felt the bottom of the lake beneath her; if she closed her eyes, she could imagine its surface, rocks piled along the soft ground and water filling the space between the rocks and her floating body.

Lying on the rock Maggie watched the clouds move across the black sky like soapsuds in a tub of water. She watched bits of cloud float across the moon, and she watched the stars flicker. She listened to the sounds of the night, the water patting against the rock where they lay, the croaking of peepers in the marshy water in the woods, and the occasional peals from a pair of loons, their voices washing over the lake.

"They sound so sad," Ivy often said, "like their hearts are broken," and she sat up and peered into the dark to get closer to the sound. Maggie watched Ivy, whose wet hair lay dark and sticking to her skull, the points of her shoulders pushed up as she leaned her arms against the rock, the outline of one round breast trembling with her gentle shifting.

"Are you looking at me?" Ivy asked, and Maggie told her, no, she was watching the clouds above Ivy's head, and Ivy said, "No, you were looking at me," and she shimmied her shoulders so that her breasts shook slightly. Then she sat forward, raised one knee, and leaned an arm against it. "It's okay to look at me, you know. I look at you too."

Maggie wanted to believe it was okay.

"It's natural to look at each other," Ivy said, and the words made sense, but Maggie shied away from the tremors she felt at Ivy's words, and she could hear Amanda's words, "Don't ever act proud of your body, it's God's gift to you and it's not to be stared at, even by you," which she had once said when she came in to the bathroom and found Maggie lying in the tub, a washcloth laid across her belly below her flat nine-year-old nipples. "Cover up," Amanda said, reaching over the side of the tub to pull the cloth onto her chest.

Ivy reached a hand over and placed it on one of Maggie's breasts.

"See," she said, "it's all right even to touch," and Maggie felt a deep pulling inside her. "Here," Ivy said, taking Maggie's arms and extending them over her head, spreading the fingers of her hands out flat. "Relax your body," Ivy said, and again she put a hand on a breast. Then Ivy leaned over Maggie and rested her head on Maggie's chest, so that Ivy's face lay against Maggie's breast. "Close your eyes," Ivy said, and Maggie did, and she took a deep breath and as she exhaled it, she felt her body give in to some natural thing.

Maggie opened her eyes and looked at Ivy's head. She started to laugh and Ivy lifted her face and looked at her. "You're not like anyone I know," she told Ivy, feeling sure of the truth.

"That's because you have no sister," Ivy said. "A sister helps you get used to yourself."

Maggie nodded, and Ivy laughed aloud, her green eyes dark as two black emeralds. And Maggie realized something deep inside her; it was just a momentary sensation, that her world was not like Ivy's, and if it was not like Ivy's, then it was like no one else's. Maggie knew there were other ways to see things. She looked up at Ivy, placed a finger on Ivy's cheek.

"I've changed," she told Ivy.

"What do you mean?" Ivy giggled.

"No, I'm not kidding. Something just changed in me."

"What?"

"I don't know," Maggie returned. "Let's swim some more." She pulled at Ivy's arm and they slid down into the water, Maggie saying, "Come on, Ivy, follow me." Maggie dove down under the water, pulled herself along with her hands outstretched and pushed up through the surface. She turned onto her back and floated. "You float too," she told Ivy, and she watched as Ivy turned over, saw her two feet resting in the water, her skin white like a porpoise, glistening, whitish blue.

Every night they swam, dipping in the water, pushing with their feet on the bottom to float on the surface, to lie on the rocks. Some nights there were no clouds and the blue-black sky stretched like silk over their heads, the dots of stars beaming out of the heavens at them. Other nights were grey-black, the clouds settling over them and blocking the light of the moon.

Maggie told Ivy she wished they were sisters, and Ivy said, "We are, Maggie, we are as much sisters as two sisters can be." Ivy told Maggie about her own sister, Meadow, who would leave for college in the fall. "You can be my younger sister," Ivy said, and Maggie had a sense of how large and ripe the world can be, how enclosed her own world was. She told Ivy feelings about Evan, about the accident, and a little about her mother. Ivy told her about a twin brother who died at five days.

"I've always felt a part of me was missing," Ivy said.

"Is that what makes you so honest?"

"I don't see the connection."

"I do," Maggie told her.

One evening they sat on the rock in the moonlight. Maggie lay as open to the night air as the surface of the water. She felt there, in the world, and her bare skin brushed the smooth rock, and she thought she was no different from the rock. I am myself, she thought, but could not find the words to tell Ivy.

"What's that?" Ivy said. "That noise?" and Maggie sat up to listen. She narrowed her eyes in the night light, and she saw Evan standing on the porch of the cabin in shadow. "It's Evan," she whispered, "he's watching us." Maggie turned her back toward the cabin, felt embarrassed. "Don't worry," Ivy said, "he's not looking at you."

Maggie glanced at Ivy, who leaned back against her arms and threw her head back to look up at the sky. Her breasts thrust out into the night, her long legs stretched out like the limbs of a birch tree, silver in the moonlight, her firm stomach as flat as the rock.

The next day at breakfast Evan stared at Ivy with startled blue eyes, and Ivy returned his stare, a thin smile across her mouth. Evan watched Ivy devour a stack of pancakes while he sipped a glass of orange juice.

"Isn't he a little old for you, Ivy?" Maggie asked after breakfast, when they were back in their cabin. Maggie placed a fresh supply of seed in Ivy's cage, stroked the top of the bird's head, ran the back of a finger against the side of Ivy's head.

"Yes, I know he is," Ivy agreed, "but there's something that pulls me to him, the same as it pulls me to you. Like I wish he was my brother," Ivy added.

"I don't think he sees you as a sister," Maggie said. "He's already got me."

The days went on like that, the girls swimming together, Evan watching, and Amanda watching Evan. "There's work to be done around here," she told him, trying to divert his attention. She asked Evan to help paint the woodshed, to replace some rotten boards on the dock, to clear brush along the trail to Chad. He did what was asked, most happily, Maggie thought, and when the day's work was done, he would find Maggie and Ivy and sit and watch.

The girls sat on the porch in the cabin and read books and played cards, mostly rummy, and Evan would rock his chair back and forth, his eyes on Ivy. Once Maggie left them on the porch to get some brownies from the kitchen in the house. She carried a small plate of Gloria's fresh chocolate brownies through the living room and onto the front porch when she heard her mother call, "Where are Ivy and Evan?"

"They're in the cabin," Maggie called. "I'm taking us some brownies."

Suddenly Amanda was there on the porch. "What do you mean?"

Maggie looked blankly at her mother, noticed her mother's hand working together at her waist. "I don't mean anything," she told her.

Amanda's eyes turned a dark grey. "Don't you ever leave him alone with that girl again." Then she turned and headed down the path.

Maggie followed behind, carrying the plate of brownies,

watching her mother's arms shift back and forth as she strode along the path to the cabin and muttered sounds of disgust. "So," Amanda announced when she opened the cabin door. "I found you."

Ivy looked up from the book in her lap, and Evan stopped rocking. From behind, Maggie gestured wildly with her hands, forming words without sounds with her mouth.

"What's the matter, Mother?" Evan said calmly, his blue eyes milky. He reached a hand to rub the back of his neck.

Ivy stood up. "Would you like to sit here, Mrs. Rhoades?" and she motioned with her arm toward the bed as her blond hair slid in front of her face like a yellow curtain.

Later the three of them discussed Amanda's behavior.

"She doesn't like you, Ivy," Maggie said, and Evan nodded, his lids falling.

"I get the picture," Ivy said, laughing easily. "I guess that means we can't ask Evan to swim at night with us," and she swung her eyes at Evan and smiled.

That night as they lay on the rock, Maggie imagined Evan in the cloudless night, swimming with them. She looked at Ivy, stretched out without any self-consciousness. She closed her eyes and saw Evan lying beside Ivy, and she saw Ivy lift her head and rest it on Evan's chest, as she had done to Maggie once. She felt herself drifting out of the scene, leaving the two of them alone on the rock.

"Do you love Evan?" she asked Ivy.

"I don't know what love is sometimes," Ivy answered, and she turned her green eyes to look at Maggie.

"I think he loves you," Maggie told her.

"I don't think he knows what love is either," Ivy mused. "We're too young."

Only once that summer did Maggie see Evan touch Ivy directly. The girls were on the dock, lying on their stomachs on their towels, their books spread out before them. Evan appeared, asked them if they wanted to go fishing, but no, they said, they were reading.

Maggie felt Evan's hand on her head. "It's cold out here on the dock," he said, and he mussed her hair.

He squatted on one knee by Ivy, reached his hand to rest it on her silky yellow hair, touched her lip with one finger, lightly.

"What are you doing, Evan?" she asked and opened her mouth and bit the end of his fingers. His eyes looked at her eyes, her nose, her mouth, every portion of her face, her neck, and they rested on her shoulder, on the white line of her skin where the blue and white checked strap usually lay, and he noticed the brown freckles along the slope of her shoulder and down across her chest, and he saw the line of her bathing suit against her breast. Then he shut his eyes.

"What are you doing, Evan?" Ivy repeated. Maggie noticed how smooth and even her face was when she asked him this, as if she knew exactly what he was doing, as if she wanted to hear him voice his thoughts.

Evan sat down on the dock, folded his legs Indian style, and smiled. "I like to look at you, Ivy," and his blue eyes narrowed as they clung to her face.

"See, Maggie, I told you he liked to look at me," and Ivy giggled.

Evan smiled at this.

"Some day you two are going to get married," Maggie told them.

"Maybe," Ivy answered, her mouth gliding into a smile, her green eyes cool and open.

"Then you'll be my official sister," Maggie added.

Evan stood up. "Want to swim?" he asked.

"Sure," said Ivy, and again, "sure."

Maggie returned to her book, her eyes sliding over the letters on the page, and she listened to the sound of Ivy and Evan splashing in the water, Ivy's high, electric giggle blending with Evan's intense tone as he repeated her name again and again. Once Maggie looked around. She saw Ivy floating on her back, her wet hair washing over her face, Evan beside her, and she saw his hand touch Ivy's stomach as his arm slid over her. She sank under the water and shrieked his name, and their heads bobbed up and down.

When they swam away from the dock, it was quiet, so Maggie returned to her book until she heard them climbing up the steps on the dock, Ivy breathing deeply. She pulled her towel from the dock and wrapped it around herself, shook her head so that strands of wet hair flung out away from her face, then clung to her head. She smiled quietly at Maggie and watched Evan lie down on the dock on his back; he closed his eyes, one hand up under his head, and the features of his face relaxed.

The three of them lay on the dock for the rest of the afternoon, Maggie and Ivy reading, Evan drifting in and out of sleep, the water all around, splashing lightly against the dock. Occasionally Maggie heard sounds from the house, a slamming door, a voice calling; once she looked up and saw Amanda standing in the doorway on the porch, her figure stiff as if she had been standing there for some time. Maggie quickly looked down at her book.

Ivy was the first to leave that afternoon. Without a word she suddenly rose, picked up her towel, and headed up to the cabin. Maggie reached a hand over to Evan, poked him in his side.

"Evan," she said. "Wake up."

"I am awake. My eyes are just closed."

"I think you'd better be careful about Ivy in front of Mother," Maggie told him. "I don't think Mother likes Ivy at all." Maggie remembered how her mother had said that Ivy was too proud, how she thought Ivy was asking for trouble. "What kind of trouble?" Maggie had asked, and her mother had closed her eyes and said it was a kind of trouble for that kind of girl. Maggie wondered what kind of girl that was, but she didn't care, because she liked Ivy's ways. Ivy made her feel like a person, as if she didn't have to wonder about everything before she did or said it. Ivy was that way, and Maggie thought she was learning to be that way too, just by knowing Ivy.

"I know that," Evan said. "I know she hates Ivy. She hates anyone I like, haven't you noticed?"

Then Maggie heard Ivy calling, heard Ivy yelling her name, "Maggie," she called, and Maggie saw Ivy running along the path, her arms waving, and she noticed the front door to the house slam shut as Ivy arrived at the dock, still calling Maggie's name.

Ivy's towel was still wrapped around her, loosely, over her checked bathing suit, and Maggie noticed the way the skirt on Ivy's suit waved up and down as she ran toward them on the dock, calling Maggie's name.

"It's Ivy," she finally said, her breath coming fast, and she raised her hand up to her chest and then to her throat. Evan sat up quickly, his eyes thin blue slits, and Maggie turned the page of her book and then closed it.

"What?" Maggie asked, "what about Ivy —?" and already she knew it was her bird, already she knew something good had ended.

"Ivy's gone," Ivy said, her eyes filled quickly with tears. "The door to her cage is open, and the window in the cabin is wide open, and she's gone."

"What about the screen?" Evan asked, rising to his feet, "what about the screen on the window, how could she have gotten through the screen?"

Maggie's face froze. "The screen?" she mouthed. "I, I took the screen off. Martin said it needed patching, it needed —" then she was up and running, gasping for quick breaths, and stumbling as she ran over roots and slippery rocks. Evan and Ivy were behind her, the three of them running to the cabin, and Maggie saying, "Ivy, no, Ivy," and she threw the door open. There sat the empty cage on the table by the window. Maggie stopped where she stood and stared at it.

"It's empty," she said, her voice low, as Evan and Ivy came up behind her.

"That's what I've been telling you," Ivy said.

"Where's the screen?" Evan said, and he pushed around Maggie, went out onto the porch, lifted the screen off the floor. He looked up at the roof, and then he stood at the railing and looked around, out at the sky, and up in the trees. "We'll find her, Maggie, she's here in the these trees somewhere, don't you worry, we'll find her."

"That's right," Ivy said. "We'll all just wait here until we find her. She's not far, I'm sure, she's got to be right around here."

"I was going to take the screen up to the house, I was —" Maggie slumped on the bed, lay back against the pillow and stared at the ceiling, felt a hollowness in her chest, a black hollow kind of feeling. "She's gone," she said. Evan and Ivy sat down on the bed beside her. Ivy took her hand.

"We'll find her," Ivy said again. But Maggie shook her head from side to side and squeezed her eyes shut.

"How'd she get out, though?" Evan said, but no one answered, no one said a word, but Maggie gritted her teeth and shook her head, knowing she would never see Ivy again.

"I told you it was bad luck to name her after a friend," Amanda told her at supper that night. "I knew no good would come of that."

"For God's sake, Mother," Evan said, throwing his fork down on the table.

"Well, it's true, dear, I told her it was bad luck."

Evan shook his head, looked at Ivy, who kept her eyes on her plate. Maggie said not a word through the meal, sat and pushed her food around on her plate. Later as she lay in bed, Ivy lay curled at her feet in a ball, and Evan sat beside her.

"I'm sorry, Mag," he said.

Maggie looked at him with fearful eyes. "It wasn't your fault."

"Yes, it was," he answered. "We all know that."

Ivy held her hand against Maggie's leg. "We'll find her," she kept saying. "She's got to be in these trees around here."

Ivy and Evan sat on the porch and wandered around through the trees until the sun set, and then early in the morning, the two of them were up again, looking, calling, "Ivy," making little chirping sounds. But a wind came off the lake, and the air was filled with it, and even the mourning doves did not call to each other, and the swallows stayed quiet.

"We'll get another bird when we get home," Evan announced after a week.

"I don't want another bird, Evan," Maggie said. "I want Ivy." She sat on the porch and read, and toward the end of the summer she did a sketch of her bird, or of how she remembered the bird, soft and round, perched on the swing with the red bell tinkling when she moved. Evan and Ivy told her it was a perfect sketch, the likeness was exact, and Maggie did a few more.

Sometimes she looked up in the trees and had a small hope that she would see Ivy, a small splat of yellow, up in a birch tree. But she never did.

"I guess Mother was right," she said on the last day to Evan. "It was bad luck to name her Ivy."

"Don't say that, Mag," he told her. "And don't believe it, whatever you do."

Evan and Ivy drifted apart, the distance growing between them, and Maggie thought that made sense.

And in the fall, after they had returned to Connecticut for the new school year, Ivy got ready to return to boarding school, and Evan began his last year, and Maggie began high school, and she never saw her friend, Ivy, again.

Ivy left by train for boarding school with promises to write to Evan and Maggie. "Sisters, right?" Maggie reminded her after they hugged good-bye, and Ivy nodded. Evan asked her to walk down to the park with him, but Ivy said no, she had to spend her last evening with her parents.

Maggie wrote to Ivy often during the first weeks after she had gone. Maggie told her about her new teachers, about Latin class which she loved, and especially about art. She was elected class artist in the first week of school and Maggie knew Ivy would appreciate that, would understand what it meant to her.

But Ivy didn't write back. Not once. In November Maggie stopped checking the mail every day when she got home from school. She herself continued to write, maybe once a week then, but she expected no response.

"I called Ivy," Evan told her at the start of Christmas vacation. "I told her we wanted to see her."

Maggie waited for his answer.

"She said she has too much to do over vacation. That she probably won't have time," he continued, his blue eyes wandering around the room.

"Not enough time," Maggie mused. "Yeah, I guess —" but she couldn't hold the anger, or was it hurt, in. "What do you mean, not have time? How can she not have time?" Maggie felt a swirling in her chest, a fuzziness in her mind. Suddenly she was mad. She kicked at the leg of Evan's bed. "How can she not have time. For me. I mean, it's not as if —"

Evan listened, his back to her as he opened a drawer of his bureau and searched for something. He pulled out a green sweater, laid it on the bed.

"I mean, after last summer, how can she not have time for me? She promised she would write, she —" Maggie was crying now, tears pushing freely from her thin lids.

Evan waited until she was done. For once, he was the calm one. The reasoner. "Mag," he said softly when she was finished crying. "Don't you see? She doesn't want to hang around here. With us." Evan's head shifted, swung at an angle. "With her."

Maggie could feel her eyes sting again. That greyness hung in her mind so, it was hard to think. She could only feel that whirling in her chest, from the hurt of it all. "But it's not fair, Evan, it's not —"

Then Evan was out of his chair. "Fair?" And his voice

boomed, his arms flinging in the air. "Fair? When the hell is anything in this house fair?"

Maggie moved out of the anger and into the familiar sense of needing to defend her mother. "Well, it may not be fair, it may not, I know, but, she tries, she —" Maggie remembered a moment, one single moment, a time when she awoke in the night, an angle of the hall light piercing the floor in her room, and Amanda was there, she was perched on the edge of a chair by Maggie's bed, and her head was lying on Maggie's bed, on the side of the bed, and Maggie saw her shoulders trembling, and "Mother?" she whispered, and her mother looked up, turned her eyes to look at Maggie square on, and her face was different, the lines soft, perhaps because of the light, so shadowed and dim it was, but Maggie saw something in Amanda's face, some affection, some small amount of love, and Maggie remembered holding on to that look, holding to the love that was there, so that in the morning when the look was gone, Maggie knew it didn't matter, because she knew she had it inside of her heart, her chest. That's where she stored her mother, she realized, in that place around her heart that felt warm at the memory of that moment, and it was that place what went quickly to her mother's defense. "She does her best," she blurted out, the words wedging in her throat.

Evan's eyes darkened. His face showed hatred in the angled lines around his eyes and his jaw. "She may do her best," he muttered. "But her best isn't good enough."

Maggie couldn't stand such a thought, turned to go.

"You'll have to face it one of these days," he told her.

Maggie closed the door behind her as she left, but she heard him yell at her through the door. "You'll have to face it, you'll have to look around."

Maggie did look around. The walls of the hall suffocated her. She returned to her room, opened the door to her closet, pulled Ivy's bird cage from a far corner, and sat it on her bed. She opened the door and reached for the water feeder. She withdrew it and held it in her hand, felt the cool porcelain with her finger. She jiggled the cage and listened to the bell ring. She closed her eyes, her finger against the water feeder, and recalled the images of the Ivys at the lake, tried to feel that warmth around her heart.

From then on Maggie thought of that summer as the summer of the Ivys.

She sketched pictures of her friend on the rock, and her bird in its cage, and her bird in flight, the yellow wings stretched across the paper. Later her art would reflect the Ivys. In art school she painted women with green eyes who floated in a lake with canaries above and below the water. She painted blue white bodies with canaries perched on golden hands.

It was her Ivy series.

⚘ TWELVE ⚘

WHILE AMANDA RESTS, Maggie sits by the fire, her sketch pad on her lap. She gazes at the owl eyes that glow in the fire, then she looks down at the pad and moves her charcoal stick quickly, sketching the fireplace in front of her. She forms the andirons with a finer-pointed oil crayon, tucking the wings in at their sides, carving lines for their breast feathers. Then she reaches for the yellow crayon, daubs golden fire eyes with a slash of black in the center.

Maggie flips the page. She starts again, with the blunt charcoal, draws a single owl, again with golden eyes. She sketches a branch under the owl, its talons silver in the moonlight. Her hands work quickly, filling in the background with the charcoal turned flat on its side. Using a white oil crayon, she makes feathers that fluff around the eyes.

"What kind of a drawing is that?"

Maggie looks up, sees Amanda standing behind her chair, her eyes on Maggie's paper. "I thought you were resting, Mother," Maggie says as she covers her drawing with a hand and then folds the pad back.

"I am about to rest, but you didn't answer me when I called. I stood right there," Amanda points a finger to the door of her room. "In the doorway, and I repeated your name several times. You didn't hear me and I was right there in the doorway."

"I guess I was concentrating, in another world."

"That's a peculiar world to be in," she says, pointing now to the pad of paper, her head nodding as her father's used to. She has changed into her robe, the belt tight around her waist. She still wears her navy socks, but she has rolled them down to her ankles.

"Will you visit Alice before evening?" she continues.

"I was going to do some sketching," Maggie answers, but she rises and puts her pad on the lounge, lays her box of charcoals on top. "I guess maybe I will take a walk and visit Alice now." She looks out the window at the late afernoon sky. The rain falls lightly, pushed by the wind against the window.

"Well, I'm going to rest now, so I won't join you."

Maggie wonders why Amanda bothers to say this. "I wasn't expecting you to join me, it's wet out, and I know how you feel about Alice."

"Margaret, the way I feel about Alice has nothing to do with it," Amanda snaps. "I need a rest; my knee is bothering me dreadfully."

Maggie pulls a rainhat from a shelf in the closet by the side door. She buttons a blue raincoat to her neck, ties the hat under her chin. Outside the brim flops into her eyes, but it keeps the rain off her face.

The rain is cold, she thinks, hunching her shoulders. Wet leaves cover the path and make it slick. Fuzzy moss lines the trail; Maggie stoops to pull a piece of moss away from its roots, holds it in her palm, studies the minute growths of green and brown, all entwined. Like a miniature forest, she thinks, and she sees an enlarged view of the moss in her painting, a multitude of red buds lying in the giant moss forest. She smiles.

Alice has seen Maggie coming, has the door open as Maggie reaches the porch. Maggie looks up at Alice, sees her brown curls hidden under a pale blue scarf, her ears sticking out from under the scarf, her brown eyes warm, as Maggie has always known them to be. Alice opens her arms to hug Maggie.

"Let me get this wet coat off first," Maggie tells Alice,

and then Alice wraps her wide arms around Maggie, who suddenly feels she will cry. "Can I have a glass of water?" she asks. "I'm so thirsty today," and she rubs her hands on her wet face, presses them against her eyes, keeps them from crying.

Alice and Maggie sit on either side of the kitchen table, which is already set for supper with the same white dishes that Maggie remembers from long ago. Martin is still in the barn with his uncle Carlton who lives with them now. Maggie drinks a second glass of water, asks Alice about people in Chad she used to know.

"Avery," Alice tells her, "he don't live here anymore. Elma couldn't stand the winters so far from Casco. They moved back with her folks a couple years back."

"What's it like to spend a winter here, Alice?" Maggie asks.

Alice smiles evenly. "You'd think it'd be awful, and I dread it come this time 'a year, but I know enough now to tell myself, once it starts, I won't mind a bit. It's different, is all. Just different."

Maggie nods.

"Snow piles up here, this end 'a the house specially, from the north, so's you can't see out the window come January. And that's a good winter." Alice chuckles, runs her hand on the edge of the table, smooths the vinyl cover with her fingers. "A bad winter, you can't see out the window come December."

Maggie smiles. "It must get lonely sometimes," she says, to keep Alice talking, to keep her own mind on Alice.

"The way I look at it, it's no more lonely than the rest of the time. Or than the rest of the world. That's a fact 'a life, loneliness is. It's how you take to loneliness that counts. I wouldn't last long in no city, no sir." Alice pulls a brown and white checked apron from the hook by the door to the cellar, ties it round her waist, smooths down the front, pulls the collar of her shirtwaist out.

Maggie remembers Jeremy saying that everything is relative and she argued with him, telling him there are some things you can't overcome, and he said, "Maggie, it's a state of mind." She nods her head at Alice, ready to consider the idea.

"Speakin' 'a lonely, how's your mother doin'?" and she shakes her head. "Both the Elliotts gone now, and your father too, so sudden like, Martin told me."

Maggie wonders how Alice gets into the heart of things so quickly. Her mind races. How to answer such a question, she wonders, as she gazes at the silver handles on the wood stove. She opens her mouth, unsure of where she will begin.

The door flies open. Martin and his uncle Carlton stomp into the room. Alice shoos them on into the mud room. "Take your wet things off out there," she exclaims, "the kitchen'll drip from your wet gear in a snap."

"Maggie," Martin says in a hesitant tone, "I told Alice you might stop by." Martin unbuttons his shirt, waves its tails. "Whew," he breathes out. "It's comin' down out there." His undershirt is damp on his chest and around his waist. Maggie looks away from him, embarrassed.

"Stand near the stove," Alice orders him, and he drags a chair over to the black piece that dominates the kitchen, still waving his shirttails as he sits on the edge of the chair.

Alice goes to the sink, rinses some beet greens.

"I really should be going," Maggie says, "I don't want to interrupt things here, I can come back tomorrow."

"Now just set still." Alice returns, handing Maggie a bowl of beets. "You scrub these with this brush while we talk, make yourself useful. And tell us, how is your mother doin'?"

Martin looks at Maggie, then down at his boots, which he starts to unlace. "These are soaked clear through, Alice."

"I keep tellin' you to get yourself some new boots, they had that sale down to Casco, last month, I was tellin' you then —"

Uncle Carlton enters the room, nods his head in greeting.

"This here's Maggie Rhoades, daughter to Amanda Elliott," Martin says. "You prob'ly seen her when she was just a little thing, two ponytails wagging wherever she went." He smiles in Maggie's direction.

Uncle Carlton nods. He unbuttons his shirt, pulls it off with some effort, hangs it on a line behind the stove, grunting as he reaches up high. He goes to the sink, pulls out a metal pan from the cupboard below, fills it with water and soap. As the spigot runs, he pulls his undershirt out of his trousers and up over his shoulders. He drops it in a lump on the floor by his feet.

Alice joins Maggie at the table, beating up some potatoes with a heavy wisk in a large yellow bowl. She sees Maggie's unease. "How're you comin' with the beets?"

Maggie has scrubbed them clean. She remembers how she used to be put to work in Alice's kitchen, both she and Evan, peeling shells off hard-boiled eggs, cutting up summer squash, picking over blueberries. She watches Uncle Carlton dip his arms in the water.

"Not hot enough," he says, so he takes the kettle from the stove, pours some steaming water into the pan, then dips a washcloth in and soaps it. Maggie studies his strong back, the muscles contorting across his shoulders as he lifts first one arm and then the other and rubs the soapy cloth around his armpits, while the water drips down his naked side, onto the counter, onto the floor, making little patter sounds.

He must be in his sixties, Maggie thinks, but the only sign of age is the roll of flesh around his middle that hangs over his belt on either side. His back still holds the summer sun, freckles lie over his shoulders and upper back. Or are they age spots, Maggie wonders. Her eyes remain on his back, on the muscles that shift long and short as he washes. He rubs the washcloth over his chest, and she can hear the different sound where the wooly hair blankets his chest. A kind of whooshing, she thinks, and she remembers washing Jeremy's chest after she climbed in a tub of water with him and knelt between his legs and rubbed his chest until it was streaked with red, and then he said, "Now, it's my turn," and he soaped the same cloth till it frothed, and he sat up straighter, and she sank more onto her knees and he rubbed under her chin first, and she lifted her chin so he could get long strokes around her neck, and then he did her shoulders, and she can feel the water drip down her arms and onto her back, and then he took the cloth and held it up to her breasts and pressed it against her and then carefully washed each breast until she lay on top of him, her soapy chest against his.

Maggie feels her face flush with blood, a tightening in her breast. She looks away from Uncle Carlton, startled by her dreaming. She listens to Alice and Martin talk about the pigs, how it's time to put them to slaughter soon, and how Alice has shifted things around in the freezer to make room for the meat. Maggie looks back at Uncle Carlton, who is still washing, and she wonders if he prolongs this bath on purpose. Or has he done it this way for years, oblivious to his action?

Once, she remembers, she followed Evan into the bathroom while he shaved. He was telling her about Sarah, the girl he'd met in the beginning of his senior year at college. He was telling Maggie what to expect in Sarah, how he was sure she would like her. She climbed into the empty tub and lay back, one leg crossed over the other where it bent at the knee, and she listened to Evan tell her about Sarah, and she watched him shave. He had his new grey trousers on, and she watched his shoulders and the muscles of his bare upper arm as he ran his razor over his throat.

"Do you ever cut yourself doing that?" she asked.

"Never," he answered. "Unless Sarah's standing behind me. Waiting."

"Do you two," and she paused. "Do you do it?"

"What do you think?" he asked and he turned a white cottony face to her, and she saw a grin spreading through the soap, and she saw the soap drip onto his hairless chest, and she laughed.

It was at this moment that the door was pushed open as far as it would go. Amanda stood there, her arms folded, her grey eyes narrowed. "What are the two of you doing?"

"I'm watching him shave," Maggie answered, sitting up, trying to hold on to the ease she had felt moments before.

Amanda nodded her head up and down, up and down.

Evan spoke through the suds. "I'm telling her about S—" and the word was muffled as he drew the razor down over his upper lip.

"It's not right, Margaret, to lie there, like that, and watch your brother like that —" and she looked from one to the other with disgust.

Maggie got out of the tub.

"Oh, Mag, come on, stay there. We're just talking, for God's sake," Evan yelled at Amanda.

"Oh, maybe I'd better go, Evan, we can talk later." And Maggie went to her room, knowing Evan would find her later. She listened to him argue with Amanda for a few minutes, something about Sarah, and she heard Amanda start in on that, was he going out with that girl again, and then the bathroom door closed, and she couldn't hear any more.

Uncle Carlton stands in front of her, a white towel in his hands, and he lifts his arms to rub himself dry. He buries his face in the towel, making a *brrrrr* sound, and then shakes his face, and the loose flesh on his chest jiggles gently. His wet hair stands on end like spears.

"You still haven't told me about your mother," Alice says.

Maggie looks at the clock, sees it is nearly three o'clock. "I'd better get back home, see how she's doing. I hope I haven't disturbed you."

Maggie puts on her coat, holds the rainhat in her hands and starts out the door. On second thought she pulls back. "Martin," she says, holding the door open, the rain splattering on the floor, a cold wind rustling the room. "Martin, would you show me that place sometime?" and her voice cracks.

Martin holds his hands to his mouth, coughs, stands up. "Well, Maggie, of course, if you want to walk up there, 'course I'll show you, but —"

"But what?" Maggie asks, feeling unsure, her china blue eyes wide.

"Well, when will you want to do it?"

Alice and Uncle Carlton stare at Maggie.

"I don't know, Martin, maybe next summer, maybe tomorrow," and she starts out the door. "I just don't know," and she pulls the door shut behind her.

"She better do it soon, that old lady has some crazy scheme about —" Martin starts and stops. He gets up, opens the back door as Maggie steps off the porch. "Maggie," he says to her. "You let me know, Maggie. I'll show you that place. Maybe tomorrow?"

Maggie stands, her hair already wet again, her hat in her hands.

"Thanks, Martin," and then, "I'd appreciate it. Maybe tomorrow will work." Maggie turns to walk back down the green, then she stops, retraces her steps. Martin is still standing at the open door. "Martin?" she asks, and he lifts his eyebrows in question. "How about now? I mean, I know it's raining, but —"

Martin squints his eyes. "We could take the truck, wouldn't have to get soaked. Rain's letting up anyhow."

"You'd do it now?" she asks, feels a shifting inside her, a condensing of something, a consolidation. It feels right. "Now would be perfect," she continues. And inside, she knows she can wait no longer.

Maggie slams the door to the truck, hears an echo inside her head. She tightens the strap on her rainhat, pulls it firmly over her ears. "The rain'll end soon," Martin announces, his hands working into the pockets of his trousers. He looks at Maggie, checking, she figures, for whether she really wants to do this. "This is the place," he says, pointing a finger to a spot behind the trees.

Maggie walks over to it. "Here?" she questions, and Martin nods.

"Martin," she says, and he walks to her side, sits on a stump. "Martin, what hunter shot him?"

Martin shakes his head, coughs, runs a hand under his chin.

"Do you believe that, that a hunter shot him?" she asks.

Martin looks into the woods. "Hunting's no good up this way," he says, shaking his head, and he looks her in the eye.

With certainty, she says, "Where'd he get a gun, Martin, where'd Evan get a goddamned gun?" She feels her eyes fill with tears easily. "Or do you think she did?"

Martin shakes his head to that. "No, Maggie. No, it was my gun."

"Your —" and Maggie can't say the word. Her lungs sting. She holds a hand to her chest.

"He must 'a took it," and he breathes deep. "I never said a word to her, figured it was better to let her tell it the other way. But it was my gun, he took it the day, the day he died. I found it," and he rises, paces over to the tree nearest them and back, "over there in the woods, buried kind 'a rough, in a hurry like."

Maggie listens to the words, to the truth. The blood in her veins pulses to her forehead, in her throat, in her chest, in her wrists. If feels good. It feels good to hear the truth.

"What else?" she asks.

"What else you want to hear?" he asks, his arms wrapping and unwrapping around his chest.

"Martin, I want to hear it all. Does Alice know?"

Martin nods, yes.

"Martin," and she reaches for his arm. "It's better to know, I want to hear it, I want to hear what you saw."

"It isn't so much what I saw happen. It's what I figured out, after I got here." Martin takes several steps backwards, toward the woods. "It was here we come through the path, me and your mother. She had arrived at the house sometime late in the morning that day, I know it was late in the morning 'cause I'd been out to Casco and back, picking out a new blade for the saw."

Maggie stands transfixed. She is there. In Martin's story, as he tells it, she is there in his house. She hears her mother's knock on the back door, her voice shrill as she calls to him,

"Martin," the emphasis on the first syllable. She can see her mother's face as Martin opens the door, the features pinched, her hair disheveled.

"Like I said to Alice, it was plain from the first moment I seen her that something bad had happened. Something mighty terrible, and I was almost afraid to hear what it was. It brought back the memory of the time with your grandfather. It was that same look in her eye, an accusing, wild look, that give me pause. Like, I wasn't going to be able to do nothing for her.

"She was trying to tell me things, pulling at my arm, telling me to come, to get the truck, to come with her, and I couldn't make out where we was to go, she wasn't making sense, but I knew it was Evan, I could hear that much, and somehow I knew."

Maggie sinks onto the ground, her legs weak. She is seeing her mother in the truck with Martin, her hands folding and unfolding, fluttering against one another. She can hear her words, "It was a hunter." Maggie can hear each word crystal clearly, each word a fabrication. "Lies," she says to Martin, "it was all lies. Wasn't it?"

Martin digs his hands into his pockets, shifts in place. "Lies? Well, it was and it wasn't."

"What do you mean, it was and it wasn't? If there was no hunter, it was a lie." Maggie makes a fist with her right hand, presses it against the palm of her left hand, over and over.

"Yeah," Martin continues. "There was no hunter. But your mother believed there was a hunter. I'm sure of that, that she believed it. She was covered with blood. All down the front of her, it was stained red, with blood. She was in shock, I'd wager. She hardly knew what she was saying. But she believed it."

"Well how do you know there wasn't a hunter? How do you know?"

Martin stops shifting in place. He takes his hands from his pockets. He points one hand toward the place where he told Maggie that Evan died. "We got out of the truck, your mother not waiting for me to open her door, like she usually did. She was out of the truck before it was a full stop. She was there beside him faster than I could see. She had her hands over her face, and she was repeating over and over about the hunter, about some damn-fool hunter. But I could tell, I could tell there was no hunter."

Maggie waits to hear the reason. It is as if she has been waiting for eight years.

"He was shot under the chin, he was. Blew off his chin, and his throat was open under his face —"

Maggie repeats the phrases in her mind, the phrases that Martin has spoken. "Under the chin," and she sees it in her mind. "Blew off his chin," and she sees Evan with no chin, just a gaping hole. She knows she will never be able to forget these images. She knows she will see them in her mind forever. Her mouth opens to form a question, but it is hard to breathe.

Maggie tries to remember Evan's face without the hole in his throat, with his chin still there. She tries to remember him smiling, to hear his voice when he called to her in the night, when they were young and shared the cabin by the water. But there is only the hole. The ruined chin.

"We better get back now, Maggie. We can talk more tomorrow. You come by tomorrow. Alice'll want to see you." He approaches her, leans over, places a hand on her shoulder.

"I guess I always knew it," she says.

"You got to remember, your mother had no choice. About what to say to people."

Maggie looks at Martin, waits for him to continue.

"She couldn't 'a told people the truth. It'd 'a killed her to tell the truth."

Maggie thinks about the truth. She realizes it was killing her not to hear the truth. She is glad to finally know the truth. ·

❧ THIRTEEN ❧

Walking back to Land's End, Maggie hardly notices where she steps, or whether it is still raining. Her mind is spinning, images flashing, memories of words, faces, moments that have clung to her, hidden, like treasures under the sea. A question keeps returning to her: Have I known this all along? Have I known that he did this to himself, that he shot himself? Did we all know? Did my father know, that day he gazed at my eyes and told me they were beautiful?

And my mother, who has known this truth, why has she kept it so? Why has she held it to her, not let me know?

Maggie thinks it through, the way her mother scurried away from talking about the accident, the hunter who supposedly shot him. Maggie remembers Amanda at Evan's funeral, the way her face collapsed, the way her lips locked together when she was asked about the accident.

And then Maggie wonders, Why? Why did she make this story up? Did she think she would save any of us the pain? Maggie hears herself tell Jeremy the truth, hears the words. "Evan was not shot by a hunter. Evan was shot by himself. He used a gun to shoot himself and end his life. And I think I knew it all along."

Maggie recalls that last time at the lake with him the way his jaw pulsed with tension, the way his eyes watered when he was staring out from the porch of the cabin to the mountains. She hears his voice, his words, the way he reminded her of the plans they once had made for their old age. She remembers telling him that things would get better when he got back to school, how he argued, how he said he didn't know. It was the thing with Sarah that had gotten to him, the fact that she had gone to England, had lied to him outright, had lived with another man without telling him. Maggie thought back to Sarah, to Sarah and Evan, to the days of Sarah.

And Maggie knows, I knew the truth. Even then.

Sarah was not what Maggie expected, even with Evan's preparation. For one thing, she was taller than Evan by several inches. For another thing she was a solemn kind of person, and Maggie always pictured her brother with someone who laughed easily, like Ivy. Sarah had striking looks: she wore her thick black wavy hair short, and her mouth was splashed across her face.

"She's sort of boyish," she told Evan.

"Not to me," he said.

Maggie thought it odd the way her hair fluffed out in front, her green eyes shining like a cat's. "Like Ivy," Maggie said.

Evan shrugged. "Maybe," he said.

Maggie only saw Sarah twice. The first time was that Christmas when Evan first told Maggie about his new girl.

"It's about time," Amanda announced to the family. "He's spent his college years in his books, I'm glad to see him have some enjoyment."

But when Evan let them know that he had invited Sarah to spend the week after Christmas with him and his family, Amanda showed less enthusiasm. "Doesn't she want to see her own family?" Amanda asked.

"I guess I can't win," Evan told Maggie later.

Sarah arrived in Hartford by train the day after Christmas, and Maggie went with Evan to meet her. Evan saw her face in a window of the train as it pulled in to the station, and he waved and pointed her out to Maggie, who stood back as Evan stepped up to the train, his arms wide and waiting. Sarah paused at the door before climbing down the steps, and Maggie thought then how somber she looked in black, not a color for a young woman, she heard Amanda say later.

"She's like a sleek black cat, her green eyes slanting in mystery," Maggie told Evan. "Ivy was a kitten," she continued, "but Sarah's a full-grown cat."

"Will you stop with this Ivy stuff?" he responded. "I'm sick of it. Mother says she looks like a bohemian, you say she looks like a cat. I say she looks like herself."

Maggie watched Evan kiss her on the mouth, and while she couldn't see his face, she stared at Sarah's open eyes until they fell on her, and then she said, "Hi, I'm Maggie," and she watched Sarah pull away from Evan.

"So this is your little sister," Sarah commented, her emerald eyes washing back over Evan. "She's not so little," she added.

Maggie pushed her hands in her pockets, watched a train arrive on another track, as Sarah whispered in Evan's ear.

"She is beautiful," Maggie told Evan that evening, as she sat in Evan's room and watched him fix the pearl studs in his dress shirt.

"I know," he answered. "Can you help me with this?"

Maggie held the cummerbund around his waist and adjusted it in back. Then she took his black coat and helped him into it. He ran a brush through his hair once again, smoothed it down on the sides, rubbed the brush on the hairless spot in back. "It still aches sometimes," he said, and Maggie took the brush and held her hand over the place. She thought it felt hot.

"I'm driving you guys to the dance," she told him, "and then you can come home with Finney when you're ready."

"Going in style, as usual," he answered. He reached for a box on his dresser, removed the top, pulled back the green florist paper, and showed Maggie the corsage he had for Sarah. It was a single gardenia, the velvet petals milky with scent.

"It's a perfect blossom," she told him, reaching a finger to touch the edge of one petal. "Absolutely perfect."

"It smells like Sarah," Evan said, covering the flower with the paper. Then he opened the door. "Let's see if she's ready."

The door to Sarah's room was open and she stood by a wall of books, scanning the titles. She turned when she heard them at the door, and the desk on the lamp glowed a dusty light around her. She wore a green Chinese silk dress, the collar high, the sleeves like petals, and it was cut to fit her slender, tall figure. Evan touched her arms with his hands, held her away from him, then reached his hand to her face, her short black hair framing her pale cheeks.

Maggie held the box with the gardenia. She pulled the top off.

"Do you want to put this on now?" she asked. She held the box, open to Sarah, who lifted the flower out and held it in her hand, then bent to smell its fragrance.

"My favorite," she said, and her eyes looked up at Evan, the corners of her mouth spread into a smile. "It's lovely, but let's leave it in the box till we get to the dance, shall we? The petals will brown if my coat rubs against them."

Evan put one arm around Sarah, the other around his sister. He pulled them to him, and Maggie felt Sarah pull back as she laid her face against her brother's shoulder. "I hope you two will get to know each other well," he said, "like sisters, Maggie's always wanted a sister."

"Or like friends," Maggie added, aware of some intrusion on Sarah.

"Sarah has no sister either," he told Maggie. "And no brother."

"You're an only child," Maggie repeated, and Sarah nodded.

"I've always rather liked it that way," she said, pulling away from Evan.

It was a cold moonless night as Maggie drove them through

the dark to the dance. She wound through familiar streets, the houses lit up with Christmas decorations. Sarah sat in the middle, her long black velvet coat buttoned high, her hands hidden in a black sable muff that Amanda insisted she borrow for the dance.

"Don't worry," Maggie told her in the car, "you can leave it here when I drop you off."

"I like it, Maggie. I'll keep it with me for the evening, thank you," Sarah replied.

Maggie drove them the long way in order to take Sarah by the Sutters' house. "There's a huge blue spruce," she told Sarah, "covered with hundreds of tiny white Christmas lights, it's a real sight every year." She slowed the car as they passed the tree, and Maggie felt the same awe at the vision, and she drew her breath in deeply. "Don't you love it?" she asked.

"Are you going through the ford?" Evan asked, "since you came this way?"

Maggie nodded, and she listened to the roll of the tires on the old cobbled section of the road that headed down the steep hill and through the ford that ran through the valley. She pushed her foot hard on the brake to slow their descent, felt the wheels slide on the slick cobbles, felt the car maintain the speed and turn somewhat sideways.

"Pump the brakes," Evan said, and repeated it.

Maggie pushed her foot down on the brake, lifted it, several times, and the car responded with several jerks, slowly, but headed for the ford at a higher speed than Maggie wanted. Usually there was hardly enough water at this spot to matter, but this night, the ford was running high, she figured, from all the rain of the last weeks. Later Amanda told them she knew the ford would be high, that had she any idea that Maggie would take them that way, she would have recommended against it. "I thought you had no reason to go that way, so I didn't mention it," she told them.

The car slid hard into the ford at an odd angle. Whoosh, Maggie heard the water under the car, and then a sputtering in the engine, and the car came to a halt and shut off. A red light blazed on the dashboard.

"Just start her up again," Evan told Maggie, and Maggie shut off the key, waited a second and turned it on, listened to the engine whine. Again she turned it off, then on, a couple more times, but the engine wouldn't catch.

"Nothing," she said, exasperated, and looked at Evan helplessly.

A station wagon driving along beyond the ford stopped. The driver's door swung open. "Need some help?" a man called.

Evan rolled down his window. "We seem to be stuck," he called back, "yes, thanks."

Evan undid his shoes and stuck one in each pocket. He removed his socks, then he rolled his trousers up to his knees. He pushed open the door on his side, and water poured onto the floor of the car. "Lift your feet, quick, here comes the water." He stepped out into the rushing water, "Jeez, it's cold," he said, his mouth open in shock. Sarah was up on her knees on the seat, pulling her long coat up into her arms. She edged over closer to the door, and Evan reached his two arms around and under her. "I've got you," he said, lifting her without effort through the door. Maggie watched him carry her through the light from the car, two black figures, and the light struck Evan's golden hair, and Maggie thought she saw infinite love in his face, his eyes dark shadows, his mouth in a grin that crossed his face; but it was the way his arms wrapped around her, enfolded her, and the way her velvet coat dipped down, exposing her slim white legs, that showed the vulnerability of his being to her.

The next time that Maggie saw Sarah was at Evan's graduation from Amherst. Sarah was already working, apprenticing with a journalist for a Boston magazine; she had left school halfway through her senior year when her father helped her to get the position. "She can't be very dependable," Amanda said, when she heard the news, "if she leaves school so near to finishing." Evan didn't argue, thought Sarah had done the right thing, thought the job sounded great until he learned that she was to be transferred to London that summer.

"Now?" he asked her. "Right now? When we're both free?"

But Sarah explained that this was her chance, that she wasn't going to settle for conventionality, and Evan realized he could not argue with that.

Sarah did come to his graduation, and Maggie thought she looked more solemn than ever, and a little older, in her navy linen suit and her wide-brimmed hat, her broad mouth painted light red, a new pair of tortoiseshell glasses on her nose. "I didn't know she wore glasses," she commented to Evan, and he told her, "Neither did I."

"She seems older," Maggie added.

"I know."

"More distant," she continued.

"I know."

The next week Sarah left for London, and it wasn't until she had been gone for a month that Evan learned she was living with another man, the friend of her father who had gotten her the job in the first place.

"I knew she wasn't much good," Amanda told him at the end of the summer. "What decent woman would allow herself to live with a man. It was poor judgment on your part, Evan, just poor judgment."

"I don't think she was your type," Maggie said, "and besides, she didn't like me, did she?"

Evan agreed that Sarah hadn't liked her, but he said he thought she would have come to like her. "I don't know what my type is, anyway."

"Beautiful, loving, and funny," Maggie told him, "is your type."

"Sarah was all those things," he told her.

"She wasn't funny," Maggie said.

Evan didn't reply. Maggie noticed the way his jaw worked,

the muscles on each side bulging and flattening. She noticed too that he had stopped shaving. "You're depressed," she told him at the lake in August.

"I hadn't noticed," he said.

Maggie is angry. She feels it billowing inside her chest. She is angry at Sarah, for deceiving Evan. She is angry at Amanda, for lying to her, for always giving Evan a hard time. It was difficult to recognize this, that she gave Evan a hard time, because she so clearly preferred him to me, she thinks. But it's true. She gave him a hard time. She accepted nothing in him.

Maggie pauses as she comes through the woods, sees Land's End before her in the dusk, the misty rain enveloping the house in a kind of cocoon. It is then that it hits her. Maggie is angry at herself.

Why didn't I ask her? she wonders. Why didn't I ask my mother if Evan shot himself? Why didn't I even ask to see the body, when she brought him home? Maggie tries to remember what was going through her mind during the days after he died. She went to work, she cooked food, she made love to Jeremy, asked him how his day was. Why was she doing all these things when the fact, the brutal fact of Evan's death, was all that should have been there?

Maggie can hear Jeremy's words, "You fool. I told you all along, you have to ask her the questions. You have to confront her." Is that what he will say to me? she wonders.

And what will I say to her? Now, tonight? What will I say to my mother? Maggie steps over to a birch tree, peels a piece of loose bark off, pulls at the layers. She looks down at her feet, which stand in yellow birch leaves, newly fallen, so they are soft and silky still, silky with the rain that wets the ground.

Maggie decides she will wait until she has spoken to Martin, has heard what he knows, so when she talks to her mother, she can be sure of the truth. She decides to wait until she and her mother have been to the grave, until that event is over. Then I will tell her, she thinks.

"Mother," Maggie calls as she opens the door. The living room is dark, the fire in the fireplace has died, and the air is cold and damp. A light shows under Amanda's door. "Mother," Maggie calls again. She listens to the rain on the roof as she takes off her jacket, walks through to the back door, and opens the door to the kitchen. Dark and cold, same as the living room, she thinks. She hangs her jacket on a hook by the side door in the kitchen, looks in the refrigerator for the fixings for supper. The ham is wrapped in tin foil still, the vegetables lie on the bottom shelf.

Back in the living room, she calls again. "Mother, shall I start supper?"

There is no answer from behind Amanda's door. Maggie knocks gently, once and then again, feeling the skin on the back of her neck tingle. "Mother?" she murmurs and opens the door.

Amanda lies flat on her bed beneath a cream-colored comforter. Her pillow is at the foot of the bed, over her feet, so her head rests against the mattress. She is staring straight up at the ceiling, does not appear to have heard Maggie enter the room.

"Mother?" Maggie whispers and walks to the end of the bed, lifts up the pillow, touches the comforter over Amanda's feet. "Mother?" again. Her voice echoes in the cold room. Inside she feels the swirling anger. It nags at her.

"I heard you the first time, Margaret, when you came in." Her eyelids close, slowly. "I heard you walk through to the kitchen and then back to the living room. I heard you every time you called me."

Maggie hears herself snap, "Well, why didn't you answer me?" Amanda does not answer. "Shall I start supper?" she asks.

"If you wish. Now that you're back."

Maggie wonders if her mother resents her being late, but

that doesn't make sense. She wonders if her mother has been sleeping, has had a bad dream. "Are you all right, Mother?" she asks, feeling a false concern that is familiar to her, a concern that is her only defense.

"Why shouldn't I be?"

"I'll build up the fires, get supper going. Shall I bring you some tea?"

"Thank you, no, dear. I'll wait until supper for my tea. But do get the fires going, it's raw in this house." Her lids open, reveal an empty look in her grey eyes.

Maggie notices the picture on the wall over the table by Amanda's bed. "Has that picture of the bird always been there?" she asks, stepping closer to see the details. "It's beautiful —"

"It's been there as long as I can remember, yes. Father said it was here when he was a boy, that it was a gift from his grandfather." Amanda sits up stiffly, stares out the window at the darkness, rotates the ring on her finger.

Maggie looks at the picture, realizes it is an owl. A woodcut, she thinks, the lines are so fine. "It looks so real, doesn't it, the fluffed feathers around the face, that one eye open, as if all the knowledge of the world is behind the eye."

"Father said the owl is the most majestic of birds." She closes her eyes, raises a hand to her breast.

Maggie studies the eye, the penetrating gaze that comes from a myriad of tiny lines worked into a circular pattern. Up close, it looks more like lines. Pulling back, she watches the eye take shape, and with it, a startling depth. "It's a combination of a human and animal eye, did you ever notice?"

"Father says the owl is not of the animal kingdom."

Maggie notices the way Amanda slips into the present tense when she talks of him. "Well, this picture certainly gives it an other-worldly kind of look, don't you think?"

"I don't know what to think, Margaret." Amanda slides down under the comforter again. "Do get the fires started up."

"You're really cold, aren't you, Mother?"

"I told you, yes, it's raw. Why don't you get the fires

going, Margaret, and stop this chattering. You stayed too long, and now it's cold as death in here."

Maggie looks again at the owl. She tries to ignore her mother's words, directs herself instead to the owl. She longs to touch its feathers, to watch it preen, to hear it call out in the night. As she leaves the room to build the fire in the living room, she carries the image of the owl in her mind. She holds it as she crumples paper, pulls out birch bark strips, lays the pieces of kindling atop the fire.

Quickly the flame reaches up. She lays two thin pine logs atop the kindling, then one large birch on top. Instantly the bark crackles with heat and flame, the room lightens, and the glass owl eyes glow in the brightness.

❧ FOURTEEN ❧

IT IS ANOTHER grey day. Rain threatens the skyline over the mountains.

"Do you think we should wait another day?" Maggie asks Amanda at breakfast.

Amanda is distracted, yet determined. "Today is the day. We'll go today, even if it rains. We'll take rainhats." She has the feeling that she cannot wait another day to get there, that the beating of her heart will overcome her if she has to wait through the night again.

The sky lightens as they head off, Maggie with her blue rainhat stuffed into the pocket of her jacket. Amanda has a silk scarf tied around her head and the hood of a yellow slicker over the scarf. They have little to say on the walk to the grave, each has her own thoughts, her own purpose ahead. Amanda tries to hold to her image, knowing that her daughter will ruin at least the part of it that allows her to be alone with her father. When she suggested at breakfast that Maggie stay at Land's End, that she build the fires during the day, that she visit Martin and Alice again, perhaps, she had met with an insistent refusal. "You could fall, or slip somehow on the path, you might need my help," Maggie had told her. "Besides, I want to go. I want to see the grave again."

Maggie imagines more of what Jeremy will say. She hears his voice, muffled as it sometimes is when he gets emotional or opinionated about something. "This explains it all," she hears him say, and she knows, he will be right.

"Nearly there," Amanda suddenly breaks into Maggie's thoughts. "Once one passes the creek, it's only minutes."

Maggie's eyes are on the ground which brightens as they enter a clearing by the lake. She sees an old orchard to the right; this is where Amanda is heading.

Near the old cemetery, a stone wall encloses what was once an apple orchard. A foundation stands on the other side of the enclosed area; it has filled with dirt over the years, and a thick birch grows right up out of one corner of the hole. It must be a hundred years since a house has stood here, she thinks.

Amanda stands by the opening to the enclosure. Pine trees tower along one end. The apple trees stand bent, slanting together to the south like a row of refugees leaning into the wind.

She watches Maggie walk all around the enclosure, watches her gaze up at the pines, run her hand along the apple trees and then peer at the forgotten foundation. On the trees are carved several sets of initials, but Maggie cannot distinguish the letters. She turns to look at her mother, sees a soft expression on her face, the eyes open wide, the brows pulled together slightly, the mouth still set.

"Don't look at me," Amanda says, lingering on the word *me*. She looks down, then up, to see if Maggie is still watching her. Maggie walks around to the opening and stands beside her mother.

Amanda holds the cane firmly in her right hand, pushes it heavily into the ground. Her other hand rests on her chest, over her heart, and she feels the beating through her fingers. A picture comes to her mind, a memory of her father. He is seated at a table with a dark-haired woman who is reaching her hands across the table to him. The woman's lips are spread in a smile over her white teeth as she speaks to him, though Amanda cannot hear what he says, is too far way, can only sense the tenderness through the softness around the woman's mouth, and the way she opens his hand and places something shiny in his palm. It is the light in her father's face that Amanda sees most clearly, the features gone from slackness to life as he studies the object in his hand. Amanda does not understand the feeling that has lingered all these years, the intense pain around her heart, a knowing that he will never be pleased with her, as he was with the woman across the table. Amanda remembers raising a hand to catch his attention, so that he would see her, and it is thus at the gravesite that she feels her left hand leave her breast and raise into the air. But he does not see her. For he is dead now.

Then she has another memory. She sees her father carrying things away from the burning barn, which rises like a wall of flame beside him. She feels herself on her knees by the road, watching him, hands outstretched, fearful that the wall of flame will fall upon him, will bury him and take him as it took the animals that cried their death cries only moments before. She hears her voice cry out, "Father," her hands held tightly and reaching out before her, and she stays that way as neighbors arrive, as the barn continues to burn, as Michael talks to people, and as her father finally approaches her at the edge of the road. She thinks he is heading her way, but as he gets closer, she realizes that he does not see her, that his eyes pass through her or over her, she cannot tell. Her mouth forms the word *father*, but the sound does not come out, just the lips make the sound, so it is hardly a whisper.

Amanda, at the grave, falls to her knees. Her cane drops to the side and falls against Maggie's leg, so she takes hold of it. Amanda clutches her hands together and reaches them out stiffly in front of her, and her mouth opens; sounds whispered from her lips fall into the air, sounds that Maggie cannot hear, as near as she is. Amanda lifts her eyes to the grave, feeds on the sight of the stone that stands erect at the head of the grave. The grass has gone on growing here, tall purple strands fill the enclosure, cover the grave, beneath the limbs of the pine trees that surround the area.

Maggie too stares at the grave, and the moment holds

them both as they remember and know what they are afraid to say, so they say to themselves the words they each would say to him if he were alive today. Grandfather, Maggie says inside, I've been afraid since you died, afraid of something, and Grandfather, Evan is gone too, he's dead too. Maggie closes her eyes and tries to imagine herself in the sky above the lake, like a bird, but the image will not come. She opens her eyes and is there before the grave.

Amanda, on her knees with hand outstretched, says inside, Father, you would not see me, and I have been unable to bear this violence. Amanda feels a hard swirling ball of crying in her chest, deep in her chest, and it starts to rise, so that her hands go to her throat to keep it down, but it rises up in her throat and she feels it like a hard ball filling her throat, and she rises to her feet to get her breath, for the ball of crying is coming up into her mouth and she feels it in the back of her throat, on her tongue, it rolls and twists like a gust of wind, and then she is standing, and suddenly she cries out loud, the cry comes out as sound, a garbled, wordless accumulation of crying sound. She feels her foot step out and then the other and she is standing on the grave, on top of her father's grave, and she kicks the stone, kicks it hard with her foot, her right foot hits the stone again and again.

Maggie's eyes widen. She cannot move as she watches her mother rage against the stone. She lowers her eyes, feeling Amanda's desire for her not to look, so she looks down at the ground, sees the cane, takes it in both hands, holds it to her, caresses the cane, and tears fall with love and sadness from under her closed lids, and she sits down on the stone wall and turns and looks at the lake, the grey expanse of water chopping with wind, and she looks to the sky and sees an even heavy grey, and she feels the wind on her face, smells the pine all around her.

Amanda steps back from the stone in horror at herself. Her hands at her throat, she steps to the side, off the grave, her head bowed. She cannot look at Maggie, and she steps to the wall and sits facing the grave, several feet from her daughter.

"I didn't look, Mother, I looked away, don't think that —"

"Hand me my cane, Margaret," Amanda says, her voice shrill but flat. She will not look at Maggie, keeps her eyes on the stone.

"Mother, it's all right."

"Shut up, Margaret," and she turns to look at Maggie with the cold grey of her eyes washing over Maggie's face so that Maggie looks away, out at the water. Amanda takes the cane from Maggie, grips the head of it, taps it against the ground, runs it through the tall purple grass.

Maggie hears Jeremy's voice in her head; he asks her why she takes it from her mother. She hears Evan's voice, telling her that one day she will have to face it, that she cannot run forever. She thinks of her mother at the grave, at the way she kicked at his stone. "Mother," she suddenly explodes, but it is not with anger, it is with confusion and hurt, a kind of despair at what she does not understand. "Why must you treat me this way?" She feels her face contort with the hurt, the shame of having to ask.

Amanda turns from her, looks at the lake, feels the air at her face.

"Look at me, Mother, will you —"

Amanda's face snaps back, her eyes like beams of silver light in the grey morning.

"What have I done to you, what is it?" Maggie asks, begging. She feels something behind her eyes dissolve, some moisture, tears, she realizes, come forth.

Amanda's face cracks. Not just around her mouth, or her eyes. It is her whole face that crumbles. "You don't know?" she whispers, a word at a time.

Maggie stares, tears filming her vision. She blinks. She wants to see her mother's face clearly. She wants to get it right, what is happening. She shakes her head slowly, feels her eyes dry. "No, I don't know. I don't know."

Amanda is not crying, but the muscles in her face are pulling spasmodically at her features, so that her nose is twitching, her eyes are squeezing shut, her mouth is opening and closing.

"Tell me," Maggie pleads. "So I can understand."

Then there are thin tears on Amanda's face, slowly marking her face which has calmed. "You lived," she whispers. "And Evan died."

Maggie pulls back as if slapped in the face. She presses her lips together, holds on to the hurt, refuses to understand. "That's a goddamned lie," is all she says, and she exalts in the truth of the words.

Amanda only stares, her face calm and dimly wet. Then she is stepping forward, closer to the grave. She falls again to her knees, sits back on her heels. She reaches out one hand, lightly, and the fingers curl, slightly arching, so that first one, and then another, and then all four fingers are moving across the top of the stone, touching the granite, the roughness of the granite, feeling the indentations in the grey stone with the tips of her fingers, feeling where white-green lichen has rooted itself into the surface, where stars of dirt have wedged into the stone.

Then Amanda is leaning forward, her face close to the granite letters, and she rests on one hand while the other traces along the letters of her father's name, into each groove where the letters are engraved. She whispers, rasping sounds.

Maggie is paralyzed where she stands. She knows she is watching her mother give in to some clinging insanity, some vestige of earlier times.

"She told you," Amanda's voice now high, "she told you not to touch me. And you listened, you did what she said," Amanda continues, little sounds, indistinguishable sounds garbled in her mouth.

"Mother," Maggie whispers, afraid to speak in her own voice, afraid to break whatever world her mother is in, but afraid to let her go on.

"Don't touch me!" Amanda cries, one hand pushing back toward Maggie, as she shuts her eyes, feels a pounding in her head, covers her closed eyes with her other hand. "You never did, not once, you never did touch me. You, you broke —"

"Mother, please," Maggie says, now alarmed. "What is it? What are you saying?" And then Maggie hears herself start to speak, to say the words, to tell her mother that she knows, that she knows the truth, that she knows about Evan, that she —

Now Amanda stands, pulls into herself. "Shut up —"

"No, Mother, I won't. I won't shut up. I want to hear you say it, say the truth, the words, about Evan, that there was no hunter, that no one shot him, that it was himself, that it was Evan that did it, I know now, Mother, I know the truth, and we've got to talk about it, there is only just us, there is no one else, we've got —"

Something about Amanda's face is changing. Some kind of shell, invisible, is sliding over the features of her face, smoothing over the lines, softening the brow, but hardening her eyes, making them like glass, like hard grey glass marbles, and her mouth is stone. "The truth?" she spits out. "You want to know the truth? About how he never really loved you? He loved me. Only me. It was always me. He just did what he was told. That is the truth."

Maggie does not know what her mother is talking about. "Evan? Of course Evan loved you. He loved us both, he —"

"He did just what my mother wanted him to do." Amanda's eyes are widening, glowing, luminous grey in the silver air. "And you ruined it, Margaret. You ruined it with your sickly sweet ways, your —" and she stops. Her heart is starting to fill her mind, the beating, the incessant beating, it will not stop, it will not let her go, it is devouring her chest and her throat and her head. Her hands are at her face now, covering her eyes, and her mouth is opening and closing, gasping for air.

Maggie steps back. She takes three or four steps back.

She looks at her mother. Inside her chest there is every feeling of pain she can imagine. And yet, to look at her mother is to know that she too is feeling every pain. Maggie watches, distant, alert, sick — of herself, of her mother, of the years, of the lies, of the lost truths. And there is nowhere to go. There is no one to run out on. No one to leave behind, to shut a door on, to close off from herself.

There can be no more running, she says to herself.

"This is it, Mother."

Amanda stops her trembling, her gasping, for just a part of a second. Her hands drop. Her eyes open.

"This has to stop." Maggie hears her voice, firm, clear, open. It is an open voice, no masks, no curtains, no hidden secret places of meaning. She feels the pain inside and knows it will not go away. Not now, or tomorrow.

Amanda bends down to pick up her cane. She points it at the stone, taps it against the granite as she stands to the side, runs the cane along the top of the stone. Now her eyes too are smooth, less clear, clouded. "I wanted only his name on the stone, only his name," and she traces the lettering with the tip of the cane.

Maggie feels herself numbing, feels herself giving in. What is Mother doing? she asks. What has just happened?

"Thomas Elliott," Amanda says aloud, her voice now calm, deep from within her chest. "There are no dates because the man is timeless."

Maggie fights the numbing, holds on to the hurt, the anger, the confusion. She doesn't try to understand. She knows there is nothing to understand. That it just is. That Amanda just is. She knows there will be no exchange, no discussion of the truth, the facts. She will not tell her mother what she feels about Evan. Her mother will not hear her.

Maggie looks into the woods. She lets her eyes go into the dark of the woods and linger there. Maybe it is there, she thinks, there in the dark that I will find it. The way to feel this. In the woods, where the shadows of the trees will hold me, will not let me go. There is nowhere to go.

There is only knowing. The first real knowing of her life. The pain will stay for now, she realizes.

The sky holds its greyness and the wind continues to rise as they return along the path to Chad. Amanda sets the pace. And later, as they climb the stairs to Land's End, Maggie feels the wind push down the lake and through the woods.

"Didn't I tell you the rain would hold off today?" Amanda says. "I knew today would be better," she continues with a wry smile on her lips.

Maggie is not listening. She is thinking of a painting. Green, bright green grass grows thickly around the base of a tree, purple clover dots the ground in small clumps. The tree leans over the edge and into the sky, held firmly into the ground by the roots. It is dawn, Maggie can see in her mind. The sky is lemon yellow, rising into pink. The sea below is purple, illuminated by the new sun that is still below the horizon. The tree limbs rise and fall in the wind, and it is sunset now, and still the tree reaches out, delicate limbs black like filigreed lace against the metal sky that shows red along the horizon.

Amanda is talking. She continues to repeat her father's name, to discuss his timelessness, until it is almost like the refrain of a hymn, echoed long and low from the next room. Maggie is in the living room, sketch pad in hand. She lays two sticks of charcoal on the table beside her. She takes the box of pastels out of her bag, removes the cover. The fire is crackling before her as she moves onto the floor, lays her pad in front of her, leans over and starts to sketch, first with the charcoal. Shapes spill onto the page, there is a movement through Maggie's arm and into her hand that is like electricity, hot and flashing as the images translate themselves onto the page.

Amanda talks at Maggie from the next room. Maggie hears the voice but not the words. Then Amanda is there beside her, talking, making plans for their supper.

"Not now, Mother," Maggie mutters. Her eyes are looking only into the image she paints, the tree, which is taking a life form.

"I want you to fix that chicken tonight. We must have it tonight or it will spoil. And besides, if we leave tomorrow, we shouldn't have food to take down with us, it's such a —"

"Not now, Mother," Maggie repeats. "I'm busy, let me —"

Amanda ignores her words, continues to talk about the chicken, how it should be baked with a high heat at first to brown the skin, then it should stay in a slow oven for at least at hour. "And there's a can of corn, we can heat up the corn, we can —"

Maggie sits upright. She turns to look at Amanda. "Mother, I'm sick of this. I said I'm busy." She has more to say, more words, more heartfelt words, but she wants to hold on to them, wants to hold the feelings behind them, let them emerge on the page. The page would do more with the feelings than Amanda would.

Amanda stares. Maggie feels her eyes waver, but she shifts instead to the image she is sketching. She sees the tree again, now the tree is sprouting new leaves, little yellow buds pursing from the tips of branches, dotting the sky with new life. Amanda is painted out of her line of vision.

Amanda turns. She walks to her room. Maggie has already turned back to her work when her mother says, "I'll rest now, then. Later, I'll tell you how to fix the chicken."

Maggie does not hear the words. She hears instead the sound of a tree growing, as its limbs outline themselves across the sky of a new day.

❧ FIFTEEN ❧

AMANDA stares into the dark of her room. She lies on her back, her hands held together over her chest. She thinks the dark moves like storm clouds above her face; she watches it shift, feels it lilt toward the ceiling and fall toward the floor. Amanda listens to the sounds, folding and unfolding her hands. The rain hits against the windows that face the lake, little sparks of sound with no rhythm. She listens to her daughter's movements in the next room, sees her get out of the rocker as its pumping increases, hears three footsteps, sees her at the fireplace, bending, pushing at the logs with a poker, then she hears the pumping again.

She listens to her heart; it pounds rhythmically like the rocker, and she sees her veins rise and fall with the flow of blood to her head and back to her heart like a river that surges with the force of God. She sees stars in the dark around her, but knows it is raining, knows there can be no stars on a rainy night, but the stars are there, little sparks of light, like the drops of rain that sound on the glass.

A picture of her mother flashes in the dark above her eyes. She sees Eleanor as she lay the last morning of her life, she sees the two faces split between paralysis and life. She sees Eleanor's green eye on her, and she sees half of Eleanor's mouth open; Amanda remembers how she watched the words fall out of the hole in her mouth like pebbles through the fingers of her hand. "I told him not to touch you." Amanda sees her mother's words in the darkness, each one a sparkling star. She squeezes her eyes shut, does not want to see the words or Eleanor's eyes on her. It is usually the beating of her heart that distracts her, but this time her heart gets no louder; it maintains a steady, irritable, but manageable pulsing. And Eleanor's words get bigger in the dark until they fill the space above her head up to the ceiling, even with her eyes closed.

So Amanda fights it. She sits up in bed, feels the darkness catch her hair, pull at it, pluck at her face, at her eyes. She holds her hands against her eyes, listens to her heart beat through her head, tries not to see the image that pushes into her mind. It is Evan, there at the foot of her bed. He is saying, "You make me sick," and one hand is pointing at her, the finger firm, unmoving. She tries to distract herself with thoughts of where she is, but the fact that she is there, at Land's End, in the place where Evan spent his last days with her, makes it impossible for her to see anything but Evan, there at the foot of her bed.

It was a night with a steady rain against the roof, a spitting, shattering kind of rain, when she and Evan were alone together at Land's End before the accident. She recalls sleeping restlessly, drifting in and out of an uncomfortable kind of dream state. She remembers listening to sounds of Evan in the next room; Evan pacing, his feet padding on the bare floor, then quiet, then pacing. When it was quiet, she would sleep. When he paced, she would awaken and stare into the dark.

At some point close to dawn she heard the front door open and close. He's gone outside, she thought, into the dark rain. Amanda sat up, feeling faint. She closed her eyes to listen, but there was no sound other than the slow steady rain. Light crept into the room, dim, hazy dawn light, and when Amanda opened her eyes, everything was in shades of grey. She swung her feet out, reached for her robe, drew it around her shoulders, and walked noiselessly to the window; she pulled the shade aside and looked into the early morning.

It was a dim world she saw. Slick bark, a slick wet path, grey slick rocks, moist drooping branches. During the night the rain had emptied the trees of their leaves; the limbs hung lifeless, the leaves wet on the ground. The surface of the lake shone silver with points of black where the drops of rain fell, and the sky was grey mist with no end.

Amanda looked for Evan in the greyness but he was not there. She buttoned her robe and tied it round the waist, put her feet into her brown walking shoes, walked through the living room and out onto the porch. "Evan," she called, but her voice fell flat in the heavy air. She walked down the steps and headed around the house. "Evan," she called.

Back down to the dock, Amanda wandered and noticed its grey surface, like ice. Amanda headed to the cabin, calling Evan's name. The windows on the front of the cabin shone black in the early light; she peered through a pane, saw the empty table in the center of the room, looked through the windows on the other side to the grey water and sky. Opening the door, she felt the skin on her back prickle. "Evan," she spoke lightly but the room was empty, and she thought of Ivy and Evan and Maggie sprawled on the beds, and though the beds were bare, she saw them on a summer day, the lilac spreads crisp in the sun. She walked through the cabin and put her face up to the glass in a window, felt its cold damp, then looked through to the lake.

At first it did not look like a person, like Evan. At first she saw the rock that rose out of the water, dark and wet, and she saw an upright shape on the rock. It took her several moments of staring to discern that the shape was Evan. "Evan," she said aloud, pressing her hands against the glass, pressing her hot cheek against the glass. Her memory jarred; she was unclear where she was and who she was seeing. For a second she thought the shape was her father's, but her eyes narrowed and her mind froze, and she remembered the sound of her own voice seconds earlier as she had called Evan's name.

Evan squatted on the rock, his feet flat on the surface, his arms wrapped around his knees. His head bent at the neck so that his face rested in his arms. He wore a green plaid shirt and khaki pants. Amanda studied the profile of her son's figure; he looked just like a bird, she thought, come to land on a rock, its wings tucked around its frame.

Amanda moved to the door and opened it, went out onto the porch.

"Evan," she called, and she knew he could hear her. But he did not answer.

She studied his posture more carefully, could see from the porch that his feet were bare, and she could see that his clothes were wet, and she knew the cold had settled in his body.

"Evan," she called louder, more like a cry. "Evan, what are you doing?" She leaned over the porch railing, straining to see him more clearly, to see his response. Evan lifted his head and looked out to the lake, then slowly up into the sky. He turned his head suddenly to face the cabin, but Amanda could see that his eyes were closed. Then he opened them. Amanda stood on the porch looking at Evan on the rock, and even in the grey morning light, she could see him look back at her.

"Evan, can you hear me?" she called.

He nodded his head.

"Evan, answer me. Can you see me?"

Evan nodded again.

"I'm coming in the water," she called as she climbed over the railing, feeling her robe pull up around her legs. She stepped on a rock, felt its slimy surface, felt her foot slip, grabbed at the railing on the porch, lost her grip, and slid into the water. It was icy cold, and the water seeped quickly through her robe and her nightgown, and she felt the quick slap of it against her skin and lost her breath. Her hands splashed beneath the surface, and she pulled up onto her knees, knowing she was wet, but unable to feel it as wet.

Turning around, she saw Evan stare at her from the rock. He had not moved from his position, had remained steady, part of the rock, but his eyes were on her, were definitely on her, and Amanda felt anger rise into her throat.

"Evan, come here, I need some help."

Amanda stood up, felt the weight of her wet nightclothes, held a hand to the porch railing to steady herself. Still Evan stared at her, and by now she felt embarrassed by his stare, seeing it as an inhuman gaze.

She knew she could not wade out across the slippery rocks to swim to the large rock where Evan perched. Holding to the railing with both hands, she made her way carefully around to the side of the porch, along the side until she reached the dry ground, and she pushed her way up through the bushes and the undergrowth that surrounded the cabin to reach the path. Back into the cabin she hurried, out onto the porch, where she could still see Evan posed.

"I'm going inside to the house now, Evan," she called. "I'm going for help. I'll be back as soon as I can get some —"

One of Evan's arms raised into the air. "No," he emitted, the sound a crack through the misty air.

Slowly he raised himself up, stood firmly on both feet, his hands on his hips. "Don't do that, Mother, I'll come in soon."

Amanda felt her wet leather shoes on her feet, the water oozing under her arches, her feet clammy and numb with cold.

"You come in now, Evan, or I'll get help. I'm going up to the house to get out of these wet things, and I expect you to be in the house by the time I am dressed. You must be frozen to the bone."

Amanda turned and headed for the house, her knees shaking, her heart racing. She disappeared into the cabin, her voice calling to him as she made her way to the house. Slowly Evan slipped into the water, the weight of his clothes like the arms of the lake's floor pulling at him. He waded through the shallow water, climbed over the railing to the cabin, stood and stared out at the lake.

A rising shiver began in his gut. It rose into his chest

and caused it to tremble, and into his arms which began to shake, down into his thighs until his entire body was a round of shivers from top to bottom. He held his arms around himself, rubbed at his sides, at his arms, his legs, but the shivering continued.

The mountains lay like sleeping bodies on their sides, encircling the lake, holding the bulging volume of water in tow. Where the mountains touched the sky, there was an outline of thin black, as if they held the sky in place with their rising forms.

Inside the house, Amanda added two logs to the wood stove. Steam spit from the iron surfaces as water dripped from the sleeves of her robe. She held her hands out flat, palms down, over the stove. She stepped out of her shoes, saw small puddles of brown water inside them, saw her blue-white toes. She removed her robe, laid it on the chair, and stood in her flannel nightgown, dripping, shivering. Her clothes rested by the stove, warming, and she felt her skin prickle as she pulled her nightgown down to her waist and stood naked, her hands warming over the stove. She dressed quickly then, drying in stages, and hung her nightgown from a hook so that it could dry.

As Amanda waited for the water to boil so she could make a pot of coffee, she looked around the room. She liked the open shelves for dishes that covered the wall to one side of the wood stove; she liked the splashes of red and blue of the china cups on the lowest shelf. She liked the large table that sat in the center of the room; Lindy had done her preparations for baking at that table, her hands working fast to knead the dough for a piecrust or for her special biscuits. Lindy had taught Amanda how to cook during the summer: soups, vegetable pies, fruit pies, and her most famous angel cake. Amanda closed her eyes and smelled the sweet coconut of Lindy's angel cake, saw the crusty top to the soft white meringue. Amanda opened her eyes, remembered the small breakfast table by the window, the wooden lazy Susan that was always covered with homemade jams, a bowl of sugar and cinnamon, and salt and pepper shakers in the shape of bells.

The kettle steamed and Amanda poured the coffee, set the pot on the stove to drip. She looked out the window over the sink, noticed the start of more rain, saw the sky darken with heavier clouds. The silver birch that stood just outside the window was grey, a dirty grey, in the dismal wetness of the morning. Once she remembered telling Lindy that the trunks of the birch trees looked to her like the legs of giant birds, and Lindy had laughed, saying she had never thought of it that way, but it was true, because all that could be seen through the window were the trunks, no branches and no leaves. "You have such an imagination, Amanda," Lindy had told her, and Amanda heard the words and started with the thought that Lindy was there in the room with her.

The back door opened, and Amanda looked into the back hall, saw Evan standing just inside the door.

"Close the door, quick," she told him. "The rain will get in."

Evan reached a hand behind him and pushed the door over, leaned against it with his back, began to unbutton his shirt.

"Let me help you," Amanda said, but he held his hand out.

"I got it," Evan said.

He dropped his shirt to the floor, leaned over to roll down his trousers, rubbed the tops of his feet, and stood up. As he came into the kitchen, steam rose from his back.

"I've got some questions," he said as he approached the stove, his narrow shoulders shivering.

Amanda saw the shaking in his legs, pulled her wet robe off the chair, said, "Here, Evan, sit down, you're a wreck. You mustn't do such a thing, it's absurd to be in that water at this time of year. You could catch your death in this weather." She watched the beads of water drip from his hair down onto his shoulders, run slowly onto his chest.

Evan sat down. His arms swung by his sides as he pushed

the chair onto its back legs and balanced it against the wall. The muscles in his chest danced with shivering, his thighs jumping to the side.

"I've got some questions," he repeated.

Amanda reached for the pot of coffee and poured him a cup. Holding it in both hands, she passed it to him so that he could take it by the handle. He pressed the cup against his cheek. Loudly, he sipped at it.

"Will you work with Martin today in this rain?" she asked.

"Mother," Evan said.

"I know, dear," she answered, "but will you work today, let's get that straight. I think you should stay in, you must be overtired, he can manage without you for a day."

"I'll see, Mother." Evan's chair fell forward with a thunk on the floor. Amanda jumped, turned away from the sink to face him.

"What is it, Evan?" Her grey eyes darkened as they drew into her face.

"It's about Sarah. Why didn't you like her?" He stared hard at her eyes, watched her look down at the floor, up and out the window.

"That's an odd question, dear," she answered. "Whatever makes you think I didn't like Sarah?" Her eyes followed the lines in the linoleum floor. "Of course, you must admit, she wasn't a good choice for you. She was too . . ." and Amanda looked up, held a finger to her lip.

"Too what?" Evan probed.

"Too," and she paused again. "Too smart for her own good. She wouldn't have been a good wife, surely you can see that now."

"In whose eyes, not a good wife?" Evan's voice grew louder as Amanda's shrank in volume and tone.

"Well, Evan, in your eyes of course." Amanda held her hand against her throat.

"In my eyes?" Then louder. "In my eyes?" he yelled at her, rising from the chair. He paced to the other end of the room to the door where he pushed at a chair with his hand so that it lifted and fell with a clatter back onto its feet.

Amanda sank into her seat, her shoulders up against her neck. "Control yourself, dear, this is nonsense, what you're saying. You're cold and wet and will probably come down with the flu as a result of that swim. You should see yourself."

"And what about Ivy?" he flung at her. "What was the matter with her?"

Amanda looked in amazement at her son. "Ivy?" she questioned. "All these years, and you're still thinking about Ivy?"

"What was wrong with her, Mother, tell me."

"Honestly, Evan, this is nonsense, sheer nonsense. That was so long ago, why I'm not sure I could remember much about the girl —"

"Tell me," he yelled and paced from the table to the stove to the table.

"Well, if you must hear it, she was too . . ." and Amanda paused to find the right words, and Evan paced. "Too full of herself for her own good."

Then suddenly Evan stopped. He pointed a finger at her, his arm stretched out in a line. "You let Ivy go, didn't you, Maggie's Ivy, that day we were all down on the dock, you let that little canary go, didn't you? Say it, Mother, you let her go, didn't you?"

Amanda lifted herself out of her chair, her hands at her waist. "Why, Evan, I believe you're sick. You sound feverish, your face is flushed." Her eyes were silver now, silver darts.

Evan's finger still pointed. "You," he said, his blue eyes still watering. "You killed that bird, and that's not all."

Amanda stiffened, drew herself up, smoothed back her hair. "Evan, you must be ill. This is nonsense. I will not let you speak to me this way."

"You have no choice, Mother. I've kept quiet all this time. We've all lied with you, lived with your lies, lived on your lies. Like Grandfather," Evan said, and he swallowed hard.

Amanda's hand cracked across Evan's face, stinging the skin on his cheek, turning his head, putting him off his balance. His body trembled, shivered, with the cold or the words, and his face flushed.

Amanda stood back and stared at her son. Her hands began to twist together, the fingers entwining, wrapping together, pulling at each other.

Then the back door pushed open. There was the sound of a knock on the wooden frame around the door, at the same time as a voice called, and it was Martin's voice. "Mrs. Rhoades?" he called in and removed his hat, held it at his waist, and Amanda saw the water drip from the brim onto the wooden floor as he stepped into the kitchen.

"I come to tell Evan," and then he saw Evan in the chair by the stove, his bare shoulders trembling, his legs jerking in spasm, his head bent forward, and Martin tilted his head, looked at Amanda, his eyes questioning.

"Martin, I'm glad you've come, Evan's sick, he took a swim, it was a fool thing to do, and he's burning up, he's just on fire with fever," and Amanda placed her hand against her heart and stepped backwards. "I think I need a doctor, Martin, it's my heart —"

Alice knocked on Amanda's door, received no response, pushed the door in. The shades were drawn, the curtains pulled, the darkness in the room hid Amanda's form on the bed. She lay under several blankets, the heavy cream comforter over the top.

"It's cold in here, Mrs. Rhoades, and time to wake up. It's nearly noon."

Amanda did not move. Pushing the door wide, Alice laid the tray with tea and toast on the dresser and pulled back the curtains, raising the shade on one window. Sunlight clambered onto the floor, reaching fingers into the room.

"It's a beautiful day, Mrs. Rhoades, sun's out, you should see the colors in the woods today."

Amanda pushed the covers back, stayed flat on her back,

no pillow under her head, her eyes closed. "What day is it, Alice?"

"It's Thursday, Mrs. Rhoades, you been resting two days now."

"It's not raining?"

"No. Mrs. Rhoades, it's like I said, the sun's out. Look and see."

Amanda's eyes opened, looked at the ceiling, blinked several times. She turned her head, brought Alice into focus, saw the tray in her hands. "I'm not hungry, Alice, you can take that back to the kitchen."

Alice did not move, stood holding the tray. Then she pulled a chair to the side of the bed and laid the tray of food on it. When she left the room, she pulled the door over so it shut hard and pushed back open.

Amanda listened to her heart. As soon as Alice came into the room, it had started up again, its uneven beat taking all her attention. The doctor had found nothing wrong with her. "You need rest," he told her, and Amanda listened to him tell Alice to make sure she rested. "There's something wrong with my heart," Amanda told him. "Mrs. Rhoades, your heart's as strong as any I've listened to, you must rest now, and I'm leaving something with Alice to help you sleep."

Fool doctor, Amanda thought after he left. What good is a doctor who can't hear the plain beating of my heart? she thought.

"I want the room dark," she told Alice after the doctor left. "I can't stand the sound of this rain, it's eating at me."

So Alice closed the shades and the door. "Should I stay through the day?" she asked the doctor, who thought it would be a good idea. She returned the next day to look in on Amanda, found her still in bed. Evan too was no better; his flu symptoms worsened during the second day, and Alice spent the morning washing him down, trying to lower the fever. The third day, his fever broke, and he lay quiet through the hours, drank a little beef broth before Alice left that afternoon to fix Martin's supper. She checked back on the fourth day.

Amanda was up, still in her robe. "What's all the fuss?" she threw at Alice, "you needn't come by today, Alice, I'm perfectly able to look after my son."

"What about you? You feelin' better, Mrs. Rhoades?"

"I'm fine, thank you, Alice, and you needn't trouble yourself over us any longer." She gave Alice nothing for her time, and Alice left without asking for anything.

The first time Amanda looked in on Evan, he was lying quietly, a wash cloth covering his eyes. She started to pull the shades.

"Leave them open, will you, Mother," and he turned his head. The cloth fell off.

"I thought the light would be too much," she said. "I thought you'd want it dark till you're better."

"I am better."

Amanda looked at Evan, felt some unease in her chest, couldn't place it, continued pulling the shades.

"Leave them open," he repeated, rising on one elbow. "I said to leave them open. I'm better now."

Amanda stood back against the window. She stared at Evan. "You've been quite ill, Alice says."

"Just the flu," and Evan flopped back against the pillow. He closed his eyes. His face twitched in different places, around his right eye, in the jaw.

"You've been ill, Evan. A high fever made you ill." Amanda held her hands stiffly at her waist.

Amanda approached the bed, smoothed the green afghan at the corner. "I made this afghan the summer before you were born."

Evan frowned, he pushed the pillow back, started to sit up against the frame of the bed. He ran his hand under his pajama top across his chest.

"I made it for Father, my father, to keep on his bed in the front room. I couldn't decide whether to have three colors or two. Mother said two is always better because it's purer. Cleaner, she used to say."

Evan watched his mother run her hand over the afghan.

She pulled at some fuzzy pieces that stuck to it, wound them into a ball between her fingers. "I do like this combination of greens, don't you?" Her grey eyes looked up as she sat lightly against the foot of the bed, held a hand to her neck.

"I'm going to heat some soup for you, dear." She looked out the door into the living room. "Shall I bring it in here, or will you come into the kitchen?"

"Will you cut this shit, Mother —"

Amanda pulled away, straightening her spine. She backed to the door to Evan's room, then lingered in the doorway.

"Alice left some vegetable soup for us, I'll mix up some biscuits, I think you're ready for biscuits, don't you think?" and as she asked the question, Amanda was pulling the door shut to Evan's reply. "I'll bring your supper in on a tray," she called to him, as she passed through the living room. "You're not ready to get out of bed yet," she called as she headed to the kitchen.

Three days later, Evan went into the woods with Martin, to do some cutting. Amanda complained that he was too weak still, that his frame had withered through the course of the flu. "You should rest more," she warned him. "You should let me take care of you, properly."

It was no surprise to her, then, when Martin appeared with Evan before lunch. Amanda was in the kitchen, fixing herself some toast with creamed chicken. She was just spooning the chicken mixture onto the toasted bread when she glanced out the window and saw the two of them come through the woods, with Evan leaning heavily against Martin.

"I knew you weren't fit to work yet," she told him later, after she'd gotten Evan into bed, after she'd heard what had happened, how Evan had overexerted, how in his enthusiasm, as he was chopping through a load of wood, the ax had slipped, had glanced against his calf, leaving a painful slash about four inches long on the side of his leg.

"I was fine, Mother," Evan told her as he gazed through the window in his room to the woods.

"You shouldn't go back to that, not ever," she continued.

"Leave me alone," he whispered, but she kept talking at him, going over her thoughts until his head settled down into his shoulders and he stared with watery blue eyes at her lips that shifted and twisted with more words.

In the morning, Evan's leg was worse. Amanda removed the gauze to check the gash and saw white streaks spreading out from the swollen place on his leg where the ax had cut him. "I'll get Alice," she told him, and when Alice saw the leg, she said right away, "We'll need a doctor, it's infected."

"I can see it's infected," Amanda replied, staring at the yellow substance that oozed from the open place, "obviously I can see it's infected, that's why I came to get you," she told Alice.

"I can give him an injection of penicillin, Mrs. Rhoades," Alice explained, "but he'll want a doctor to look at it." Already white streaks fingered their way up to the knee. "It must smart," she commented to Evan.

"Like hell," he answered, his brow sweaty, his eyes wide with fever or pain.

Amanda wound her hands together as she watched Alice clean the area around the wound. Her eyes riveted on the bloodstained gauze that lay in a pile on the floor. She stared at the flesh on his leg, where it was separated in a bloody line, as Alice ran a patch of gauze over the opening.

Alice prepared a cup of broth, held it to him. "You must drink," she said. "Your face is looking some green now."

"I'm afraid I'll vomit," he said, and turned his face to stare at the window. "Can you pull the shades down more?" he asked, his hand going to his head.

"You rest," she told him, and to Amanda, "he'll be all right with this penicillin till the doctor gets here, that should be late this afternoon. And you might want to move him into the other room, near the fire. He might be happier out there, warmer."

"How do you manage here?" Amanda asked Alice before

she left. "Without a doctor nearby, it must be —" and she left the sentence unfinished.

"We don't have emergencies these days, Mrs. Rhoades, just —" and Alice paused. "Just the regular things, nothing serious. It's not so hard to get out now, with the road," she explained.

The pus in Evan's leg began to drain within twenty-four hours, and some of the swelling left after the first dose of penicillin. The doctor recommended rest, but he said the leg should heal quickly. Evan sat in a chair by the fire all day, reading. His complexion continued to pale, his eyes dark blue in their sockets as the days passed. Amanda brought him trays of soup, stew that Alice made for them, eggs, bowls of peaches. Most of it he let sit on the trays by his chair.

"I'm just not hungry," he told Amanda. "I can't force it," he went on, rubbing the back of his head with his hand. He was tired from not sleeping well, from the night sweats that woke him, the dreams that made him cry out.

"You're not improving," Amanda told him finally. "We must leave, soon. We've stayed too long." She lowered the two shades over the windows in his room that faced the woods where the shadows darkened, pulling her eyes into the spaces between the trees. She fluffed the calico quilt, laid it smoothly over Evan's bed. He lay with one arm behind his head, his eyes watching her.

"In Connecticut we'll have a proper doctor see you. These country people don't know what they're doing, they patch and press, but they don't know enough to be exact," she repeated, smoothing the quilt with her hand. "And your father returns in two weeks, you'll want to be settled, you'll want to be back on your feet, he'll want to know your plans, about graduate school, and —"

"I don't have any plans," Evan said, flatly.

"Yes, I know, dear, not until January, but you need a plan when we get back, you'll think better, you'll know what to do; all you need is to get back there where a proper doctor can look at you and —"

"What I'd like to know, Mother," and he closed his eyes as he took in a breath, and his other arm slid up and under his head, "is how Grandfather drowned. I've been thinking about it, and I can't make sense of it."

Amanda felt the mattress shudder. She stood up, smoothed the legs of her navy wool slacks, and heard a sound from outside.

"What was that?" she questioned, holding her hands to her waist, turning her head to the pair of covered windows.

Evan opened his eyes, shifted his position, sliding up against the headboard. He leaned on one elbow. His face flushed pink, his eyes watered, and when Amanda turned, he was staring fully into her face.

"Did you hear that?" she asked, her brows raised together in an innocent stance, her grey eyes liquid, pooling.

Evan's eyelids fluttered slightly. His head began to nod, a barely perceptible nodding at first, but as he waited, as they stared each other down, the nodding grew deeper, so that his head tapped the headboard with each upward motion.

Amanda sighed, hard and fast. She looked down at her hand, wiggled the thumb. "You don't know what you're asking me to do."

Evan said nothing, just stared at her.

"Is it because of Sarah that you've got so sick?" she queried, shifting the focus.

Evan's brow quivered.

"I knew she was no good for you, I could see it in those green eyes of hers, I knew it from the first moment, her eyes showed it, Evan, and it was your bad luck to be taken with her."

Evan's eyes trembled. One lid lowered over his right eye.

"You've had bad luck all along, and I've tried to make amends. Sarah was just one more piece of bad luck, I knew it would turn out against you, I knew —"

Evan's face paled to a yellowish grey. Suddenly he was thrown forward as he vomited onto the bed, bits of sandwich and yellow mucus, lumps of peach, and then he vomited again onto himself, two more times, and with each heave, a cry was emitted.

Amanda's eyes widened but she remained standing at the end of the bed. As she averted her eyes, he let forth a final cry and raised himself from the wet mess on the bed. His hands came to his face. "Jesus," he said, and again, "Jesus, Jesus, Jesus, Jesus," he was chanting louder until Amanda spoke his name with a harsh tone and told him to hush, he was sick, he needed a doctor, she told him, they would leave soon. But his chanting grew louder, and she backed away from him to the door, until she was up against it, her back flat against the wooden panels, and then she pulled open the door with one hand, and as she slipped out, he yelled, "You make me sick, can't you understand that —" and then the door was closed, and she fled to her room, closed the door and sat on the chair by the window and peered into the dark night, not a star or a moon to shine on the lake, not a sound of a loon, just the slow rising of the rain.

Amanda did not undress. In the dark she found the bed, fell into it, pulled the covers over her head, turned onto her back and lay there, flat on her back, her arms stiff by her sides, staring into the dark, sleeping for minutes at a time and then wakening with a stiffening of her arms under the covers. When the first light of dawn spread through the cracks under the shades and onto the floor, filling the room with a fine grey dimness, Amanda jerked awake and opened her eyes, felt the relief of the new light. Her heart began its racing anew, and she swung onto her side and sat up, holding her hands hard against her heart, wishing it would stop its rapid pace. She sat like that, letting the light grow, until the room was more than shadows, until she could see the pattern of roses on the curtains clearly.

Rising from the bed, she went to the window and looked out at a grey morning, but the rain had stopped, and the air looked cold against the drying bark of the trees, and a low breeze swept up from the lake, and Amanda knew it was cold. Then she realized the cold in her room, and it seeped into her skin, the cold did, and she rubbed her arms and breathed out deeply. She opened the door to the living room, stepped onto the bare floor with stockinged feet, and saw the door to Evan's room ajar. She could see the foot of the bed that was his, could tell the bed was empty, went to his door expecting to see him in the other bed, but it too was empty, and his own bed lay unmade, the stink of his sickness lying in the bedding.

In the kitchen the fire was out and the room held the new cold. She reached for some kindling, began to ball up some paper when a thought came to her. He's gone to cut wood with Martin, she thought, and it nagged at her heart, made her angry. That fool, she thought, he's so sick he doesn't even know what he is doing, and that fool Martin won't know enough to bring him in. She dropped the kindling on the floor, pushed it with her foot, decided she would go after him; he was too sick to know what was good for him. "It's time to leave Land's End," she said aloud and felt the cold in her hands and against her face.

Though Amanda had never been up to the orchard in the woods behind Land's End, she knew about where it was, and as she pulled a hat over her head and buttoned a heavy navy wool jacket, she pictured Evan with an ax in his hands. She could feel his weakened body, could feel his throat dry and sore from being sick, knew for certain the lack of force in the slap of his palm against the ax handle as he reached to hold it, as it hit his leg. Damnable fool, she thought, and again registered the thought that he needed a doctor. She considered heading first for Chad and then up through the woods, for she knew there was a shortcut, but she was tired of the people in the town watching her life, so she headed to the trail behind the back woodshed. For a moment she wondered at her own strength, thought of her own failing health, the joints in her hands and knees swelling in the cold damp, the weakness of her heart, but all of that felt far away in her anger, and she knew with a sense of mission that she needed to get to Evan as soon as possible before he swung the ax into his leg again or before he collapsed from weakness.

She hadn't noticed the time when she left, but she was startled by the darkness in the woods. As the trail started up into the thick pines, she wondered if it was earlier than she had thought, but this washed out of her mind and was gone with the image of Evan, so she walked steadily through the wet forest, water dripping still from the branches, the ground slippery beneath her feet. Her breath formed thin clouds of mist in the air as she panted from exertion on the places where the incline was steep. The minutes passed quickly as the image of Evan pulled her through the woods, and she rehearsed the words she would have for Martin, a man whose lack of judgment and decent sense gave Amanda more cause for anger. She thought back to Martin's handling of her father's death, knew of his sneaky ways, and her heart was fueled with irritation and disgust for the people of Chad.

At the first plateau on the mountain, she could tell she was near the orchard. Turning to look at the trail behind her, she realized she could not see the lake from this place, all she could see was the trail descending behind her like a tunnel, and she felt her balance shift, felt herself sway backwards, thought she might fall back, pictured herself sliding down the mountain and into the lake, all in one motion. The wind was rising beneath her and above her, a gentle whistling through the trees that dried the woods slowly from the night's rain. The sky was brightening, and Amanda again wondered, Perhaps it is much earlier than I had thought. She heard no sounds of work in the woods. She felt a trembling in her knees; looking down, she could see them shaking, and for a moment she thought it would have been better had she gone to Chad first, to make sure that Martin was up at the orchard.

A little farther on the trail, she felt the sun break through the mist as the air brightened more. The woods were thinning, she realized, wondering if this was the clearing Evan had spoken of. A few more steps and she saw a cluster of rocks and behind them an orchard. This was smaller than the ones that she had seen down by the lake. Only six bent trees stood hunched together, and Amanda fancied they looked like wartime soldiers marching to an execution. Her breathing came now in short gasps and she sat against a rock and breathed in deeply, held her hand to her throat, listened to the sound of her breath as she stared at the trees.

It was the sound of a shot behind her that twisted her up and around from her place on the rock. Amanda's mouth opened wide, formed a black hole in her face ready to scream, but when she saw Evan standing on the other side of the orchard, and in his hand was a shotgun that pointed to the sky over her head, his name came to her lips, and she cried out, "Evan," and then she wondered, Where did he get that gun?

The features of Evan's face were lost in its pale whiteness. Locks of his golden hair hung damp against his forehead, but it was his posture that drew and held Amanda's attention. She stared at his bent shaking legs, at his bare feet, at the gun that he clutched against his chest, one hand rubbing the wooden stock unevenly in a jerking motion. He held the gun still poised in the air, and then he pulled it up and looked through the sights, aimed it somewhere over Amanda's head, and she watched the shaking in his legs work into his chest and into his arms, so that the muzzle of the shotgun weaved in the air. He looks drunk, she thought, and called, "Are you drunk, Evan?" and then, "Where did you get that gun?" She took a step in his direction. Instantly the weaving of the shotgun stopped and it held firm in his grip, aimed over her head.

"You stop," he said, his voice high and thin like a child's. "Right there, you stop," he repeated. He locked his knees to stop the shaking.

Amanda noticed he wore the T-shirt he had worn to bed, and there were stains of vomit across the shoulder. "Evan, it's cold, you're sick, you shouldn't be out here like this, you'll catch your death —" and she stopped as she saw the two black holes of the gun stare at her like the beady eyes of a bear, set in deep. "Where's Martin?" she questioned, looking around, her eyes darting behind him and into the woods and back to the black eyes facing hers.

"I said stop, Mother, and I mean stop, stop every-thing —" he said, his voice rising in pitch. "Stop talking," and the barrel of the gun jerked up and focused on her again. "Stop thinking even."

Amanda felt her breath hold in her shoulders. She stood up taller, breathed in deeper, felt he was surely out of his mind with fever. "Evan," using a harsh tone that she hadn't intended, "this is nonsense, where's Martin, where's —" and before this question was finished, she heard a large crack, it was the gun, and it lurched upward as she felt the air beside her head move, and she realized it was a shot, a burst of pellets passing by the side of her face. She froze, her mouth still open, her legs planting firmly beneath her, her eyes darting.

"I'm sick of it," he said suddenly, clutching the gun as it started to tremble in his hands so hard that his shoulder twitched.

Amanda remained frozen. She watched as he started to cry, as his frame shook with a violent kind of shaking, but still those black eyes glared at her, wavering up and down, and then he spoke again, said, "Do you know what it's like to be in a box," and with these words his trembling ceased and he grew still and firm again as the eyes of the gun pointed at her belly and stayed there, unmoving. "My bones hurt in this box, it hurts to be in here —"

An image of her father came to Amanda's mind, an image she had lost for many years until this moment. It was the image of her father standing in the lake, the barrel of a gun pressed into his throat, and she felt the bark of the tree against her face, the tree she hid behind as she watched him, and standing there before Evan, she reached her arms out and fell to her knees at what she saw in her mind.

Amanda thought she might faint. She felt a shooting of pain into the back of her neck, and her eyes were losing their sight, so that instead of clearly seeing those two eyes of the gun, instead of seeing Evan's face all white and featureless, looking like a child, a faceless child, she saw only light and dark. Where Evan was, she saw dark, just a dark patch before her eyes, and above, when she lifted her eyes skyward without moving her head, she saw light. But it wasn't sky and sun pouring down, there were no clouds, it was just a lighter shade of the dark in the patch where Evan stood.

Then she heard another shot and in the space of time after the sound of the shot, as she knelt waiting to feel the impact in her chest, where somehow she knew the gun was aimed, she heard her father tell her that he would never forgive her, and in that space of time she saw his face in her mind's eye, and she knew he was gone from her forever, and even though he had been dead for some twelve years, it was not until that moment when she waited for the shot that she knew he was gone from her, that she had lost him. And she knew it was her own fault, that she had turned him away by being there in his sight at the moment of his lunacy in the lake, by being even alive herself.

And in that space of time as she waited, her eyes remained open, still seeing only black and white, dark and light, and after what seemed a long period of time, she began to see a color, and it was the color of red, and she thought the frame of her line of vision was edged in red and then filled in with red, and it was a bright red, it was the color of bright red roses in a garden of only red roses.

And then she knew it was the red of blood. It was the red of blood as she had seen before, the red of blood in her father's face, and this time she knew it was her own blood, but when she looked down at herself, when she put her hands to her face and then to the back of her head where it hurt so much, when she touched her hands there and then looked at them, she saw no red, and then she knew.

"Evan —" she cried, and again, "Evan," this time louder, the two syllables blending into the name of her son.

And then her vision returned, and there was no longer

only black and white, only dark and light, but the scene was bathed in red, and the red covered Evan's face and ran down his body, over his chest, and the tree he stood near was red, and the grass was red, and she knew she wanted not to see what was there before her.

She stood there staring at him, lying back against the ground, the gun lying beside him, the muzzle resting against his hand now, and she could not move. She stood just staring, and though only a matter of seconds passed, it was for her the whole of time. It did not get dark and night did not come as she waited. Finally she whispered his name, "Evan," she whispered, but he did not answer, there was only a gurgling kind of sound in his throat, and she wondered if he was trying to say something, the gurgling sounding almost like words, and so she waited.

Amanda knelt on the ground, fell down onto her hands and knees. She crawled over to where Evan lay, unmoving, the trembling stopped. She rested her face against his chest and felt the cold metal of the gun touch her arm, but his chest was warm with the heat of life, the heat of his own blood, so she lay there against him until there was no more warmth, no more life. Until his chest was as cold as the metal of the gun, and his blood was as hard as the ground beneath him.

❧ SIXTEEN ❧

Margaret," Amanda shrieks into the dark as clouds of ashes heave into her mind. She squeezes her eyes shut, then open, then shut, to escape the pictures in her mind, as one after another image crowds in, the faces blurring, the horror growing, the feeling of herself shrinking under the aura of too many memories. Her heart flaunts its rapid beats so that they become part of the images she tries to escape, so that a single lurching beat of her heart entwines with the vision of Evan in his blood-drenched death, so that the next lurch of her heart shows the hole she dug in the woods to hide the rifle, and the next beat rings through her throat with the words she cried to Martin, "He's been shot, he may die, he's been shot by some fool hunter," knowing that Evan was already dead, his blood a shroud that covered his body and the ground around him.

A triangle of light spreads into the room as the door opens and Maggie leans over the doorjamb and says nothing. She is not sure that she heard her mother call, and she waits with her hand on the knob to see if Amanda is sleeping.

Amanda turns her head when she sees the light. "Margaret," she says, "I need some light in here."

"Shall I leave the door open, there's enough light from the fire, and I can build it up some more, and then some more warmth might come in here, it's freezing, and you —"

"No, I want the door shut, but I need a light," and

Amanda feels uneasy asking Maggie for this. "Just a dim light, a little light, a candle would be all right," and she closes her eyes and waits, listens to the sound of Maggie's feet on the floor, to the sound of a drawer pulling open, and then a new light floods above her as Maggie places a lighted candle on the bedside table.

"Bring me another candle, though, in case this wears down." Amanda slides her hand back under the covers.

"Are you okay, Mother?" Maggie asks as she lays a second candle on the table.

"I was dreaming, it's nothing. I just need a little light —" and Amanda turns to face the wall.

The door closes and Amanda opens her eyes, takes a deep breath, moves her eyes over the ceiling, over the walls, at the windows that face the lake, at the bureau that sits between the two windows, the mirror reflecting the picture over the table by her bed, the print of the owl resting on a branch, its one eye seeing the world. Amanda closes her eyes, falls instantly to sleep.

Toward dawn, when she wakes, she opens one eye and sees the owl eye again. Eleanor's eye, she thinks.

Turning, she sees the candle's flame. She studies it, her eyes absorb the silky glow of the golden fire. She stares into the base of the flame, the blue-black lip surrounding the charring wick. Amanda leans up onto one elbow, moves her face closer to the candle, can feel the heat from the small flame. She exhales a slow breath through her lips and the flame jerks, wiggles, and returns to its original position. Her face moves closer still, her eyes level with the black night. Amanda notices a loose thread on the cuff of her nightgown; she pulls at it sharply so that it breaks, and she holds it close to the flame. The thread waves gently in the air from the current of heat. When she lowers it, there is a tiny sizzling sound as the thread contracts, pulls up, blackening into a shred of smoke.

Amanda swallows, moves her head slowly from left to right, her eyes on the light. And then an image comes. She knows when an image is about to happen, and she squeezes her eyes shut again to fight it, and her heart leaps in new rhythm, but the image comes. It is the vision of the burning barn, and her ears ring with the sound of such volume of fire, and her heart sinks at the remembered sight of the swirling black rushing clouds of smoke that filled the air, dropping ash over the ground. Amanda focuses on the beat of her heart, but instead of taking away the image, instead of feeling that fear and anger at her own beating heart, its rhythm carries her closer to the vision, until she is a young girl, a fourteen-year-old girl, her long brown hair under a brown cotton cap, her hands outstretched and clutched together, and she feels her knees strike the gravelly ground as she falls onto the roadside, and then she hears again the cry of burning animals, a death cry so close to human crying that she wondered if there were people inside, and she now wonders if it was her own life that was in the barn, alongside those animals. Images of their wild eyes, their shifting fearful bodies, their flaring nostrils, and she cries with them for help, wordlessly, with animal sounds. Her eyes see the space around her fill with dense curling black smoke until she cannot see the wild animal eyes any longer, can only hear their chanting cries.

Amanda rolls onto her stomach on the bed, slides off until her knees hit the floor with a crack, her arms stretched out over the mattress, her fingers twining and untwining. Out of the corner of one eye she sees the eye of the owl, a black shining eye, and in the image her eye is drawn to the rafters of the barn where an owl screeches, its beak opening and closing, its talons tightening on the rafter, its wings fluffing and flattening, and Amanda can see all these things from her place on the floor of the barn where she rests on her knees. Through the whorls of smoke she watches the owl lean into the rafter and then lift its wings, she sees it leave its place as it swoops through the sky of the barn, from one end to another and back to the middle where it finds a higher place, a rafter close to the peak where a thin shaft of light cuts the smoke. The owl opens its beak but now Amanda cannot hear its cry, the billowing flames create such a roar of wind, and again the owl leaves its perch, dips low over the animals, by the space filling with flames now along with the smoke, and the owl climbs upward until Amanda can no longer see its wings arch through the smoke.

"Take me with you," she cries to the owl, reaching one hand up, feeling flames slide around her feet, but the owl is gone up in the smoke, up to the rafters where she cannot go, and as the cry of the animals reaches a higher pitch, she knows she cannot escape, she knows she is with them. The smoke wraps hot arms around her, the flames pull at her legs, the cries cushion her head, until she throws her arms back in a gesture of surrender.

Her right arm knocks at the candle that has burned un-wavering, creating the vision and now the experience. Amanda does not hear it knock against the table, does not see the hot wax spread onto the linen table cover and does not see it start to smoke and does not hear the air crackle. She falls back onto her knees, bends her head, knows she is safe, knows the comfort of this conflagration, feels held in its softness where her own hands can no longer strangle the wind of her rage. She opens her eyes and sees the golden satin sheen of flame slice the space before her eyes, the soft golden sheen rubs her eyes, brushes her cheek, and she feels its velvetine softness, the softness of flame, the odor of dead flame now living, it lingers, and she lies back in the velvetine space as the glass in the frame by the bed cracks with heat, and the owl bubbles from its place on the branch.

It is still raining, Maggie thinks, as she listens to the steady patter. It is almost dawn, and she knows she will not get back to sleep.

Maggie pushes back the covers on the lounge and sits up. She pulls an orange blanket around her shoulders, slides her feet into the slippers that rest on the floor, pulls up the socks that have kept her feet warm these last nights. Gazing out the window into the black night, she wonders if the rain will last through the next day. It is too wet, she thinks, too cold to stay much longer. If it dries up, it will be okay. Indian summer, she thinks, and remembers telling Jeremy how much she wanted to see the lake in October. But this rain is awful, and she pads over to the fire, lays another log on top, listens to the bark sizzle.

Reaching for a sketch pad, Maggie has an image. She sees the woods in full color, blossoms of red and gold against green, whole clusters of trees like single blossoms. Her pastel moves across the blank page, flowers form, orange and yellow lilies rising from the green woods background. She flips the page, starts again, drawing single trees in clusters, trying to give them the illusion of being single flowers. Again she flips the page and stares at the white of the next page.

Maggie thinks of her mother flailing at her father's grave that afternoon. She thinks of the place where her grandfather is buried, beneath the pine branches and near the lake's edge. She sketches the sight, the apple trees leaning, the solitary stone with no dates, no words, only a name, the pine trees reaching with protective hands over the ground. She remembers when he was buried, how she stood by her father's side, his hand on her shoulder, and she watched her mother, recalls the expectation that Amanda would faint or scream or collapse, but she did none of those, and Maggie was relieved, though she knew she had not experienced the funeral itself, had instead experienced her mother's grief.

Jeremy often told her she spent too much time paying attention to her mother, not enough time paying attention to herself. "What's to attend to in me?" she asked, and they argued.

"If you don't know, I can't tell you," he had said, and she pondered these words often but could not feel how they applied to her. After her grandmother's funeral, she complained to Jeremy that she felt nothing. "I know," he answered, and she felt a shock from his words.

"What do you mean, you know?" she asked.

"I just know," he answered. "I could see it in your face. There's lots you don't feel anyway."

"Maybe I can't," she defended herself. "Maybe feeling is too much for me."

His eyes probed her, then jumped away. "It's your life," he finished, and she chose not to pursue what he meant. It was several days before she could ask him.

"It's like your not wanting me to come to the lake with you," he answered, though Maggie wasn't sure it was the answer she sought.

Now she thinks about his words. Am I afraid to let him see? she wonders, thinking of Amanda, how Amanda holds herself in. Do I not want him to know the truth about me? Maggie stops. The truth about me, she thinks. The words echo, the truth about me, the truth about me.

Maggie flips the page in her book. She draws another sketch of the grave in the orchard. This time she sketches in a bird perched on the stone, a little sparrow, grey with black eyes, and its claws form on the page out of proportion to the body, the talons reaching down almost to the lettering of the name. It makes Maggie shudder. All this time I've blamed only her. But what about me? I've helped it happen. Haven't I?

The room has filled with early morning light as she has sketched, so that when she looks up, she can see the dawn. The rain is slowing to a distant murmur, she can hardly hear it. At the window Maggie looks to the lake. The world is bathed in grey. Two black dots on the water catch her eye. Loons, and she opens the door to step out onto the porch, pulls the orange blanket closer around her shoulders. The cold air hits her face, a wind is coming up from the water. A front must be coming in, she thinks, hopes the rains will stop, that new sun will come.

Maggie sits on the steps, rubs her eyes, feels her tiredness. She sees the roof of the cabin, slick black amongst the slick wet trees.

Evan was right, she thinks. He knew. That's why he got so angry all the time. And then, she realizes: That's why he killed himself. He tried to save me, but what about him? Who was going to save him? Tears form, slow lonely tears, tears of missing her brother, tears that she cannot tell him what she is learning. Evan, she thinks, it wasn't just her. It was you. And me. It was all of us. I didn't realize. Not till now.

Maggie feels a straining, flashing ache in her chest. She lowers her face to her knees, rocks gently against the step. God, she thinks, if Jeremy were here, maybe I could tell him, maybe I could tell him about this pain, this thing that wedges inside me. I know I have run from this, have been afraid to let you see.

For if you can see, then so will I. But I think that might be better, not to be alone with it anymore.

Maggie stands up. She walks down to the water, feels the pain follow her, bombard her, as her eyes dart over the water in search of the loons. Here one minute, head dipping, one loon disappears, only to reappear in another spot. It calls and its mate sinks below the surface, emerges in another place, calls.

She heads toward the cabin, feels the wind hit at her face, tightens the orange blanket around her again. Into the cabin where she feels Evan, calls his name, goes to the porch, through the door and calls his name again, knowing he cannot, will not answer. She feels a hard black ball in her stomach, pushing into her chest, filling her lungs. On the porch she leans against the railing, closes her eyes, sees herself and Ivy on the rock, Ivy telling her that a sister makes a girl know herself, that Ivy would be her sister if she were here today with her. Looking up, Maggie glances through the branches of the low-hanging trees, half expecting and hoping to see her canary appear, as the loon appears after sinking and dipping in the water. But Ivy does not appear, and she is not on the rock and Ivy, her sister, is not there. She is alone on the porch, a grey mist rising slowly off the water as the breeze picks up. Across the lake, edging the water as the mist lifts, Maggie sees the red and gold remnants of autumn, what is left after the hard rain.

A picture of the watch that her grandfather gave her

comes to Maggie's mind again. She remembers how he opened her fingers to place it in her palm, how he closed her fingers over it, and held her fist between his hands. She remembers watching his face, the line between the brows deepening. The softness of his voice was like a whisper from God, and the gift was the gift of life. Why does this come back to me? she wonders.

Tears spring to her lids. Memories come. Memories she has pushed away flood into her. Tears come harder. She hears Jeremy's words, she hears her grandfather, and suddenly the black ball rises into one cry and the sound washes around her, fills the porch, spreads out over the lake, echoing.

"Mother," she cries aloud. "You did not want him to love me." And then louder, "But why?"

The sound of her own voice startles her. She looks around. The smell of smoke cuts through her thoughts. Is Mother up? she wonders. Has she made a fire? Is it so late?

Another bird pierces the air. Maggie looks up. A blue heron approaches the shore from farther down the lake. It glides, wings spanned, in a current, its great choppy neck stretched long. Maggie follows it with her eyes, up over the cabin, then above the tree line of the woods.

That is when she sees the smoke. A thick black curl, it weaves into the sky, twists over the trees with the wind. Oh God, the words form in Maggie's mind.

Out of the cabin, up the path, and in that short minute, she stands just forty feet from the house, sees the front room, Amanda's room, frothing with smoke and flame, and the smoke billows like a cloud, then thins again with the shifting breeze.

"Mother," she cries and stands frozen to the ground as the window in the living room cracks, as flames move as fast as lightning through the structure of the house.

Maggie runs through the brush around to the side where her mother's room is. The ground is still wet, she slips, her face cracks against a wet sprawling root, and her foot twists under her. On her feet again, she tries to get closer. "Mother," she calls, and then much louder, "Mo-ther," but the fire is louder now than her voice, and she cannot hear herself cry out. A wall of hot wind hits her face as she tries to get closer still, and she backs off, feels her skin prickle around her eyes. She sees the windows in the next room crack and splatter glass onto the ground. Before her there is no longer the corner of the house, the clapboards painted green up to the shingles that were stained grey do not exist. There is no room here, she thinks, no windows. There is only solid fire, and it spits out onto the ground, tiny bits of flame, blackened bits of charred house, it all spatters, like vomit.

Next, a large crackling breaks the roar, and Maggie falls backwards as she watches the front half of the roof cave in like two pieces of paper bent and dropped in the wind. The crash is accompanied by a roar of wind and heat, and it pushes out away from the house toward Maggie who gulps smoke and wet ash. On her hands and knees she crawls back, gets up, runs through the trees to the back of the house. The back door is locked. She looks for something to smash the window by the door, picks up a rusted piece of pipe that sticks out from under the porch, and *smash*, she breaks the window, and *smash* again, she pushes at the remaining glass, knocks at the wooden strip in the middle.

Behind her someone calls her name.

Maggie looks, cannot see who it is, "Help," she cries, "you must help. My mother is inside," and black smoke starts to come out the window she has broken, and black smoke is washing down over the roof as the breeze pulls it up and over. Another crash, and the rest of the roof goes, and with it, twisting smoke rushes against the windows which crack, one after another. Maggie is thrown back off the porch steps. She gasps for breath again, is not conscious of the searing of her lungs, knows only that Amanda is still inside.

"She's trapped," Maggie cries, rising, "she can't get out, she'll die in there," but her words are lost in the bellow of the fire.

Someone pulls her away, saying, "No, nothing you can do," and pulls at her arm, wraps an arm around her shoulder, drags her back. There are others coming through the woods, three or four, and Maggie recognizes Martin.

"Martin," she screeches, and then she coughs, deep from her chest, and she feels the burning in her throat.

Martin runs to her. His face is twisted, his eyes like bullets, they are so hard, and his mouth is working, but Maggie cannot hear the sound and she cannot distinguish the words, she can't think through her coughing. She points to the house, coughs the word, "Mother," and Martin takes hold of her, gestures to the others, and they spread out around the house. Martin pulls her back, away, holds her facing away, and he holds a hand to her cheek and Maggie sees black wet soot on his palm as he pulls it away, and she holds her own hand to her cheek, and it too is black when she pulls it back. Her mind jumps from her face to the remembrance of her mother.

"She's trapped," she whispers to Martin, "trapped in there, she can't get out," and she coughs, and Martin tells her to hush, and then she cries, "But Martin, she'll die." Martin pinches his mouth up, tightens the lips.

Martin looks her right in the eyes and shakes his head from side to side.

Maggie feels another wave of windy heat press against her back. She turns to see the house a solid volume of flame and her mouth drops open. The main corner beams stand a dark golden shade of fire, the rest of the house rises in waves of yellow fire. "Oh my God, my God," and she covers her mouth, feels sickness coming on, falls onto her hands and knees.

The others come around the house as several more men come through the woods along with Alice. Maggie listens. "Nothing to do now," one says, "and if that wind don't come up more in the next twenty minutes, we'll be okay." "How's the girl?" another one says, pointing in Maggie's direction.

"Maggie," Alice calls and bends to her knees beside her.

"Stay with her, Alice," Martin says, heading out front.

Maggie folds down onto Alice's lap. She rocks her shoulders forward, she holds her hands over the back of her head, and she rocks against Alice and coughs and then grows quiet. Alice strokes her arms, runs her hand across Maggie's back, murmurs over and over, "It's okay now," and moves with Maggie's rocking.

At one point the fire whistles. Maggie looks up, watches the flame rise and then, as if the air were let out of a balloon, the flame deflates and there is only black smoke. Alice leads Maggie around to the front and down toward the water. The smoke rushes into the woods as the breeze grows.

"Will it catch?" she hears Alice ask Martin.

"We'll thank the Lord if it don't. We can be glad for all that rain we got, it'd be wild now if we hadn't got the rain." He looks at Maggie, turns back to face the fire.

And then there is no more fire. There is steaming smoke, whispering into the sky. There is a half-collapsed chimney, blackened and steaming, there are some beams laid across each other, sizzling, there is a partial wall on one side of the kitchen. Mostly there is rich black, like the black of charcoal, Maggie thinks, and remembers her sketch pad.

Finally she stands. A bitter, putrid stink reaches her nostrils. Again she thinks she will be sick. Alice has wet her apron, is rubbing it against Maggie's face. "It's just soot," she says to Martin, "I don't think it's burn," and Martin nods.

"What. About. Mother?" Maggie finds the words, one at a time.

Alice bites her lower lip, shakes her head.

Martin looks down.

"You sure she was in the house?" Alice questions.

Maggie frowns. "Of course."

Maggie turns, sees the mist has risen off the lake completely, sees a few patches of mist in the mountains. She looks over to the rock where she and Ivy spent that one summer. She looks over to the roof of the cabin, sees streams of new sun on the shingles, some still glistening black with the wetness. "My God," she says, and a low cough echoes from her chest. She holds a hand to her throat.

Alice and Martin turn to face her. Alice spreads her arm

around Maggie's shoulder again. "The warden'll be here, Vance has gone to send for him," Martin says.

"My God," Maggie repeats. She knows something horrible has happened, knows the horror of this fire. But she can feel nothing.

"It was prob'ly the smoke that killed her, Maggie, you can't let yourself think on —" Alice adds.

"No, you don't understand," as she realizes it herself. "You don't understand," and she coughs from within, tastes a sour odor. She shakes her head, her hands slack by her sides. "I should have been in there with her, I should be in that black mess with her." Still she can feel nothing.

"Now don't say that, Maggie, it won't do no good," Alice tries.

"No, you still don't understand. I, me," and she raps a finger on her breastbone. "I should have been in there, asleep. She didn't know I'd gone down to the lake. She'd have killed us both." Then she remembers the look on Amanda's face in the night when she went in to put the candle by her bed. She had not wanted to linger, had not wanted to listen to her mother, but now, standing before the remains of the house, now she could remember Amanda's face, how small and child-like it had looked, how alone, how very alone. And though her words had been short, Amanda herself was there in that bed. It was the real Amanda, Maggie realizes, and though the same old words came out of her mouth, it was Amanda, the girl, under it all, under all the pretense. Oh God, she thinks. Let me see her one more time. Let me tell her, just once, just for a moment give her to me for a moment, God, so I can tell her. I see. I see her now. I understand.

"It was an accident, Maggie," Alice says. "Your mother never knew just what she was doing, 'specially that last time I saw her, with Evan. She was just, just somewhere else all the time. You must 'a known that about her."

"Oh, God," Maggie wails, and for the first time Maggie can remember, she needs her mother. She wants her mother's arms around her, the way Betsey's mother used to enfold her sometimes, the way mothers enfold their daughters. Inside Maggie, things are folding up. Her insides are coming apart. She is that tree on the edge of the precipice, but she is falling, the roots are giving way. "Oh God," she says again, "Let me see her just one more time."

Maggie bends in a spasm of coughs. She holds the wet apron to her face. "Don't you see," she begs, pulling the apron away, now black from her hair. "I need her, I need to tell her," and she stares, knows there is no answer, that she cannot tell Amanda anything, that her own complicity is for her alone, that her life will be lived with that complicity, and she will have to find a way to live with it. Jeremy, she thinks. She hears her words to him. I didn't realize, she will tell him. I've been doing it too, haven't I, I've been hiding.

I don't want to hide anymore, she thinks, as she looks up at the place where Land's End had stood only an hour earlier, maybe less. She follows the trailing smoke with her eyes, searches the sky for the words. Jeremy, she will say, help me with this. Please help me with this.

Maggie turns, heads to the charred steaming refuse. She stands close, notices the small pieces of wood that spattered through the windows and burned partway. Slowly she starts around the perimeter. One step, then another, until she goes all the way around. Heat rises from the pile, and the air is stiff with a dead flame odor. Maggie shudders. As she comes to the final corner, where Amanda's room was, she squats on one knee.

Her throat tightens. A child cry comes from her throat. She searches with her eye to find the place where Amanda might have lain to die. "Mother," she says, and another child whine is emitted from her throat. "He gave me the watch because of you. Don't you see?" and her tone is gentle, mothering. "He gave it to me because he loved you. He just didn't know it though, Mother. Like you. You wouldn't believe the truth."

Maggie lifts her eyes. A blue heron, and Maggie fancies it the same one she saw from the cabin porch, comes in flight over the trees from the mountain. Maggie follows its flight, as it veers away from the rising steam from the house, around to the north, swooping on a current, until it flaps its wings down, a slight bend partway on the wing, and up, and the heron surges over the treetops to the north.

"It's a little late. But it's the truth," Maggie says, feels the tears behind her eyes, in her eyes, on her cheeks. "It's the truth."

Maggie does not sleep. Her lungs burn with each breath. She does not want to lie down flat, does not want to rest, so she sits in the rocker in Martin's kitchen by the stove, a warm glow touching her legs. She rocks and she thinks, and with each breath, the pain makes her know what she has feared.

In the morning Alice appears in the kitchen in a blue quilted robe. Maggie does not speak, stares out the window, rocks. Alice places a mug of coffee on the table near her, and Maggie nods, picks it up, and sips. Martin comes in; he wears a pair of heavy wool pants and a blue work shirt.

"We'll pick through what's left," he says, his eyes hard.

"You mean, find Mother's bones," Maggie replies flatly.

"You'll want to have a funeral, you know," Alice says. She places strips of ham in a frying pan.

"We need bones for that, you mean. I guess we can't bury an empty box." Maggie stands up, wheezes.

"You need to be checked for that, Maggie. I can take you down to Willis today," Alice says.

Maggie nods, yes.

In Willis the doctor examines Maggie, tells her she will continue to experience discomfort for a few weeks, but there is no serious damage to the lungs or larynx. Then she calls Jeremy from a pay phone at a gas station.

"It's me," she says when she hears his voice.

He can tell something is wrong, waits over the crackling line in silence, can hear her wheeze.

"Are you sick?" he finally asks.

"No, I'm all alone," she answers and begins to cough.

"You are sick," he says, "I can hear it, are you all right?" he persists.

"No, I'm all alone," she repeats. "I mean, really all alone. There's only me now. Mother's —"

Jeremy waits for the word.

"Dead," she whispers hoarsely. "Can you come?"

"What do you mean?" he asks.

"Jeremy, don't ask questions. Later, ask them. Just come, now."

"Maggie," he says, "I don't even know where you are."

"I'm at Land's End. Or what's left. Get to Willis. I showed you that on the map. Ask directions to the lake from there. It's an hour or so from Willis. They can tell you."

"What's the name of the lake again?"

"Carter," she whispers over the crackling. "Carter Lake."

"I'm on my way, Maggie."

"I just can't talk now. Just come, Jeremy," and she wheezes good-bye into the phone.

It is the smell of coffee from Alice's kitchen that awakens Maggie the next morning. She sits on the edge of the bed, looks around at the walls of the little room where she slept. Alice's sewing machine sits by the one window in the room. One of Martin's plaid shirts is laid across the back of the chair and some blue fabric is stretched under the needle of the machine. Alice had laid the piles of clothes that were on the bed on the floor by the door when she made up the bed for Maggie the night before, and though Maggie had thought she would not sleep, she had retired to the quiet of the room shortly after dinner, had fallen asleep, still dressed, on top of the covers. Sometime during the night, she had climbed under the covers, after she had grown aware of the cold stiffening of her limbs, and she had slept through until the morning kitchen smells sifted under the door.

Maggie hears gentle talking sounds through the wall that

separates her room from the kitchen. It is Martin's voice, soft as the rustle of leaves outside the window. Maggie pulls on her shoes, laces them, and stands up. Her head swims when she thinks of what is to come in the next days. And of what has been. She turns and pulls the covers straight, smooths them out, fluffs the pillow.

Alice and Martin are not in the kitchen when she opens her door. The breakfast dishes are drying in the rack. A tin coffeepot rests on the back of the stove, a thin steam rises from its spout. Maggie heads for the back door, steps outside to a crisp October air and a blue sky. She wonders how beauty can go on in the midst of what has happened, how her mind can still notice it, how her heart can feel it. She walks down the hill to the town's dock, feels the early sun on her back as she reaches the open green near the water's edge. She finds a place on the stone wall to sit, feels the cold surface of the granite rocks with her hands. The lake is calm, blue, a soft and deep blue. Maggie remembers the feel of the lake at her face when, as a girl, she would dive into its icy waters and push her way to the surface, how the water was thick, yet light, against her skin, her hair, her open eyes. How there was some escape in the surge of water around her as she emerged with a shout to the clean air.

The sound of a car pulls her attention to the road that comes from the woods to meet the green. It is a car she knows, it is Jeremy's white Saab. Maggie can see the shape of Jeremy through the windshield, and her heart wavers as she sees him step out and stretch his arms above his head. His blue shirt is wrinkled, the sleeves rolled up to the elbows, and his grey corduroy slacks are loose and rumpled. Maggie watches from her place on the stone wall as he pulls a jacket out from the back seat, and a scarf, the red one she gave him last Christmas. Then he turns, and as she waves her arm, he sees her.

"Your hair's sticking up all over the place," she says as he approaches.

"I drove straight through, I —" and he stops. Jeremy

smooths down his hair, stares at Maggie with open dark eyes. "Maggie, I don't know what to ask, I —"

Maggie notices the car door still open behind him. Then her eyes pull back to his gaze. "I don't know where to begin," she answers.

Jeremy reaches out for her hands, pulls her to her feet, touches her hair, pushes it back from her forehead, touches her face, her neck, her shoulders. Then she is pressed against him, her face burrowed in his shoulder. She tells him the events, just the events of the last days: the walk to her grandfather's grave, her mother's anger at the stone, her own anger and then understanding of her mother, the long restless night, and the final morning. Her voice catches as she tells of the ashes that floated through the air in the day after the fire died.

"What's next?" Jeremy asks. "I mean —"

"I'm going today with the warden. To search —" and she pauses, hesitates for the right words, "for what's left. To see if —" and she cannot go on.

Jeremy loops his fingers around the belt of her slacks. "What?" he asks. "To see if what?" He pulls her closer.

"To see what's left. Of her," Maggie says, and she feels a sickness in her stomach, in her throat.

"I want to go with you. To do that," he tells her.

Jeremy waits for an answer. There is a pushing and pulling of the air between them, a tension in Jeremy's hand at Maggie's waist, and a trembling in Maggie's face at his shoulder. Then she pulls back and looks him in the eye.

"I want you to come with me too. To do that." And as she says the words, she feels a knowing inside of some kind of shift, some loosening of her inner walls. "I, I want you to help me with this."

Jeremy nods. He takes her hand, half smiles at her. With her.

"You must be tired out. From the drive," she says.

"That's one hell of a trip," he tells her. "Up through those mountains. It's like coming to another world."

Maggie knows. She knows it is another world. It is a world she has loved for a long time. For all of her life.

During the night at Martin's, Maggie had imagined picking through the fire's refuse. Martin had suggested she wait with Alice at their house, that he could do what was needed, but she told him, no, she wanted to be there too. She had in her mind the thought that she might find the watch that her grandfather had given her, that it might be somewhere near her mother's bones. She imagined its charred surface, the silver burnished black, and she heard the chimes when she opened the cover.

So when she and Jeremy accompany the warden, the sheriff, and a team of deputies to the fire's remains, Maggie is certain she will find the watch. The deputies follow her instructions and wade in through the chunks of wood, the burned pieces of wall. She shows them where Amanda's room had been. They sift through, making piles of metal pieces, piles of objects that Maggie might be able to identify. Jeremy keeps himself at a distance as Maggie hovers around the edge of the house.

"Here," one of them cries, and the deputies circle, lower to their knees, a low flat rectangular box set beside them. A black something is laid in the box. A bone? Soon it is full. It is a pile of black shapes, long and thin, slivers of tusk charred black, Maggie thinks.

My mother's bones, Maggie says to herself, and her stomach turns, causes a fit of coughing.

Maggie describes the watch, tells them to look carefully. The sun streams onto their backs as they bend and pick, bend and pick, and Maggie rests on a rock near the path where she can see, where the sun can fall into her face. She cannot escape the raw fire smell and the fine black ash that covers everything. It sifts through their hair, their noses, their skin, so the deputies are as black as the bones after a while.

"Are you sure you want to stay for this?" Jeremy asks as

he kneels behind her, his eyes scanning the charred mess. "This is pretty, well, pretty bad, and —"

Maggie does not take her eyes from the deputies, but she answers him, "I have no choice. I have to do this." She coughs some more.

"You should leave," Martin tells her.

"Not yet, I want to see if they find the watch."

Jeremy waits there, behind her. He watches her shoulders rise and fall with her breathing.

They find no watch, though, but Maggie knows she will search some more, will ask Jeremy to help her. She feels the autumn sun on her face, turns to feel the lake breeze, to look at Jeremy. She is glad he is there, though she cannot tell him so. Not just yet, she knows. His unshaven face, his dark tired eyes tell her it is time to go back to Martin's. He needs something to eat, she realizes.

Maggie watches the deputies, sees one of them lay something oblong into the box, it is about the size of — "Her skull?" she asks, and feels her stomach turn. Oh God, she thinks again, as she imagines raw flame at her mother's face, sizzling at her grey hair, singeing her lashes. Oh God, she feels it again, that want, deep in the core of her, for her own mother. All those years, she thinks, all those years when I was a child, hid from this feeling, ran from the pain of it, made it so that it didn't exist, listened to Evan, felt his hatred, my own hatred, but did not feel this, this wish, this simple wish for her to be my mother. Mother, she wants to cry out just once, just to hear the sound of want in her own voice, that sound of need and want that forever was locked within her and now is filling her breast, running into her veins, Mother, she hears inside her, and then she hears her own voice, it is Maggie's voice, and it cries, "Mo-ther," once, and then again, and then more times, and Martin is there watching, and Jeremy is there, and the deputies, and the sheriff, but she doesn't think of them, does not know they are there for there is only the sound of the girl, Maggie, calling out to her mother.

"Maggie," Martin says low, at her side. And Alice is there, her arms strong as they wrap around her shoulders, pull Maggie to her, hold her tight to her breast, and then Maggie is crying, gulps of crying, for herself, for her mother, for Evan. For all of them.

Later that afternoon, after Jeremy has returned with Alice to her house, for rest, Maggie still waits at Land's End while the others search.

"Time to be getting back," Martin tells her when the sun is behind the trees.

"Martin," Maggie starts. She is afraid to leave the place that once was Land's End, the place she loves.

"I know," he answers. "It's better to go, though. This time will be the hardest. It always is." His dark eyes are soft, warm. "Your young fellow'll be waiting for you."

"It always is," Maggie repeats the words. There is an always she has never known. This is the first always, for Maggie. Though the sun is lower, the air quieter, there is a warmth against her back. It started when the sun came through, late morning, drying the birch bark on the trees, thinning the air, loosening the ash piles.

"What'll your young man think of all this?" Martin asks, and Maggie knows he means all of it, from Evan to her grandfather, and to her mother.

"I don't know," she answers. "Well, he'll have a lot of questions," she goes on. "He'll want to know."

Martin nods, as if content.

The moon is full. Maggie's room shines with the moonlight when she wakes in the night with a sweat covering her body and a wedge of scratching in her throat. She leans onto an elbow, looks out and up at the night sky, sees the sparkling of stars in the velvet black sky. She coughs, feels the rawness in her throat, the fire smell in her nostrils, the odor lodged there in her face. With each breath, she can remember the sight of Land's End as it rose in flames, as it smoked through the afternoon hours and into the next day, the fine ash film covering the surrounding birch trees and the yellow leaves on the ground.

Maggie gets out of bed, finds her sweater in the silver light, pulls it over her head. She feels along the floor for her socks, pushes her feet into them, steps into her slippers. She opens the door to the kitchen, touches the black wood stove as she passes it, runs a finger along the cold metal edge. At the sink, she pours a glass of water, drinks it slowly, holds the water in her mouth each time before swallowing. The pain in her throat is eased somewhat, but she takes a biscuit from the covered plate by the bread box and chews off a corner. It is hard to swallow, but she thinks it will help.

Moonlight stretches in through the two kitchen windows, as she tiptoes across the room and into the parlor where Jeremy is sleeping on the horsehair couch.

"Jeremy," she whispers. She kneels by the couch so that her face is level with his. She spreads her hand over his shoulder. "Jeremy," she whispers again, closer to his ear. Then she nibbles from the biscuit as she feels him stir. When one of his eyes opens, she tells him, "My throat hurts. I can't sleep."

Jeremy rolls onto his side, lifts the blankets. "Climb in," he tells her. He pulls her back against him and she lies with her head on his arm, her body next to his, so that where his knees are bent, so are hers, against his. His other arm is wrapped around her and his hand strokes her chin, softly. "Your skin is soft," he whispers.

"Can you smell the fire?" she asks. "I can't stop smelling the fire. It's in my nose, it's all through me."

"It'll take a few days," he answers. "Are you cold?"

"Not really," she tells him. "I was sweating, woke up in a sweat. Not because I was hot. It was a dream or something —" She turns onto her back, looks at Jeremy's face in the night light. She touches his lips with a finger, feels the stubble on his cheeks with her palm. Jeremy's eyes are dark holes in his face. "I can't tell if it's my lungs that are burning, or if it's something else."

Jeremy waits for her to say more. His arm pulls her closer.

"It's like something inside me is gone," she says, then stops. "I don't even know why you love me, can love me."

"It's those hairs at the back of your neck."

Maggie feels his breath at her neck, warm. She wants to ask more, but waits. "Want to walk down to the dock?" she asks, feeling restless.

"Now? You want to go outside now?"

"It's nice out — the moon's full. I just want to see the lake in the moonlight."

Once out of the house, they don't whisper. They speak in low tones, though, and they hold hands as they step carefully across the path to the green. Everything is grey and silver, as in a dream, Maggie thinks. At the water's edge, they stand and look out at the black expanse. "Maybe a loon will call."

"I've never heard one in person," he tells her. "I've never been in a place like this."

"I know. Let's wait," she says. "Maybe we'll hear one."

Jeremy and Maggie stand on the flat part of the green near the dock. They start to sway back and forth together. They stand like that, swaying, Maggie in front of him, his arms around her waist.

"It's so silent," he whispers.

"The silence is all there is," she tells him. She reaches an arm back, around his neck. Then she turns and faces him, and they rock from side to side. Maggie grows soft inside, remembering the feeling of needing her mother. It hurts to remember it, to feel it. She tells him about it, what it was like to need her mother that way. "You ever feel that way about your father?" she asks him. "As if you're still a child, and you need him?"

"Sure," he tells her. "You think that's supposed to go away?"

Maggie says she doesn't know. "It's a new feeling for me."

"I need you," he tells her. "But you know that. There's a lot we could do for each other. That we don't do now."

And then it happens. A loon calls, a low wail followed by a high eerie pitch. And again. They stop swaying, turn to look out at the water, can see nothing but the night against the black silvery lake.

"Jeremy," she starts, a crack in her voice. "How'm I going to get over this. So much gone —" She sees the moon, full, a solemn glow above them. "It's going to take forever."

"What is?"

"The dreams," she answers. "Finding new ones." She starts to cough, bends against him, cries some.

Jeremy waits until she is quiet. "Maybe it's not a matter of finding new ones," he tells her. "Dreams, I mean. Maybe they've stayed with you all along. Maybe you've been so afraid of losing what you had, you never took the time to know what was there. Like me," he suddenly adds. "You always come close. And then — you're gone."

Maggie listens to his every word. Something inside her doesn't fight his words. Something inside her just listens. She looks around at what surrounds them. There are the shadows of the mountains against the sky. There are the pine trees along the green, silent and tall. There is the lake, oily black and calm. She looks at the way Jeremy cocks his head, to listen to the silence.

"The air's not so cold," she states. "I think we'll have an Indian summer." She reaches her hands behind his neck. "It'll be warm today, you'll see. You'll have to talk to me a lot today. Tell me things. Things you've probably already said before. I want to listen," she tells him. "I really do."